THE BROCH

THE BROCH

MARTIN ROSE

WITH KATHLEEN WARD

This is a work of fiction. Names, characters, businesses, places, events and incidents are either the products of the author's imagination or used in a fictitious manner. Any resemblance to actual persons, living or dead, or actual events is purely coincidental.

Matador
9 Priory Business Park,
Wistow Road, Kibworth Beauchamp,
Leicestershire. LE8 0RX
Tel: 0116 279 2299
Email: books@troubador.co.uk
Web: www.troubador.co.uk/matador
Twitter: @matadorbooks

ISBN 978 1800463 196

British Library Cataloguing in Publication Data.
A catalogue record for this book is available from the British Library.

Printed and bound in Great Britain by 4edge Limited
Typeset in 10.5pt Baskerville by Troubador Publishing Ltd, Leicester, UK

Matador is an imprint of Troubador Publishing Ltd

Visit the author's website at www.grahambullenauthor.com

FOREWORD

I've never been a big fan of forewords.

Even now, I harbour resentment for those ponderous Penguin Classic introductions of my adolescence. Intimidated (or simply bored) by them, I'd close many a book before the tales they lionised even uttered their well-crafted openings.

But I recommend you read *this* one.

I can't make you, of course. But I owe it to Martin (he will make his own request soon enough) to try.

It's true that his story will not be seriously diminished if you skip these pages, or those of my similarly presumptuous afterword.

But I'd appreciate it if you gave me just these few extra minutes to explain.

I first met Martin on a creative writing course, high up on the Scottish moors above Loch Ness.

He told his fellow students that he'd taken an early exit from the world of work in order to test himself against the driving ambition of his youth: to be a writer. He'd become a reader well before pulling on his first pair of school trousers, taken on the train every two weeks by his mother to the local public library. Upon his initial ownership of an adult lender card, his habit grew at pace. "A true '70s bookworm," he said. "It was like being given a day pass to everywhere."

Feeling, at the end of his college years, that he might after all chance his hand at composition, he instead grasped tightly onto a series of accumulating excuses not to do so. Work. Marriage. Mortgage. Children. Each one more legitimising than the last.

Then, he told the group, the chance to "call my own bluff" had presented itself in the form of a severance package from his employer. One by one, thirty years of alibis washed away.

His enthusiasm and curiosity during that week, and the excited support he offered his peers, are what I remember about him the most, that first time. The short pieces he brought with him were of some merit, though lacking in any real direction or craft. But he was desperate to learn (and oh so easy to encourage).

Over the next two or three years, I learned of his progress through evenings shared in Inverness at the local writing salon (a lot less exclusive, and more fun, than it sounds), or by virtue of pieces circulated via that initial course mailing list.

He then began to attend the monthly writers' group I still host back on the moors. His enthusiasm there was, if anything, even greater than when I'd first encountered him. His writing, while still often uneven, had grown in confidence. And he had a voice. A style and a way of seeing things that I felt, and still feel, were uniquely his.

We explored how he might bring his first novel, *The Quarant*, into the world. Over the months, his conviction that he could successfully court a major publishing house diminished, but his productivity remained impressive. During that first course, my fellow tutor had told the group that the only way to learn to write is to write. That Margaret Atwood's professed goal, to 'fail better' with each attempt, was both noble and useful. Martin, with more time than many of his peers, took this fully to heart. He took the plunge and self-published *The Quarant*, and his second novel, *The Puppet Master*. Put together a modest but appealing website.

Then we lost touch. He remained on the distribution list for our monthly meetups, but stopped circulating work. He simply stopped coming.

It was almost a year later that Caitlin turned up at my door.

She'd called me from Martin's home, and then driven over the Kessock Bridge to my own home in Fortrose. Together we walked the short distance to IV10, the cafe on the corner by the cathedral, where she passed me an iPad and a folder of papers taken from Martin's writing desk. Over the course of three lattes and a tasty plate of local mackerel, I learned how they had met on Harris, and the events she had stumbled (yes, she used that word) into.

She seemed nervous. Worried that she would fail to grab my interest, or perhaps simply let him down.

Before the end of that evening, back at home by the fire, I felt myself shift from intrigued listener to full co-conspirator. The next morning, I began to move things around in my mind; bend and twist plans to make space for whatever this new project might be.

I'll say more in the afterword about the events that followed, but allow me a few more moments to explain how this book took shape.

Firstly, Martin's experiences on Harris were pretty much as he records them. It's true, I parsed some passages through a more sober, less hurried lens than that at his own disposal. His intensity rarely falters, but inebriate pace, in life as much as in prose, requires the odd benevolent intervention to keep the ball from spinning off into the gutter. The tone, I hope, remains his own; Caitlin's recollections have helped considerably.

The short pieces punctuating each chapter are drawn from older files and papers. If their selection or sequencing disrupts or disappoints, that's down to me. To my mind, they offer some insight into how Martin came to leave home that first Saturday. An origin story, of sorts.

I've honoured Martin's choices concerning the sequencing of his reminiscences of earlier times. They feel too strongly tied to his frame of mind at key points in that week to warrant any editorial interference. As for his own introduction, I've left it untouched. It's so suggestive of the man I knew, humble and self-deprecating, and I wish to offer you the same opportunity I had to react to his early request, and to make your own choice as to whether to take his journey with him.

I take full responsibility for the prologue and Chapter 8. It will become obvious to you that Martin was in no position to conclude his story himself. Having spoken several times with Caitlin of that last day, I have chosen to tell it in my own words, while hoping to remain true to Martin's own take on the world, and his beliefs about his place in it.

On a final, personal note, I confess to having not yet fully worked through my own thoughts and feelings about how this book, rather than either of his first two, has been the one to sail onto the bookshelves.

The angel's share of Martin's memories continue to hover and swirl in the air above me. I hope their tang somehow mellows his sons' feelings for him and, by extension, your own.

Sláinte.

Kathleen Ward,
Fortrose,
Summer 2019

Score Chart

0–50	*Nothing short of absolutely diabolical*
51–64	*Nasty and well worth avoiding*
65–69	*Very unimpressive indeed*
70–74	*Usually drinkable but don't expect the earth to move*
75–79	*Average and usually pleasant though sometimes flawed*
80–84	*Good whisky worth trying*
85–89	*Very good to excellent whiskies definitely worth buying*
90–93	*Brilliant*
94–97	*Superstar whiskies that give us all a reason to live*
98–100	*Better than anything I've ever tasted!*

(Jim Murray's Whisky Bible 2007)

'Cause that's all we can have, yes it's all we can trust
It's a hell of a ride, but a journey to dust
And there's nothing pathetic listing clothes she'd wear
If it proves that I had you, if it proves I was there
Say, "I remember that."

(Prefab Sprout, 'I Remember That')

PROLOGUE

SUMMIT EDGE, THE CLISHAM

SATURDAY 27TH OCTOBER 2018

Do you see me?

There, at the top of my fall, pinned in motion against the deepening pink of the afternoon sky?

My shadow's safely back in my pocket, lifted from the last scraps of grass on the cliff's edge. Breezes pass under me on their way from the sea to somewhere more substantial. More solid.

I'm just here. See?

Look across and beyond the painted stretch of damp yellow sands that lie beneath your feet. Cast your gaze up and over the three bays between us. Along the steepening ridge, beyond the splintered boulders. Just below the summit, where the shallow dome cuts away into glistening granite drop.

Wait. I'll twist a little, wave an arm. Sketch myself against the jagged sea-blown cliff. There. Do you see me better now?

See my curled and beckoning hand, slicing through the chill, damp air to greet you. I see you, *just inside the curve of the bay, wrapped against the promise of October rain.*

See Borrum's breath coming up to grasp me, climb past me, impatient to see my tumble through the startled Hebridean air.

I hear the expectant call of the ground below, its plane frozen within my first rotation. It swallows down hard. Jaws widen to welcome me, to take their first full feed of my release.

There. I'll rejoin my patiently waiting arc, no longer alone. Lean in with me. Hear the whoosh and cry of air plucking at my coat and legs.

Look closer. Please.

The tear in my eye is not one of sorrow. Rather, my happiness at your company, at following this through, overwhelms me.

Do you see the urn? The glints of gold and turquoise, prehensile seahorses flicking forward and back. Brief glimpses of shining glaze, washed by the tide of approaching dusk. Do you feel its weight?

I'll pause again while you approach. Here, hover beside me. We've got to know each other well, this past week, so no need to be shy now. Especially now.

It's true, the land below notices me too, and yearns for me to join it. But I'll not rush. The remaining moments can be savoured.

I savour them, and all the moments before; good, and not good.

My arm tightens around the empty urn.

What's that, you say? My lips? Ah, yes. Their thin grey coating, each grain of ash ornamenting my smile. Can you taste them? The bitter chalk and grit of the last spoonfuls, still betraying the last drops of peaty Islay malt?

My tongue and throat hold the last ounce of her.

The urn is all air too, now. A hollow instrument, searching out its first and final notes. Brought into my chest, beneath my coat.

You frown still, I see. Censure. Berate. To no avail.

It is done; Trish, I am both of us now.

No longer frozen, I fall a further length, so push on your gaze, or we will part.

There, I'll turn. Look back up at where you stand. Grip my arms around my chest.

The ground conforms to my disdain, its claim already struck.

You still frown, I see. But allow my smile to melt your rebukes. To wash them away.

I am coming, my love. We join the earth together, embracing as we once joked we would, in our defiant, deliberate plunge into inseparable warmth.

POLITE INTRODUCTIONS

Death doesn't just cross my mind for three hours a day; pop Its head around the door, asking after my health; approach only at my invitation.

No. Rather, It barges in, presses me into the unyielding ground, demand I name It with each constricted, lung-emptying breath. Its foul exhalations invade; insult my throat with oily fume and rank, burnt air.

Twenty-one hours a week practising this, or for that matter *anything*, you'd soon become an expert, right?

Imagine, then, Death's prowess at torment, these past ten months. I'm conducted masterfully; every muscle and sinew, scarred with proofs of loss and absence, tuned to the next brutal sweep of Its hand. It can do it all, without assistance or safety net.

So I keep It close. Deny Its fists the backswing needed to further bruise and puncture. I cling to the ropes, just one blow from the canvas. From torment's end.

The sad clown look fits me like the proverbial.

Deep breath, Martin. Too much, too soon. Don't get carried away.

Sorry. It's hard enough to make our first conversation fun, with all this (my) talk of Death and Its skills. How many friends have *you* ever made after facing such an initial barrage of melodramatic self-obsession? Not many, I venture.

Anyway. How can I put this?

Today, I'm reaching out. But it's you who has made the first move. You who hold this, *these words*, in your hands.

My empathy for fellow humans has tended to zero this year, but I have always been able to divine in others a need to be cheered up. Sadness signals *me* as a slowly sinking Elastoplast in warmed Pacific waters beckons the shark. Even across the current distance between us, I feel it there.

Something ails you. No? Are you sure? Be honest – why *did* you pick up this book in the first place? The cover blurb is unlikely to attract the carefree and untrammelled.

I may have you all wrong, of course.

Will you stay with me for a few more pages? Perhaps if I speed up a little; offer a few more concrete facts about my whereabouts or circumstances, before you bring the covers together, or relegate it to that part of your tablet that holds other rash and (in hindsight) mistaken purchases.

We might already be off to a bad start, you and I.

Yet this, *these words*, are a most important part of our beginning. The beginning of *us*. That quantum hook that might (eventually) return you to your happier life, and me towards the end of mine.

Let's agree this right now, then. I'll never be the one to break our gaze. No matter what you say. What advice, welcome or not, harsh or gently spoken, you might offer; or how unsettled or conflicted by it I might feel. I won't flinch. And I'll do my best to ground my musings and wanderings in forms both tolerable and clear.

And in return? I'm not sure. Perhaps you'll keep reading; grind and gnash your teeth in a determined effort to honour your promise. Offer me the benefit of your doubt.

Don't get me wrong. This is no trivial enterprise. The moment you put this book down, you'll leave me screaming alone into the abyss. That's how much I need you. How much it matters that we get on.

I'll make my skull glass. Snap and part my ribs for a glimpse at pulsing and pumping walls. Explain their every beat. I'll hide nothing.

So perhaps you could withhold judgement for a while? Could that work?

Great.

So how about you and I start again?

Hi. My name is Martin. In the nine months or so it's taken to eat the ashes of my wife, I have become a recluse. And a barely functioning alcoholic.

There. It's said.

I'm torn, I admit. Sitting here, looking out over the dark Atlantic shoreline, telling you this straight out of the gate. How does one introduce oneself without frightening one's new friend? Before even learning their name.

If a slim(mish) middle-aged man, all white goatee and tremoring left eyelid, approached you in Debenhams or Waterstones and quietly, apropos of nothing, spoke those words to you, would your first instinct be to lean in, eager to hear more? No. You'd tell him to piss off, or, silently controlling your disgust, glance around for the nearest shop assistant.

Would you find it easier to take if the same words came from an old friend? A fellow worker, or old school chum? A lover? Would learning of these things from *them*, the eating of wives and the drinking of alcohol, after years of uncomplicated, reciprocal friendship, give you any less pause? *Hmmm.*

So you see my dilemma. How *should* I state these two dominant and inescapable facts without seeing my story dissipate upwards and into anaemic, lonely air?

No. I want to feel that you'll listen. Take an interest. Maybe even forgive my worst actions and thoughts, or at least empathise with me for doing and thinking them.

You might, right now, decide, *No, this is one seriously screwed-up man, and my life will be richer, maybe even longer, for turning and walking away.*

I would get that. Really. But wouldn't it be a shame?

Trish, to be fair, would have little truck with any of this probing. She'd be telling me to get on with it; stop messing around. "There could be a few people prepared to listen to you, but none of them will hang around if all they get from the start is you bleating and pleading. Man up," she would say, "and get on with it."

That was her all over. As I am to sadness, she was to bullshit: detected it, but then took no crap from anyone.

Well, from no one but me.

So if, after these first thousand words or so, you choose to walk away, revulsed, repulsed or just plain bored, and complete your journey to that heavily made-up woman in perfumes or the bespectacled young man at the bookshop counter to raise the alarm, then go ahead.

But it would make me sad.

No. That's not right.

Sadder.

CHAPTER 1

SATURDAY 20TH OCTOBER 2018

. . . there ain't no journey what don't change you some.

(Zachry, *Cloud Atlas*, David Mitchell)

BEGINNINGS

That whole 'early morning' thing. Hated, but unavoidable.

The recent pattern continues. Bed. Sore eyes on waking. Salt-encrusted lids.

Two weeks since the first time. And since then? Every night.

To be fair, it's only on those nights when I leave the cork in that last bottle that I mewl in my sleep. That should teach me.

Either way, Gallagher's done with his nightly work. Beaten the crap out of my right shoulder while I'm out cold. Sodding silverback. And his even more sodding bat.

I've yet to stumble upon his refuge. But they – it and he – are here somewhere.

That punched hole in the air is still there, too, chiselled by his advances and the swing of that bat. If you lower your face to the thick beige carpet, signs of his passing appear. Echoes of weight and its careless malice.

They do nothing for my back, though, these early morning searches. Twisting and turning – hurting like a bugger – is my new alarm call. But if I delay? All tracks vanish, lifted into the same air that conspires to hide him.

Then again, what would I do if I *did* find him? Mock his girlish lashes; his poor articulation of bilabials and consonants? Or simply throw him the finger? *I favour that last one.*

I roll and shift weight onto my left side. Two stacked pillows face me, their uncompressed surface a full three inches above my eyeline. The air above them is empty too. In direct contrast with my mood, lines of sun bleed down each side of the curtains. Aluminium rods refract a band of light a foot or two into the ceiling.

I so wanted the weather to be crap. For the escarpment above the house to be masked by river mist. To hear the insistent timpani of rain on the zinc roof of the en suite. But no. A sunny morning. *Terrific.*

Beyond the curtains, between the house and the waters of the Moriston, Napoleon emits the next strangled squawk of his post-dawn garden strut, optimistic as ever that one of his harem will finally turn from their contemptuous indifference and permit some early morning canoodles. Predictably, a second later comes the thrash of wings as he attempts, the effort of his call spent, to stay on his feet. No female, haughty or otherwise, appreciates a mate who loses their balance while calling attention to themselves. Stupid bloody bird.

Anyway. Here we go.

Bed – up and out.

Slippers – on.

Phone – detach from overnight power source.

Eye contact with bottle and glass beside the clock alarm – avoided.

Dressing gown – enrobed.

Lansoprazole (dose recently doubled) – blister-popped and swallowed, by way of a slow, angled dip beneath the tap.

I grip the sink edge on rising. Wait patiently, eyes closed, while the Faraday cage of my skull does its job.

The toilet cubicle and a slackening sphincter beckon. Nowadays, of course, eating pretty much bugger all, I raise only the odd 'plip' in the pot. Still. Better out than in. *The Brexiteer mantra.*

I remember what day it is. Saturday. But not just *any* Saturday. A red-letter Saturday, deserving of a special welcome. Some heraldic fanfare or crowd-lined parade. Ticker tape. Elegant secretaries hanging out of windows, fated to swoon as it swings into the glen. *Jesus, so soon?*

Plip. The day, you'll be pleased to hear, has now fully arrived.

Back in the bedroom, two bright yellow Post-it Notes sit on the bedside cabinet, joined evenly into a single mass. Their large, underlined title ('Stuff to do THIS MORNING, nob!') is legible even without my specs. I chuckle at the epithet. Donna deploys it with Steve to great comic effect, whenever she thinks he's being argumentative for a laugh. She's always been funnier than she lets on.

I haven't spoken to Steve for weeks. His last WhatsApp volley, a dozen or so messages, remains unanswered. I think he might have given up.

They don't know about Trish. Never had the heart, or guts, to tell them. They're six hundred miles away, so I haven't had the same trouble with them that I've had with others.

Anyway, the list is a brief one:

~~*1. Make sure whisky is safe in the boot.*~~

1. Up, dressed and packed no later than 9.00. Check into ferry at 13.30 for 14.10 depart. Allow 3 hours' drive.

2. *Trish.*
3. *DVDs, drives and books.*
4. *Letters to boys.*
5. *Make sure whisky is safe in the boot.*
6. *Lock everywhere up and post spare keys to Steve.*
7. *Check fuel and paperwork in car.*

Choosing not to dwell on how reactions to posted keys might play out, I attach the Post-its to the bedroom door.

I'm great at lists, even now. *Is that the final skill to go? Just after bladder control (intermittently failing), but considerably later than any willingness to spend time with others (long bloody gone)?*

The case is next. Clothes and wet-weather spares, wrapped around hard drives and box sets. Toilet bag.

I retrace my steps to the en suite. A brief glance in the mirror at the lower half of my face confirms last night's shave. And the glass looks clean. *Good man.*

That's one of the first things you need to know about me. I'll always adhere to standards if observed. Unwatched, all bets are off.

Ah, but now, a last-minute quandary. What books to take? Trish's favourites are musts: *Rebecca* and *Everything is Illuminated*. A quick wander along the lounge bookshelves and in they go. And for me? The Salinger, of course, and *A Rabbit Omnibus*. There's no way I'll read them again; I just want them close, to be discovered amongst my final accoutrements. Imagine the posthumous gossiping of a last-minute lapse: "Yes, the deceased's powers of discrimination were clearly lacking in his last days; he had been thumbing through *The Da Vinci Code* and, God forgive and save us all, the venerable Ms Rowling." Imagine. Thumbing Ms Rowling; a final act as tasteless as it is (probably) illegal.

Bellow teeters on the brink, but fails to reach escape velocity.

Too articulate, when I can barely transpose a postcode to an envelope without error. That said, there's room for a small McEwan. His earlier, nastier stuff.

In tribute to our early days of romance, I return from the snug with *American Psycho* (don't worry, I'll explain that one later), and single copies of *The Quarant* and *The Puppet Master*.

If you were an hour from leaving your home for the last time, what would *you* take? Would your choice be driven by times shared? If so, shared with whom? By moments that speak to your best days on the planet? Times when the universe was oh, so definitely on your side?

And what of the moments themselves? Do you hold *them* close, keep *them* tight? Plead with them to stay? Once gone, they'll taunt you from beyond your reach; and some days, if you recall them at all, you'll wish they were never yours.

Hark at me. *A horny pheasant isn't the only pompous thing living here.*

I pause and, out of habit, rotate the platinum band on my wedding finger. The ring moves freely now; one of the more convincing signs of my recent weight loss. *See, Trish, I can shed pounds if I put my mind to it.*

I make a fist. Grip it tight.

The next few minutes pass without note. The house is in a condition worthy of any later keyholder, and I've made my peace with all I leave behind.

Whiskies in the boot – check. Trish on the worktop by the sink – check. Envelope containing spare house keys (addressed and stamped) – check. Letters for the boys – ditto.

It's then that things go decidedly wanky.

I'm placing the case at the door. Then I'm flat on my back on cool lino. Gallagher's nowhere to be seen, so I can't blame him. Some cunning-person, then, casting a last-minute curse? My legs feel filleted.

A couple of minutes, and I half-sit, half-lie, leaning into the sink unit. To make matters worse, here come the sobs. I *was* fine – or what passes for it – but now I'm its opposite.

Consolation, token though it may be, comes with the relief that my breakfast tipple probably retains some anaesthetic properties. Enough to salve the worst of the Barnes Wallis head-bounce across the utility floor, anyway.

Have *you* ever experienced such rapid transitions (as someone claiming adulthood, that is)? Babies pull it off with ease. Bawl, smile, bawl again. Each fleeting stimulus replaced by the next.

I look up. The corners of two envelopes extend just beyond the edge of the worktop.

OK. Enough said.

Do you have children? If so, how old are they? No – that's not the right question, really. Age has little bearing. Better to ask, how well you think they know *you*. How they *feel* about you; about your efforts to bring them up. If you knew you had one final chance to speak to them, to offer an explanation of yourself, to characterise your relation to them, would you find the right words; ones you'd want to feel would endure? How might it feel to search for them? To pin each one down?

Mine, with Trish, were "See you later. I'll put the dinner on when you get back"; no one suggesting for one moment, helpfully, that her death was pencilled in for later that morning. God knows I've tried to think through what I would have said to her if I *had* known (apart from "Don't visit Geraldine today"); how I would have explained to her all she meant to me, how much *us* meant to me.

But now, with the boys? I'm still talking crap. *That bloody knock to the head.* It's not about whether you've got kids yourself; it's about how much of your own life as a child is still accessible. How you felt, still feel, when recalling those unthinking put-downs or instinctive actions of a flustered mother or distracted father. Those unremarked moments that, for the first time, caused you to question your place in their priorities and affections. They're there. Dormant. Compressed and built over by each new layer of adulthood, yet surging like magma escaping its breached chamber.

A delayed birthday card. The casual, unintentional slight lurking in the most innocuous of parental conversations, passing entirely undetected by others. That chance remark that undermines the Ambrosian fondness of a cherished childhood event.

In a week's time, two suicide notes from a self-obsessed, negligent father will be opened. Words will spill out and stain undeserving minds.

I reach up for them.

Confessions to months of deception. Wishes for their well-being, and an oblique hint at my imminent (or, by the time of their reading, recent) demise at my own hand. What else should I say? Perhaps less, or maybe even nothing at all. Just tear them up. Replace them with callous silence.

No. Better they learn of events from me, albeit after they are settled. Support their ability, with the delayed arrival promised by the use of second-class stamps, to feel that they had no way to stop things. That they are not responsible.

Hell, I stopped thinking straight months ago. *Who knows what's best?*

More sobs.

Frankly, nothing I've written will help. Twenty years after walking out on them the first time, I'm doing it again.

Maybe I should just torch this place, and have done with it.

This is getting out of hand. Tell me to shut up and move on.

Ignoring the supply of candle matches above the worktop, I bend and take my flask from the case. Three long swigs, and back it goes. My scalp a little tender but otherwise undamaged, I congratulate myself on the fact that Gallagher and his bat will have no means to follow me, and start pulling myself together. Tap my back pocket for the ferry ticket, like Bilbo with The Ring.

What's that?

You're right. 'Wanky' doesn't even come close.

BURNING BRIDGES

Ten minutes later I'm in the car, pulling onto the Skye road. Trish, envelopes and a bottle of Jack occupy the passenger seat, above my last-ever clinking empties bag. (Just clear glass. Drained malts and Jack only.)

I leave the gate in its customary open stance, having already positioned next Thursday's recycling bin on the roadside paving. See? Like I was saying. Standards.

Napoleon, mid-strut on the front lawn, is the only witness to my departure.

I keep my eyes low on the road. Just another car on the A887.

At the village centre, the near silence of letters and keys dropping into the postbox outside the corner shop grates more than the sound of shattering glass. The image of Kieron and Conor bending to pick up their mail in a week's time almost sees me filling the nearby ornamental tub of winter heather with a partially digested bowlful of Fruit & Fibre and a backwash of Jack; a less than dignified final bequest to our neighbours.

I think we can agree it's been a challenging start to the day. Three deep ujjayi breaths go some way to quell the rising panic.

At least the rusted white tab on the front of the postbox cooperates.

Time of next collection: Monday, 16.45.

I know it's daft, but I really was expecting some kind of Wagnerian chimes; the swelling of strings and brass at this last action before leaving. Bend into the breeze with me, palm cupped around expectant ear. I've not missed it, have I?

No. Just faint sounds of traffic from beyond the final bend out of the village and, from the other side of the river, the plaintive buzz of a chainsaw. Logs for next spring?

Let go. Step back. It's done.

Thoughts of the ferry rise from nowhere.

You might now hear a small but anxious squeal of tyres upon my leaving.

There. See? I can change moods just as quickly as any bloody infant.

TWO SINGLES TO HADES, PLEASE, MR CHARON

My next test beckons as I travel back down the Skye road. Sron na Mhuich looms to the south of the house, its sun-dappled slopes and mile-long escarpment marking the head of the glen just beyond the river. Another hundred yards further down the road, and I'm back looking at it over the Ballachulish slates of The Schoolhouse.

A voice in my head recites all the things I've probably forgotten to do prior to leaving. But I can't go back. I'd be lost for good. Sunk.

I allow myself a smile. The house sits there, nonchalantly resigned to its fate. *My master was here, but now he is gone. Do with me as you will.* I'll leave it to reminisce on our time spent here in its own way, in *its* own time. Next spring's bats can return to a loft under different ownership.

I drive the further half-mile to Ken's house, and park up a few yards into his drive. It's empty, his car obviously in the garage to the left. The walk up the slope to his front door is long enough for second and third thoughts to rise, but I tamp them back down. Folded cracks run across the asphalt surface, littered with wild grasses. Mind your step if you're coming – I don't want you to stumble so early into our journey.

I stop about two feet from the door.

In random, sweat-drenched nights, or doomed mornings when still trying to write, the image of me standing in this spot, inches and moments from 'the responsible party', was a regular torture.

Watching news footage of the latest distraught family standing outside court as their solicitor read prepared statements of grief, or of relief at the conviction for rape and/or murder of their daughter or son or wife, we would turn to each other and single out more appropriate punishments, administered by the survivors. We imagined the righteous release arising from each such blow; the feeling of justice when parading the severed testicles of their daughter's rapist for the cameras, or the still-warm heart of their son's killer. "Arseholes," we would say. "They deserve to die for the lives they have stolen," we would say.

I've day- and night-dreamed my way through every variant of this kind of vengeful act, standing, in each episode, exactly where I stand now.

But now, as the door finally opens, and I'm seen through rheumy, watery eyes, I have no idea what to do or say.

He's feebler than I remember. Spindly. In a worn dressing gown. The dip between top rib and clavicle catches light like paper-thin cracked enamel. Three chest hairs poke from his unbuttoned pyjama top. One pyjama leg, dishevelled, hovers just below his knee. His shin and blue-veined calf appear to have been grafted from a distressed, malnourished pony. Below, slippers, cut from the dull red of a faded Chesterfield displaying an emblem that might have once held meaning, sport now only a pasty grime.

I lift my gaze from his feet. He is trying to make sense of this visitor at his door. And then… there it is.

There.

His eyes widen. His head rolls back slightly on his neck.

There are so many things I want to say to that face. So many feelings demanding a way out of my chest and into the open.

Yet here we are. Silent still.

I see threaded red lines papering his nose and sunken cheeks. His hands tremor as they rise to his face. His mouth opens, but words won't form. Instead, there is a kind of quiet cheeping. An arm lifts in my direction. *I'm on the set of Invasion of the Body Snatchers. That final scene.*

I reach forward. Gently lower his outstretched finger. That strange noise continues; a fledging bird looking back up at its nest from the failed end point of its first flight, knowing it might not live to try a second time.

The truth of it. The bald truth of it. This man, this brittle, sad shell of a man, is me. He's as big a wreck as I am. Just in different slippers.

You might think my retreat back down the drive a little ungainly. Cowardly, even. But if you've ever spent months building up to something, and then bottled it… no, *reconsidered* it in a split, last-minute second to be pointless and petty self-indulgence, and looked into eyes that reflect your own inadequacy, you'll forgive me for wanting away.

I've got a long road ahead, barely half a bottle of Jack to hand, and less than three hours of the clock to consume both.

GO WEST, YOUNG MAN...

A hundred miles to Uig, and I manage less than ten before pulling over.

My legs are shaking, and anything close up shimmers with an intensity that blurs all detail. Ahead, beyond the next bend in the road, stands the autumnal profile of Carn Ghluasaid, and its smaller cousin, Meall Dubh.

I've no choice but to pull into the next lay-by, this one birthed from an imposing slab of bedrock, the hills lost behind battalions of larch.

I think back to that doorstep. There he was, submissive in a way I could never have imagined, yet I couldn't get a word out. Just stood there, frozen inside the arc of that quiet, strange mewling.

Years ago, on a day out at the football in Norwich, I stood in *The Coach & Horses* on Thorpe Road with Paul, a good friend from work.

We were having one of our 'days'. Beer, burgers and the footy; male bonding of a type made even more enjoyable by Paul's wicked sense of humour, his coarse Anglo-Saxon turns of phrase, and occasional glimpses of passionate humanism.

He'd just been to the pictures with his wife to see *Titanic*. His eyes filled up as he spoke of his shock at how the crew had ruthlessly prioritised the safety of the wealthiest passengers. "It was so bloody blatant! That people could be so callous! I could hardly watch. The lights came up, and I must have looked like a right blubbering cunt, walking out with all the other women still crying at your fella going under."

The match tickets, won by either one of us through the works' raffle, were a passport to a different version of myself. Enlightened pub chat (see above), surrounded by the yellow and green of other City fans, seemed a mile away from life with Carol, and several secretly cherished steps closer to an imagined, more comfortable variant.

I spoke about my anger regarding a situation at work, describing the behaviour of some middle manager that week; a man (and they were almost all men) who epitomised the brash muscularity of those who built gas platforms in the North Sea at a rate no longer seen. I claimed I would confront him when I next had the chance.

Paul snorted messily into his pint. "Oh, come on. Really? You'd really do that? I don't fucking think so."

I looked up from my own glass.

"Martin. It'll never happen. *You're a sheep in sheep's clothing.*"

And here I am, thirty years later, lacking the balls to properly confront my wife's killer. Shame burns with the ferocity of a street-side immolation.

I look across and down at Trish, leaning her weight against the torso of the JD. I'm not sure if my apology makes any sense to her, or even registers. She's heard so many over the past year. It probably just drops into the dark, watery depths.

Just like DiCaprio.

Everything's happening way too fast. *Bring things down a notch.* At this rate, I'll never make it out of the glen, much less be allowed on the ferry.

When was the last time you had that fluttering in *your* chest? Air struggling to get in, starlings fighting to get out? Mind leaping from the now into inescapable future horrors?

Yep, this is definitely *the* Saturday.

When this type of thing kicks off at home, I reach for the headphones and Harold Budd. And a smooth glass of Speyside; an Aberfeldy or a Cardhu. Here, in the car, I settle instead for a chug on the Jack, and a blast of Lloyd Cole. Nothing that a sunny North-West Highland drive, accompanied by wry, close-to-perfect songwriting, can't begin to treat. '*There for Her*' (the best song Nilsson never wrote), and the shimmering 6/8 of '*Margo's Waltz*'. Trish joins me in the choruses.

I'll add at this point that music held a special place in our relationship. Nurturing and grounding and, along with books and movies, part of the soil in which our early love took root. I date our deepening relationship as much by albums (we met in the year we jointly discovered *Parachutes* and *White Ladder*) as by calendars. Music's divisive too, of course; even now, I may be pushing you away with each selection. If so, perhaps you can substitute our favourites with meaningful music of your own.

So. West once more, and the scenery reasserts its magic. Am Bàthach's flank reaches out to newly laid, pothole-banishing tarmac. Narrow burns flash and spill down the flanks of the South Glen Shiel Ridge in the low-angled morning sun.

I look down to Trish and murmur, "Watershed" as I top the pass and begin the long drop down to Shiel Bridge. Habit again, I'm afraid. One of following an initial recognition of a landmark or feature with ritualised, ironic repetition. The rules by which some entered the canon while others dropped away remain unclear. "Watershed" here (Trish had noted the precise location where waters exercise their last free choice of travel: east to Loch Ness or west to Loch Duich); "Chinese, anyone?" on our journeys across The Fens to visit the boys (the restaurant's Dragon Gate entrance arch stood alone in twenty square miles of reclaimed marshland and shit-scented crops). And let's not forget the bellowed exclamations of "The Horn!" (this accompanied by mandatory sexual leers), on each encounter with the uniquely curved exterior of a cafe stop midway between Dundee and Perth.

Glen Shiel's an extraordinary place. Home to eighteen Munros, all welcoming grassy flanks and, for the most part, generously wide ridges. I smile at the memory of standing on the summit of Sail Chaorainn, exchanging looks with Trish as a solitary walker materialised from a sleet shower, his radio relaying *Test Match Special* from The Oval. Crowds basked beneath a high urban summer a mere few hundred miles to the south while we, amid the ever-changing Highland weather, took shelter at the closed-in summit.

Back in the car, I salute the Forcan Ridge, turn up the Glenelg road and park up at the Mam Ratagan viewpoint. So here I sit, Trish on the picnic bench, the car a few metres behind me on the other side of the road. *Are drivers in the glen below distracted by her glint?*

Beyond the Five Sisters lie the open, broader peaks of Affric. Another ritual rises unbidden: our assertion that this place, despite its utter impracticality, would be the site of our forever house. I didn't plan it, but that's how urges work, I guess.

I place an unopened Highland Park on the picnic table, undo the urn, and pull out a spoon and a Ziploc bag marked '#20/10'. The breeze at my back, I work carefully to open the bottle. I'm on a tight schedule, but I'll do this properly.

So. Join me in my only innovation in the face of overwhelming entropy: the Malt Ceremony.

Back in February, aware that both the days and the single malts ahead of me were (quite literally, as it turned out) numbered, I sought advice from the best. Mr James Murray, drink critic and author of *The Whisky Bible*, offered solid guidance on how to pay final tribute to the master distillers. Needless to say, the finer points of cork and stopper handling have suffered in proportion to my growing consumption, but this week? This week I'm redeeming myself and returning them to their purest form, with the most indulgent of malts.

I pick up Murray's *Bible* (the 2007 edition) and turn to page 127. With my free hand, I run my thumb over the raised moulding of the bottle's Celtic-styled insignia. I read aloud from Jim's summary, taking care not to push my right thumb too far into the slim volume's binding (the old librarian in me still brings out my need to treat books kindly), and savour his descriptions of **n**ose, **t**aste, **f**inish and **b**alance:

> **Highland Park 25 Years Old** *db* (**96**)
> **n**24 *nectar. Hang on? Is nectar this good? Honeycomb and toffee-apple combined and lightened slightly with a squeeze of tangerine and a near perfect stratum of delicate smoke. As I once apparently famously described a younger HP: not a jagged edge to be found...;* **t**24 *sits on the palate as if owning the place and sings: the weight is perfect so both the big barley notes are at full throttle, yet remain on the lightish side and heavier oaky-nutty-marzipan offers the weight. Meeting in the middle are warming spices and a swirl of smoke.* **f**24 *the age shows, but as if botoxed. There are no cracks to the sheened honeycomb and in the balance, as any great HP should be, the bitter-sweet battle is won hands-down by the sweetness.* **b**24 *HP Ambassador Gerry Tosh's hitman has got me and I've gone to heaven... this is the best bottling of HP25 I've ever come across, in this form eclipsing the astonishing 18. You have to work overtime to find fault with this. I suggest you grab a bottle and try.* **50.7%**

The clock's ticking, and I've left my dram glass in the car. So be it. I raise the bottle to my nose and seek out the faint citrus scent. Ironically, the open air is helping; the competing smell of my clothes and skin is muted by the breeze.

I lower the bottle to my lips and take a first full nip. After the Jack, the texture and smoothness on my tongue is extraordinary.

I hold it in my mouth, and feel its heat grow. I'm proud of this new-found restraint (don't laugh). Looking across and down at Trish, and the enamel shine of the seahorse on her closest face, I finally allow it to pass down my throat.

While the heat moves down to my chest, I reach over to #20/10, lick the spoon to moisten it, and ease it gently between the thin blue plastic seals at the top of the bag. When I draw it out, the spoon is dulled by a fine coating of ash.

I raise it to my mouth.

Close my lips down on it.

Draw it gently back.

I recite the usual words in my mind, slowly and with care, then bring the Highland Park back to my lips for one more pull.

At the next swallow, my mind races back through the glen, past the dam and along the Moriston. I'm back home. Hear Trish's barefoot tread on bare, black oak floor. Feel the movement of air as she passes me, reaches out her hand, inviting me to the bedroom.

But then? Then the smell of burning paper, the charred ruin of a donor card. A stained plate by the kitchen sink.

I shake my head free and look across the head of Loch Duich. In front of me, ridge follows ridge, geology folding into the same familiar patterns we toasted together for years with flasks and filled rolls. Wisps of cloud hover a few hundred metres above Beinn Fhada, but otherwise, the tops are completely open.

Just the right amount of beauty for two. But I'm alone.

To preserve the isolation of the moment, I bring it to a close. Cut it off, seal it, before any intrusion materialises from the glen below. I return sachet and spoon to the urn, and press the cork back into the bottle. I cross quickly back to the car.

That's it. Me, Trish, and the Five Sisters. And no one else. I've shared her far too much as it is.

My throat tightens as I look at the clock on the dashboard. No more stops allowed, or I'll be late. Only time for glances now.

The shoreline at Eilean Donan, dark seaweed greens and browns exposed by the low tide beneath the causeway; the view back east from the Skye Bridge; gyppo caravans still blighting the lay-bys north of Broadford; the imperious Sgurr Nan Gillean over the moor from the Sligachan turn-off. I continue west to the junction of the single-track road to Carbost, The *Old Inn* (our favourite walkers' pub on the island) and the Talisker Distillery.

Another memory – the outrageous and unexpected tattie-bogles punctuating that route, beginning with 'The Stig' standing with crossed arms and opaque-visored crash helmet. Life-size scarecrows, dressed as zombies, ballet dancers, even Cybermen. Bloody brilliant! Take a look on Google Images for yourself. Borne of that same spirit in which the public voted to name a new polar research vessel *Boaty McBoatface*. (When the authorities lost their nerve and plumped for the safer *Sir David Attenborough*, I came close to defacing my passport.)

The last thirty miles pass without incident, me finishing the Jack while Trish sits in the front seat, choosing to ignore any occasional lapse in my driving. Not that she can see much, her eyeline being at least nine inches below the dashboard.

The drop down to the CalMac ferry terminal, viewed across Uig Bay from the high eastern approach, still feels new. We only came here twice before; each visit a poor man's 'Plan B' for unclimbable, weathered-in hills.

Befitting late October, traffic is light. Passing the Mace store and the terminal ticket office, I slow for an inspection of booking papers and pull into Lane 3. One less conversation left to navigate. Just the store at Tarbert and the housekeeping staff at Borve to go (your good self excepted).

Protected from view on two sides by camper vans, I nip out of the car and raid the boot for my last bottle of Jack. It's a good job there's no customs checks to worry about – the malts in the boot exceed the value of the bloody car.

The vehicles ahead of me are empty, their passengers no doubt taking advantage of the fine lunch menu at the bar on the pier head. Good luck to them. We went there for food when we were here several years ago, attempting to redeem our lost day on the hills celebrating my fiftieth with some unplanned calorific comfort. One of the many unspoken rules between us was *'When on the coast, eat fish'*; so, "Haddock and chips twice, please." What arrived, a full thirty minutes later, would not have looked out of place in the Blue Boar services at Watford Gap, circa 1960. The batter alone had a half-life extending well beyond the Demise of Man.

I glance to left and right before bringing the JD to my lips for a quick slice. Ahh. Whiskey with an 'e'; the number-one choice of daylight hours.

Half an hour later, I sport a most considered and sincere smile for the young lady in her orange high-vis and bright red lipstick just at the boarding ramp. Access secured, I glance down to Trish and accept her quiet congratulations on not making an arse of myself.

If it's all the same to you, I'll skip the details of the 'roll on, roll off' part of the journey west; mainly due to there being none. Unwilling to mix with my fellow passengers, and with no one with whom to share any view, I simply stay in the car. *'No view, no point'* (Rule #250 or so?).

Three hours later, I point the car up the ramp and onto the Harris mainland.

Right. Provisions.

While researching this trip, I fell in love with Munro's Store. It had posted news of a recent meat cabinet malfunction on

Facebook. Accompanying the apology was a confirmatory photo of shiny-steeled emptiness. What's not to love about a place like that?

I park up near the tourist information centre and complete my food shopping. Cheese, bananas, bread, coffee. Local eyebrows rise when I point behind the counter and ask for six bottles of Jack, but I guess a late sale of alcohol before the obligatory Sunday shutdown is too good to challenge.

Job done, I point the car to the steep rise south out of the village. It's not as if I haven't studied the route multiple times. But the nerves kick in anyway.

Have you ever felt that things, cosmic things, are on the verge of getting their own back after a recent run of unexplained or undeserved good luck? Maybe an unsolicited phone call offering you a cancellation at the hairdressers, followed by the surprisingly successful conclusion of a conversation about salary. Or maybe the logging chainsaw, stubbornly resistant to your usual exhausting attempts to start it, screams into life on the first pull of the cable, followed later by a highly satisfying session in bed with a loved one. It doesn't have to be the big things. No; just the feeling that, with luck running just one or two notches above the norm, the Great Leveller lies in wait around the next corner, preparing to tear organs from your body and feed them to swine.

I don't mean to overdramatise here (despite having just done so), but if there's one recurring nightmare that invariably plays out for me in real life (and the reason why it continues to be so resilient to all efforts to dream better), it's how useless I am at navigating while driving. Over the years I've developed a pretty good sense of direction on the hills, able to judge height and distance to summits or other landmarks with uncanny accuracy. But put me behind the wheel *to pretty much anywhere new*, and I'll let myself, and those with me, down every time. Every bloody time.

So here we go. Cue the A868/A859 junction, and my essential aid to nerve-free navigation (aka the next bottle of Jack).

I'm immediately in rock-strewn heathland. Passing places (for my money one of the ten most important inventions of the modern era) outnumber dwellings; mostly crofts and slightly neglected roadside bungalows. I shudder to imagine the fun to be had behind those doors on the Lord's Day. *Scrabble, anyone, but no double word scores for 'blow job' or 'tit', remember?* A small Perspex bus stop, complete with tattered computer chair, proclaims its repurposing as a tourist information point. Hilarious.

Four miles on, the road takes a distinct inland turn. The moors are truly rugged, dominated by outcrops of ancient Lewisian gneiss, their bent and twisted geology exposed like a giant brain freed forever from its primeval owner's skull.

The air around me darkens with the loss of glinting sea. Still no trees; nothing except contorted rock scraping the underbelly of the sky. The road widens, then shrinks back to the width of the car, edged above the worse corners and gullies by low Armco barriers.

Then I get my first sight of the North Atlantic. The monopoly of greens, greys and browns is broken by a strip of gleaming lead blue nestling, about a mile further on, in the shallow gap between two low hills. Power and telephone lines weave from the hillside to join the road, suggesting the real wilderness is over. I'm jarred back to the twenty-first century by a clattering cattle grid and the incongruity of screaming yellow plastic above another bus shelter. Boundary fencing and gates return. Double track, a narrowing causeway, and then back to the width of a large car or small lorry. Far off to my right, under an area of darker sky, are the flanks of the North Harris hills. *The Clisham's in there somewhere.*

Then come the first hints of golden sand. I can't help myself. "See, Trish? See?"

Michael, a friend who offered me the single most definitive and clinching advice on retirement (*"The day you ask yourself, Have I got enough? and Have I had enough?, and answer, Yes to both, is the day to quit"*), regularly described how much he loved his weeks up here, walking the moors with a gillie to the most isolated and atmospheric lochans for freshwater quarry. But it was when he moved on to describe the beaches that his eyes shone.

I've seen pictures, of course, but always had my doubts, living in the Age of Photoshop and an overachieving, faintly suspicious VisitScotland marketing team.

My pulse quickens. I snap off another mouthful of Jack. I was wrong to doubt.

Nearly there.

I reduce my speed in deference to the increasingly frequent and nonchalant wanderings of sheep. Closing in on Borve, I mute the music, telling myself to sharpen up.

Past a primary school (Sgoil Sheileboist), and the dunes are a mere arm's length from my door.

Past a campsite and burger van (refreshingly absent the forced signwriting humour of '*Burger, She Wrote*', '*Only Food and Sauces*' or – most cringeworthy – '*Phat Phuc Noodle Bar*' of the more world-weary mainland).

Past a cottage garden, the fractured image of a toddler pedalling a bright red car stop-motioned through a flicker of fence slats.

The sign to The Broch instructs from an impressive drystone wall. Beyond it, a narrow gravel track rises up the hill before disappearing beyond a hairpin some fifty metres on.

I indicate left, to no one in particular, and pull the nose of the car off the road.

I reach over and place my palm on Trish.

Neither of us feels the need to say anything.

LOOK THE PART; BE THE PART

The place does not disappoint. Three soaring storeys of yellow sandstone and grey-and-lilac granite. Curved and smooth, huge base stones support smaller, more intricate masonry below a circular turfed roof. And the final touch on this side: a footbridge over a dry trench offers access to a huge wooden door.

I giggle (yes, *giggle*) as I walk slowly from the car, phone to ear, and peer further around the structure. Rhododendron plantings and other small trees mirror the curve of the rising stonework, challenging the more barren hillside to do its worst.

And then, there it is.

It's as if someone's taken a peerlessly sharp blade, cleaved the place from head to foot, and then resealed the insulted structure with the most beautiful and polished crystal. Nine enormous windows plunge down the length of the tower, reflecting the dusky outlines of the bay at my back.

This is the feature that excited Trish so much.

"Hello? Borve Estates? Just to let you know I've arrived."

While I wait, I make myself respectable. Crunch several Extra Strong Mints; push myself into a heavy, full-length tweed jacket, unworn until this moment and intended to bestow upon me the required trustworthy air of a man who does *not* stink of alcohol through every hidden pore. I clear the front seat into the boot, hoping that Trish will recognise the need for, and forgive, her brief loss of liberty.

Mr Fraser ("Please call me Robert") arrives with the key a few minutes inside the promised ten. A tall man wearing a field jacket and khaki trousers, he steps from his Land Rover with a confidence that only those at ease with the land around them can ever possess. I immediately envy and fear his unapologetic self-assurance.

We approach the entrance together, all small talk and journey inquiries.

"Yes, that's correct. The booking was for myself and my partner, but I'll be spending the week alone."

Robert receives this news with what I imagine to be his customary delicacy; yet also with a slight but noticeable increase in the pace of his delivery. *Nothing like a bit of masked emotional discomfort to cut down the man-to-man chit-chat.*

Inside, he points out the luxury Highland hamper, the size of an Alsatian's dog basket, sitting on the small dining table in the kitchen, but flounders noticeably a few minutes later when showing me around the master bedroom with its boutique chocolates and crystal flutes. "Ah, yes," he volunteers, "the two bottles of Bollinger are downstairs in the fridge."

I nod knowingly, wrestling with how Trish must have placed these additional orders without my knowledge (the extra dozen bottles of Innis & Gunn's Gunnpowder IPA present less difficulty for both Robert and me, given their dramatically lower levels of conjugal symbolism).

Instructions and keys delivered, my host recrosses the moat (ha!), leaving me to wave from the door, preparing to bring everything in.

Let's get this hideous bloody coat off, and shut the rest of the damned world out.

THIS PLACE!

Trish would have loved it here. *Does* love it.

First, the extravagance of the room layout. Ground floor: utility room leading to kitchen-diner. Middle floor: lounge (sea and hill facing) and bathroom. Top floor: master bedroom. Glance up to the high, twelve-panelled ceiling, and you'll see the skylight promising access to the unpolluted night sky – right above the bloody bed! This whole place for just two people.

Does interior design press your buttons? Trish was hooked. Kelly Hoppen design books under the coffee table. Magazines. A Sky Box full of George Clarke's Geordie catchphrase – "That's *oonbelievabul*!" – and Sarah Beeny's knowing glances at resistant, laughable clients.

She spent years shouting at couples on those house-building and renovation shows, taking mock offence (well, taking the piss, actually) at their errors in design and project management. She particularly loved to hate those folk who, having sought to appear on national TV, ignored advice, made a complete hash of things, and ended up with a rubbish house and the credit-card debt of an unrestrained caviar addict who'd just paid off his deposit for the first tourist space flight to Mars. Trish's 'thumbs down' at the end of each show (there were more failures than successes, to her mind) carried the weight of a Caligula or Nero. This would be followed by her summary of what they *should* have done, to the sound of road traffic and the occasional drunk wandering beneath our modest IKEA-furnished top-floor Aberdeen flat.

Empowered by her conviction that she could do a better job, even without the help of experts, she took the plunge (and when she plunged, you had to stand back, or the backwash of her entry into intended waters would knock you off your feet), negotiated a career break, and bought first one, then a further property to gut, restore and sell. Wageless for fourteen months, she sold each for a profit exceeding the salary she'd forgone, returning to work vindicated and a stone and a half lighter. And my love for her, already at its highest high point, soared further still.

So, three trips to the car and a couple of ascents of the underlit beechwood treads of the spiral staircase, and I'm done.

Cheese and bread are enfridged with the complimentary smoked salmon; bananas and whiskies are recumbent with the equally complimentary oatcakes on the worktop.

My toilet bag, a faux-leather hangover from my days at the Aberdeen B&B, looks out of its depth in the luxurious bathroom. The gleaming roll-top freestanding bath will remain, I suspect, sadly parched, given the competing luxury of the adjacent walk-in shower, completely at home in its proudly self-conscious, slate-backed elegance.

In the lounge, my favourite dram glass sits on the coffee table between the sofa and the TV, next to Trish and a buff cardboard folder. I rotate her slightly, until my favourite of the four seahorses turns to face me.

The box sets go next to the Blu-ray player. My manbag, holding what used to be my portable writing studio (iPad, charger, earphones, notebook and pen), but nowadays functions only as a portable movie screen, sits on one of the two chairs angled to take advantage of the landscape outside.

It's approaching six, and the huge panels of glass frame each end of the faint, stubborn ribbon of light that runs the length of the horizon, joining sea with darkened shore. Raised masses of land, a few miles away to left and right, complete the scene.

I pull out a biro and two sheets of paper from the folder, and stand barefoot on the underheated oak flooring, six inches from the monumental panes. I've already worked on List #1: each whisky paired with a day and date. I don't need space for notes, but it should still be easy, each morning, to assign a confirmatory mark against each line. Knowledge gained, item procured, whisky consumed. A well-managed list keeps the stars hung in the sky, don't you agree? Holds them in place (to hell with gravity) with the scaffolding of an ever-growing number of 'ticks'.

I've read and reread Jim Murray. Twelve bottles of malt sit on the floor at the edge of the room (I want to say corner, but all the rooms reflect the circular exterior of the building), purchased from specialist shops and websites. This leaves two bottles of Highland Park (one already opened), Trish, and my tumbler of choice (heavy pewter base, all stags and thistles) on the coffee table.

So, then. The Ceremony. The full one.

Like any other ritual, no matter what's being enacted or what that action signifies, it's the thoughts and motivations of those conducting it that fascinate most. Even heinous and unforgivable behaviour has its origin point somewhere, right? We should always remain curious about *that*, even as we might turn away in disgust or despair. I guess what I'm trying to say is that, while not wishing to apologise, I'm hoping I still have your attention and that you'll continue to think of me kindly.

So first, I lift the glass and take a full mouthful of the golden liquid. In a repeat of this morning at the Mam, I hold it in my mouth, feel its burn build on my tongue, then swallow.

Misery has never tasted so good.

I force my eyes open, pour a second measure, and place the glass on the table.

I turn to Trish, reach inside and remove the remaining sachets from the urn, setting each one down and sorting them by their numbered labels. This step used to take bloody ages. Just eight left now, and it's done in seconds.

I return all but one of the sachets to the urn ('Trish' again, once the lid is back on), orient the bottom edge of #20/10 with the closest edge of the coffee table, and lay the spoon next to it (concave side upwards, the handle stretching away from me).

The sachet betrays nothing of its earlier use.

I close my eyes. My first ujjayi breath since Ken's driveway.

What shall I focus on? Yoga teaches an emptying of the mind at such moments, but my ritual demands the opposite. I need cheering up. So it's Trish, standing in the lounge, imaginary microphone in hand, impersonating Macy Gray and all her wonderful phrasing and gravelly, just-woken-up-after-a-night-filled-with-wonderful-sex voice. One of Trish's finest sexifilarious moments of recent years. It always does the trick, bringing a smile to my face. Even now. It's right up there with her Elvis.

I open my eyes, manoeuvre the remainder of #20/10 onto the spoon, lift it slowly, respectfully, tip its contents into my mouth, and close my lips to remove any remaining residue. Before the tears come, I swallow, count to five, and then reach for the glass. I wash her down in one.

James Murray makes no reference to the resulting balance of flavours and nose after a mumbled "I love you" and the salty onslaught of tears.

I move on, relaxing a little in the knowledge that List #2 has within it the solution to the rest of my evening. Seven TV shows that Trish and I rated 'The Best'. What more evidence of twenty years together is needed than that we had little trouble reaching agreement on them?

Seven shows. Seven nights in The Broch. Perfect. Assuming, that is, I can assign each show to a day. I just need to work out how. Do I match them to my best estimate of my mood as the week progresses? Or (like a hoarded Malteser with a Dalwhinnie eighteen-year-old) perhaps to my expectations of the match to the whiskies? It's a tough one.

Here's the list:

Battlestar Galactica
Breaking Bad
Justified

Sons of Anarchy
Sopranos, The
True Detective (Season One only)
Wire, The

What would be on your list? Perhaps you're not a fan of what is now referred to as 'long-form drama'. Perhaps your list would comprise the movies you've most enjoyed with a loved one, or just those you would most want to experience when you know you have a week to live.

At the risk of an informality bordering on flippancy, I decide to say to hell with it – they're all good. In the interest of time, I ask Trish. She immediately suggests *Justified*. I top up my glass and sing along, with all of our customary actions, to the theme tune as Episode One begins.

Later, bringing the second bottle of twenty-five-year-old closer, I pause the player for a few seconds to consider the wisdom of combining two bottles and my manbag with the staircase to the bedroom. The four-poster is glorious, no doubt, but I can't remember if there's a TV in there.

Easily solved. I err on the side of personal safety and open the second bottle, confident that before dawn I'll make it to the end of Season One on this lovely, comfortable sofa.

G'night, y'all

HOME VISIT
EARLY AUGUST 2018

"Just one more second. That's it." Another photo of the boys; this time with their partners, Lauren and Anna, and his little granddaughter Mia. "Trish'll really love that one." He pockets his phone, and then switches to his stupidest talking-to-a-toddler voice. "Isn't that right, Mia?"

The little girl pulls the last piece of paper napkin from her hair. Her new teeth flash, and are then outdone by her impish grin.

They're in The Jolly Sailors, perched about ten metres from the cliff edge overlooking Pakefield Beach. Clouds still threaten rain, but there's been nothing yet. He's managed his walk along the seafront with Kieron and Lauren pretty well, with only a few simple untruths thrown into the conversation to keep Trish embedded in their present.

Sitting opposite Conor, he adheres consistently to the story of Trish's parallel visit to her own parents and sister back in Aberdeen. "'Two birds, one stone' is how we think of it," he tells them, pausing only briefly to consider the implied slight. "Trish is so busy, she's not been able to take any leave for months, and what little she has, apparently, she prefers to avoid spending on long days in the car."

One of his more credible deceits.

Travelling down by train offers perfect cover for Trish's possession of the car. It also avoids him driving anywhere with friends or family on board. Doing no harm to others is perhaps his last remaining moral precept.

He's dependent on lifts between Steve and Donna's, where he's staying, and the homes of his family. This consequence, an abuse of goodwill, he chooses not to dwell on.

Later, he sits with his parents in their small bungalow nestled in the grounds of the residential home. Previous visits offered him or Trish the chance to share photos of their recent holidays on his tablet, or pictures of The Schoolhouse's garden; something both parents seem to enjoy.

Family, in its growing number of generations, has always been everything to his parents. Their interest in Trish shows no sign of diminishing. His lies to them are louder than most others, given their deteriorating hearing.

Steve and Donna welcome him back every evening. In their guest bedroom, he reaches to his rucksack by the bedside. He withdraws his nightly sachet and one of four half-bottles of Glenmorangie, again navigating carefully around any threatened breach in his ritual. He does all he can to maintain his appearance of happiness. It is his last visit, after all.

He cherishes every moment of his time with the boys. Watches their movements, the ebb and flow of the space between them and their partners. Takes every opportunity to praise them, pump them for every storied detail of their recent lives. Clings on, as long as he can, to their greeting and parting hugs.

When his train pulls out from the station to head back north, he has just two or three minutes to compose himself before the guard asks to check his tickets.

He'll try his best to write this down.

CHAPTER 2

SUNDAY 21ST OCTOBER 2018

I may not know a lot about a lot of things,
but I do know how to blow shit up.

(Boyd Crowder, Justified)

A SURPRISE MATTRESS AT AN EVEN MORE SURPRISING ALTITUDE

I don't know how I got here, but, well, here I am, supine, inside the deep oak corners of the emperor-sized bed. Either those stairs aren't as dangerous as I thought, or my dormant scrambling skills, honed on several of Scotland's tougher peaks, are yet to entirely desert me. If I remember later, I'll look for crampon marks.

But I made it, yes? Through *Saturday*.

My promise to Trish, my promise to myself, still breathes and stretches. I'm pretty smug, actually.

The trick now, though, is to surrender to the full, unhurried ache of a week here. I don't feel it yet, but I think I will; that urge to jump (no pun intended) to my finale.

I don't think I'm made that way, but if I were, such an act would be a betrayal. A mortal sin of dilution and cowardice. Or is getting this all over with quickly the braver option? I've no idea.

Do you believe in shortcuts? In their value? How many have you taken, only to find that reaching your destination or outcome quicker somehow deprives it of its attraction; cheapens its original purpose, or the taste of its achievement?

I still have a bit of the old Victorian work ethic knocking around inside me somewhere (thanks, Mum). If you earn it, you enjoy it more – something like that. Hard work and focus trumps, or at least masks, any lack of natural talent.

I have many natural lacks, actually (thanks for asking). A number of them material. They, rather than my surpluses, have shaped my life profoundly. e.g....

Staying power. *When the tough get going, I peel off from the pack and look for something more comfortable.*

Competitive spirit. *If someone is willing to hurt me to get the ball, I'll allow them to have it (so, yes, Paul was right all those years ago).*

Belief in the absence of an afterlife. *Although convinced of the bullshit of religion, I sometimes feel variations in internal pressure that suggest that perhaps, after all, we're all more than mere skin and bone.*

No; if I work to make this week happen the way it should, I'll get my reward at the end. That's one of the reasons I need you with me: for you to see my next error taking shape, and distract me from its path. I might not even know what you've done, how you've helped. But *you'll* know.

In the days when I had friends, I'd spend hours apologising for emails sent after my second Jack. I'd read indignant reactions to each erroneous claim or poorly worded sentiment, and feel like crap until able to follow up each panic-written apology with a face-to-face one.

If you'd have sat next to me in those times, gently but firmly lifted my hands from the keyboard, looked me knowingly in the eye? Well, imagine the difference you would have made. Even now – *particularly* now – if you see me about to do anything especially stupid, just stand at the edge of my sight and raise a hand or finger in warning. Give me reason to pause and shave off some idiot risk.

Do you have someone who does that for you, as Trish often did for me?

Raylan and Boyd wove their way through similar challenges of friendship and duty by the end of *Justified* last night. Walton Goggins, while just one of a cast with great lines, delivers every word he's given with a wide-eyed conviction and truth that blew us away. He knows himself, exploits each of his weaknesses to get what he wants; yet, in a triumph of writing and acting, remains deeply vulnerable and capable of love. I'm still, I admit, sorely tempted by the possibility of 'being' Boyd Crowder. Such a swagger.

Trish sits next to me, on the bedside table. Glaze shines off her body and lid, caressed by light from the bay and the gentler illumination of the skylight. The heavy cloud cover of the previous evening has blown over, and there's more than a suggestion that grey will shift further to blue. The irony of promised sunshine.

Today, the 21st, is Trish's birthday. I head downstairs to the bathroom, mentally rehearsing what I'll do to mark the event. Other than burning this place to the ground.

PEEL OFF THE SCAB, AND SEASON GENEROUSLY

The dead are stubbornly hard to reach, but they respond to our cries best when they arrive overbrimmed with anguish or its opposite. This morning is probably going to involve a lot of the former, and pretty much none of the latter.

You have been warned. If you're not in the mood for this, I understand. Really. Hearing of other people's grief is like listening to tales of other people's children. That said, I lack the stamina to keep this up all day, so maybe just skip this part and rejoin me this afternoon. But I'd love you with me, if only to force me to complete what's needed.

It's not a case of turning a glass upside down on a flat surface and going through the whole pantomime of asking for messages. Or of palms clasped, beseeching the mercy of a God that claims to care. I can still distinguish between grief and imbecility, and anyway, death simply doesn't work that way. Never has.

I'm back on the sofa, with one of my hard drives hooked up to the home cinema. On my lap are perhaps two dozen photos, each liberated from their frames. Trish features in them all. Wedding day (ours). Family gatherings (hers and mine). Wedding day (Kieron and Lauren's). And at the bottom of the pile, the one of Trish and The Gimp.

I should probably say more about that last one. If she hadn't looked so bloody gorgeous that day, I would have left it at home. But there's something else; something special about how she looks out from that picture. It's perhaps the photo that most captures her day-to-day persona, or attitude, or (cheese alert) essence. It was taken at a photographer's on George Street in the early noughties (her aunt had given her parents a ruby-wedding gift of a studio shoot).

I think we'd been married for about a year. Yes. Yes, that's right; it's my wedding suit. Here, look. Her left hand reaches across and rests high on my right arm as we both look into the camera. Her eyes, her face – hell, her *everything* – is lit up. She just *glows*. Her make-up is light and she wears her hair short, shaped beautifully to follow the curves of her face. I, on the other hand, stand there in a manner that has given birth to arguably my least attractive nickname.

The Gimp.

It was taken in the summer. Hay-fever season. Trish looks immaculate in a slapped-baby-pink satin off-the-shoulder cocktail dress. I, face swollen, eyes almost shut, smile apologetically and weakly, looking like a moron. A self-medicating fifteen-year-old picked up from a methadone dispensary, asked to dress up in grown-up clothes that don't quite fit, and told to make a happy face.

Oh dear. Let's move on.

I lay out the prints on the coffee table, creating a mosaic that, mercifully, hides my own ruinous image.

The next hour goes by, TV remote in one hand and Jack in the other, moving through the hard-drive collection of our pictures. The photos on the coffee table remain at the edge of my vision as I scroll down the screen.

The first collection, from summer 2001, shows us hosting Mum and Dad on their first visit north. Trish sports a denim jacket, jeans, and a smile that could knock jumbos from the sky. One, taken on the sea wall at Aberdeen harbour, reminds me of how, thirty minutes later, the six of us scurried back to the car after John, Trish's dad, keen to show us his intimate relationship with The Dons, forced a door at the back of the Donald Stand and set off the stadium alarms.

More follow. Our first holiday together in Tenerife. Our first trip to the North-West Highlands.

It's when I reach August 2002 that the morning hits the skids.

Trish, posed with one outstretched hand on the upright of an ornate four-poster, swathed in gold evening dress, a delicate silk shawl dropping below one shoulder and around the other, a matching clutch bag in her other hand, looks out at me from the screen. Moments before our wedding.

It's the first time I've seen it since her death.

How is it that my heart doesn't just up and fail?

They talk in Formula 1 about the gravitational forces that drivers invite as they brake and accelerate. Four Gs, five Gs. Multiple times a lap. But they train for it. They frankly, I think, live for it. But I've spent most of the past year doing everything I can to *avoid* situations that conjure those disruptive and burdensome forces.

Not speaking to people.

Not looking at photos.

And here I am, pushing myself around each blind corner with every nudge of the remote, without flame-retardant overalls, or stewards standing by to pull me from the inevitable wreckage. *Where's the damn safety car when you need it?*

Jack and snot dribble down into my beard. Months of drinking to forget, and now this. Scrambling to remember. *I told you it wouldn't be pretty.*

The TV goes to standby, fed up with waiting for a next command that doesn't come.

A couple of years ago, I asked Trish what her own most treasured moments of our time together were. I was convinced they would be a small number of what we referred to as our 'red-letter days'. Our first visit to Paris together? Sitting on the ridge of Stromboli after dark, watching and feeling the shock of constant explosions around us? Walking in the Sacred Valley, or escaping the hubbub of Cairo to sit in the desert and look back at the pyramids? Adventures captured on film, or digitally.

Her answer surprised me.

"I don't know. But I don't think they're the obvious ones. Of course, I've loved our holidays. Our wedding day; that was brilliant. But it's not them. It's snogs. Our lazy Saturday mornings in bed. And that time when we were both really stressed out over the divorce, when it just seemed like everything was getting on top. That day when you said to me… do you remember what you said?"

I shook my head.

"I was really freaking out, and you put your arm around me, and you said – you looked into my eyes and said, 'The only two people in this relationship are you and me.'"

So. Not one of her favourite moments has been captured on camera. That's partly what makes this exercise so bloody hard. Perhaps that should always be true. For everyone, I mean. Maybe cameras and phones come out at exactly the wrong moments.

Trish cried the day we completed the Inca Trail; my image-packed camera stolen hours later from an innocent-looking Aguas Calientes bar. Maybe, looking back, that mattered less to each of us than we realised. Maybe, somehow, all our photos have always been for others, not for us. They exist, so I brought them. Yet if we had never taken them in the first place, how different would I feel sitting here now?

I'm too upset to work that one through.

Does any of this ring true for you? What parts of your own life, your connections to the lives of those around you, are cemented into place through your collected visual record? You might consider simply closing your eyes, just now, and seeking out those unrecorded moments that mean the most.

When I next raise my head, I look out and up. Clouds are being shifted at some pace around the sky, suggesting that if rain is anywhere near, it will be here soon. The wind is starting to play its symphonies around the outer stones of the building, racing in and out of deeply recessed windows.

I need a break, so head to the kettle on the ground floor. I make sure to leave room in the coffee for a finger of Jack.

It's barely eleven, and the sky is definitely darker. I still need to calm down, so out comes the iPad. This place has great Wi-Fi, so I open YouTube and find the extended loop of Harold Budd's '*A Minute, a Day, No More*'. Have you ever listened to any of his stuff? The man's a genius, and I love his collaborations with Robin Guthrie. Trish was never a fan, but I've always found his music incredibly soothing.

It works well enough to allow me to sit back in the sofa, and retrieve the piece I wrote a couple of years ago about our first visit to the *Shahbazz*, up on Rose Street. The moment when I took perhaps the biggest chance of my life. At least once, you see, I was a man of courage.

I'm within touching distance of equilibrium when YouTube interrupts Mr Budd with a bloody Jason Donovan advert for Cadbury Darkmilk. Bastards! I've lost it again.

I have to get out.

HOW TO GET WET AND INFLUENCE PEOPLE

Ten minutes later, my backpack reassuringly weighted down with Trish and a square-bottled litre of Jack, I turn to look back at The Broch, rising impressively into brooding skies.

I'd like to say I ventured out because walking clears my head, but that doesn't happen these days.

There *was* a moment, around Easter, when I sought to re-enter our hillwalking past. I'd have a go at a Munro or two. The nearby peaks at the eastern end of Glen Shiel were an obvious choice. I made it to the summit plateau of Carn Ghluasaid without too much problem, despite the wheezing and my acid-drenched legs. It was approaching the summit cairn that screwed everything up. No Trish to urge on those last few steps so she could be the first to tap the cairn with the end of her walking pole. In the five minutes that followed, I drained my hip flask, willing a feeling of emptiness back to one of awe (you can see eighteen other peaks from that spot; gorgeous in lilac-hued late spring air). But I had no such luck. When I got home, I just dumped hiking; added it to the list of activities headed 'Things I Did Only With Trish That I Will Never Do Again'.

If *you'd* have been up there with me, warmth wrapping its arms around you on each easing of the corrie breeze, you might well have offered me some kind of opposing argument; stopped me cursing myself for inviting such painful heartburn (from equally bilious excesses of whisky and reminiscence) while still three hours from the car.

I should have known better. But back then, a mere four or five months ago, there was still a part of me that wondered if there was a way back, a point where the world would regain its normal orientation (at low moments, as is still the case now, I could feel myself sliding off), and if I deserved to reach it.

Instead, now, I avoid everyone. Remove myself from the possibility of that suggestion, no doubt well meant, of 'getting back into the world'. Anyone close enough to say such a thing deserves my gratitude (it's not easy, I suppose), but I still retain the odd uncharitable thought that it's for their own benefit if I stop wallowing in my peculiar and pervasive brand of misery and remove any risk of contagion around the village. A tad harsh, perhaps?

The sky here still looks ominous and the wind has definitely got up from yesterday, but it feels surprisingly mild. I follow the track down to the main road and cross to face any likely traffic. Sunday at midday – should be fine. The only people about are probably already flocked and penned in the free churches at Northton and Leverburgh, or back across at Tarbert.

Remind me to toast them from the sands on their return. I respect their right to worship. And my double right to raise the demon drink to them on the Lord's Day and avoid any unpleasant contact with the vehicles transporting their newly chastened souls.

Breaks in the roadside fencing elude me. Shoreline fields hold small gatherings of sheep (the real sort), their fleeces marked in a manner suggesting any number of trips through Red Arrows air-show contrails. But how to reach the dunes beyond them? I don't trust myself to leap the fence. My physical ineptitude is lore among walkers across Scotland; where barbed wire's involved, I'm lucky my scrotum remains broadly intact rather than hanging, indelicate and bloody, from any number of estate fences.

A little further down the road, tree plantings and a grand sweep of ornamental stone advertise the entrance to the Estate House; a large white building sitting on the ocean fringe.

I should have asked Robert when I had the chance. But The Broch is expensive. Exclusive, even. A brief use of the estate drive should be OK, right?

Decision made.

Gusts of drizzle accompany me past the walled garden and the main house. There's no one around to challenge me. From the gate at the back of the property, it's a short few steps to the bank of the narrow estuary. Five more minutes (the drop from the main road looks even worse from this side) and I'm on the coast proper, four or five feet above the beach on the raised surface of machair.

And what a beach! It stretches perhaps a quarter-mile. A pure, unstained cream, retaining its pale luminescence even when submerged at the shoreline.

Trish and I once walked together along the Morar coastline, returning home from a couple of days' remote walking in Knoydart. We stumbled upon a pair of newlyweds, fully kitted out in their wedding finery, having supplementary wedding pictures taken. Despite our deep sense of intrusion on walking out from the wooded path onto *their* beach, the violation of *their* private moments (*'Hi. I'm Just Cause, and this is my wife, Impediment'*), it's the shock of the sand I recall most.

But this stuff, a few feet below me, is of a different order. In fact, let's just call it white and have done with it. The same colour as that girl's shimmering wedding dress. The tourist board would love me for that.

You tempted yet?

That said, as I half-drop, half-slide down to the beach itself, I feel a second handful of moisture, thrown this time with a subtle increase in power. I pull my hood up, shrug the backpack off my shoulders, remove the Jack, and head south in the direction of the darkest clouds. I feel a drop in temperature on my thighs from the breeze and light rain, as the denim on them begins to darken. The sand, of course, remains stubbornly bright.

Flipping the bottle between each hand in time with my steps, I move further along the bay, hidden now from the road, but on full display to any creature popping its head above the North Atlantic.

Ahead of me, a couple of miles away, is the hill I saw from The Broch last night. Another day, who knows? When the weather's better, I might try it.

Five more minutes, and I've had enough. There's more sand ahead of me, but it's hard work ploughing through rather than over it. The firmer stuff nearer the waterline would be easier, but I like having the shelf of the machair above me.

As a student, driving across Lowestoft Harbour Bridge to begin a night shift at the local Birds Eye factory, I remember how guilty I felt passing the police positioned at either end, seeking to prevent Kent miners from travelling to join pickets in the Nottingham coalfields. I had nothing to hide, of course, but my presence alone generated in me a sense of implied criminality. Looking determinedly straight ahead, I would nervously check for any suggestion that an intercept message had been sent to the far end of the bridge. *Sheep in sheep's clothing again, I guess.*

There's a small outcrop of thick grass protruding into the beach, and I drop down onto the sand below it. Not entirely comfortable, but out of the wind, and a smaller target for the strengthening rain. I'm a little out of breath, truth be told, and it's good to take a moment or two.

Brushing off my hands, I twist the lid of the bottle and take a good long slug. I pull out my phone, resettle my earphones, and scroll to Radiohead. Thom Yorke's voice floats off to the horizon, and the Jack goes down easy.

I look again at the hill to my left, the one that drops down to the sea. Then across to the far right, where the bay is framed by the island of Taransay, itself boasting a further three bright patches of sand on its facing shoreline.

Sitting low, I get a sense of the roll of the ocean. The surface seems relatively peaceful, but I know it's not always this way. Bad weather can be an October staple, but Trish and I agreed to simply hunker down in The Broch through the worst days, feeling great at the prospect of being *in* looking *out*. We'd been on enough Scottish hills to appreciate the unique pleasure of watching extreme bands of rain or snow approach as if to swallow us, only to veer left or right at the last minute. The spectacular glass panes of The Broch looked like a perfect sanctuary, and we looked forward to spending some of our time together on the sofa.

Anyway. Let's change the subject.

An obvious question, then. Have you ever visited this part of the world? Maybe you only picked up this book because you're familiar with the area, and want to see how someone else describes it. You may already be sitting there, brows knitted, lamenting the deficiencies in language and observation I inflict upon your affection for the place.

Or was I closer to the truth when we first met, when hinting that we may have something else in common; a shared emotional landscape? I genuinely don't wish such things on you (I've long since stopped running from the dark, unforgiving corners of such a place); yet, it's true, we're both human. We must share *something* beyond the delight of the first chocolate Hobnob of the day, or the wonder at a perfectly timed retort from Christopher Hitchens. (As an aside, my favourite Hitchslap is from a public debate in which he was challenged on the subject of prayer by a venerable cleric. When confronted with the question of whether he, a self-proclaimed antitheist and libertarian, had ever prayed, he happily conceded that yes, once, he had done so. For a hard-on.)

It's when stationary, with a bottle in hand and a chance to reflect back, that what little empathy for others I might still have bleeds briefly back in.

So I must ask. How is your own relationship with Death? With the dead? Age is a coarse predictor, of course, but I'm happy to speculate that if you're anything from your early twenties to perhaps your mid-sixties, you'll know of these things. I've always thought it odd that it's those with the most loudly expressed conviction of life after death who grieve the most, and have the greatest difficulty in accepting the inevitable. If their beliefs are sincere, and the recently departed failed to commit any but the most unforgivable sins, then surely they should rejoice at their loss? So their grief, or their kind of it, suggests to me either a dim view of said departed's chance of heavenly tenure, or (and I sense this is more the case) a slight dent in the shiny gold alloy of their belief. Each passing like the careless drop of a spanner onto Tutankhamun's polished death mask; scuffed, and bent out of true.

I hope I'm not prying too much (*he said, continuing to pry*), but how have your own brushes with death been? What have they taught you?

It's the *process* that Death employs that craves most of *my* attention, rather than Death itself. The wishing it would stop at the cemetery gate. But when it arrives, accelerated by external agency, it takes years to slow down, pull over and park up. Declare itself done.

It's true, isn't it? Each year you and I pass by the future anniversary of our end, oblivious and uncaring, while we inch closer to it with every sunrise. And that's OK. It's the deal our parents make, wittingly or not, when they unleash us on the world.

It's when a twat with a car in his hand intersects with a lifeline designed to be so much longer that I struggle.

I raise my Jack Daniel's to the horizon. *So here's to you, my friend.*

As if to offer a suitable accompaniment, the rain's set right in. My outstretched hand comes down wet, and my glasses refract multiple blurred images of the seascape. It's not cold, though, and I'm not ready to go back yet.

I don't think I've mentioned it before, but I love 'weather over water'. On the hills, arriving weather fronts can demand the hurried recalculation of plans; choices that rarely result in a decision to just stay put. They can be exhilarating, but at the same time cause genuine and warranted fear. But by the sea, short of tsunami or total immersion, I've always found staying still, becoming an integral part of things as they develop, little short of mesmerising.

As a teenager, at the onset of a storm I'd cycle down below Pakefield cliffs and take up a position by the sea wall. It helped if the arrival of low pressure coincided with my own form of adolescent depression; the kind of self-pitying mood that I was so talented at conjuring. Such safaris possessed a hint of the primordial. If I'd been brought up on the American plains, I would have chased twisters at every perceived slight or romantic rejection. Crops would be more likely flattened by my careless and frequent steps than by any cyclonic arrivals. I guess, in those years, it was my equivalent of those F1 corners again. Pulled by the rage and tear of that type of gravity that feeds off teenage life. Playing chicken with the lightning.

Here, looking out over the Atlantic, there's little threat of extreme weather. I can already see the back edge of the rain system that's been passing overhead.

But I like it here, away from all those photographs. The wind blows, the sea's rhythm remains unbroken. Birds aren't falling from the sky. Hungry quicksands appear singularly absent. Time simply passes.

It's almost upsetting to feel so not upset.

But I think I can engineer a version of the rest of the day that allows me to occupy The Broch without resorting to violence against property.

Oh, and PS: the Jack's finished, so I need to get back.

I'm a bit wobbly getting up, but I'm quite chuffed that I made the effort to get out (let's you and I forget about how it was really a form of cowardly escape). Whenever Trish gave me the choice of a drizzly walk around the head of the glen or an hour with a coffee and a book, I'd often summon the guile needed to deprive her of some exercise, and stay indoors. So this afternoon's fresh-air option, irrespective of the reasons for it, puts me a couple of brownie points up.

I pat the backpack gently, alerting her to the virtue of my actions, and turn back along the beach. My steps up the damp sand to the firmer layers of wet machair are not amongst my most elegant, but they do the trick.

I'm just back on tarmac when a figure approaches me from the house.

His eyes drop to the empty bottle of Jack hanging from my hand. Instinctively, I shuffle the bag from my shoulders and hurriedly place it next to Trish. Pulling my earphones out in readiness, I wince at the clink of glass against ceramic, and the possibility that the sound carries any distance.

It's not Robert, but this younger man exhibits that same sense of confidence. I envy him, truth be told.

"Hello, sir. Can I help you? Are you lost?"

On an existential level, the answer is a pretty definite 'Bloody right I am!', but his question scans more as a euphemism for an assertion of private property rights. I offer a brief, contrite statement of my hope that a stay at The Broch might somehow waive any restrictions he might deem prudent, flashing my front-door key as credentials. That should help – *not.*

I can't fault the boy's politeness. Or his assertion that visitors might want to declare their presence at the estate office on arrival. Every feathered occupant on the estate, he explains, continues under notice of seasonal slaughter, and the opportunity to hunt and shoot hinds commenced this very morning. "We wouldn't want any kind of accident, would we, sir?"

This last fact must come as some bittersweet relief for the local stags, knowing they've dodged the bullets of their own four-month culling season, only for their partners to wander into the crosshairs. I've certainly not seen any of them putting their hooves up on the hill behind The Broch, shooting the shit of their near escapes over a fraternal pint.

I mumble my appreciation of the warning, promise to observe all notices, and continue on to the road.

So much for doing everything I can to safeguard my stay for the week. No one's searched my bag, but I think I've just gone to the top of the local watch list.

I'm back at the 'moat', my back turned to what is now driving rain, but wanting to take in a few more views of this stunning building.

It's amazing. Really. The first broch built in Britain since the Romans left. Are you familiar with these structures? Most of them now are little more than scattered blocks in the bogs and clifftop moorlands of Caithness or Aberdeenshire farmland. Erected by itinerant builders, they were the swankiest buildings in Britain three thousand years ago. Barratt and Bovis (the Beavis and Butthead of today's construction industry) they were not. You can't help but respond to structures like these. Or to the motivation to build them.

I've left some of the lights on inside. Although it's still a couple of hours before dark, the building is even more impressive against the undulating moorland than on my arrival yesterday. Darkened glass surfaces, above and below the warmly lit lounge panes, offer abstract reflections of the surrounding countryside, conjoined by a thin, pervasive blanket of wet Atlantic air.

Back inside, I discard my waterproofs in the utility room, and take the stairs slowly to the top floor, stopping off briefly to pick up Mr Murray's assessment of tonight's malt. Laying down in the centre of the bed, I pull the duvet over from Trish's side, and settle down to read what he has to say in his entry on page 118.

> **Glen Moray 1986 Commemorative Bottling cask 4698** *db* (**96**)
> ***n**25 take your time over this: like a week or so! The bourbon notes are unmistakable (nosing blind, I might have plumped for Kentucky!) with a series of rich and sharp blood orange/kumquat notes*

interlaced with dark chocolate. A peculiarly coastal saltiness has also crept in. Amid all this can be found a sharp maltiness. Just one of the great noses of this and many other years; ***t****24 spectacular bitter-sweet arrival on the palate shows a glorious harmony between the malt and bourbony oak. Beyond this gentle spices abound, as do mouthwatering candy-fruit riches;* ***f****23 one of the longest non-peaty fade-outs since 'Hotel California'… the ripeness of the malt, enriched by the most fabulous of bitter-sweet molasses lasts until finally replaced by a toasty vanilla;* ***b****24 Ed Dodson hand-picked this cask from the warehouse to mark the opening of the distillery's visitor centre in late 2004. Ed has retired but – and this bottling proves the point entirely – he should be brought back to the distillery, as Elmer T. Lee has at Buffalo Trace, and be given his own named brand. You simply cannot buy the experience and natural feel Ed has for Glen Moray. This astonishing single cask proves the point with a delicious and unforgettable eloquence.* ***64.4%. ncf***

I think I've probably drunk more Glen Moray than any other whisky over the years. In the year of Guillemots' gorgeous *Walk the River* album, it became a staple of my whisky bar just as much as the sight of their Elgin distillery was hardwired into my weekly route into Aberdeen. Even now, I can't understand why their base brand is so cheap, lacking nothing of the smoothness of its Speyside peers. These Commemoratives ran to £260, but remain comfortably the cheapest of the week.

I put the notes down, and I'm out like a light.

When I wake up (or, perhaps more worryingly, *come to)*, it's dark outside, and a faint, deep, irregular thrum comes from the window. The wind has got up a bit. I walk over and place my palm flat on the cool glass. Reverberations, each distinct from the last yet part of the same low voice, rise through my arm. Turning to sit, my back to the glass, I peer through the glass dome above the bed. Similarly dark, and absent any celestial glimmerings. I like it here. Sitting here. In this place.

Later, I'm downstairs with Trish, reclaiming my glass from the draining board and then clearing away the photographs from this morning. The sofa offers an already comforting familiarity.

Time for three deep breaths, the pouring of the Glen Moray, and the lifting of the lid. I place the remaining seven sachets on the table, move them delicately around by fingertip, and slide #21/10 to the base of the glass. With my first draught, I search for vanilla and molasses with the raw, flensed endings of what used to pass for my taste buds.

I complete The Ceremony. Trish is happy to hear of my day, despite her collusion in all but my recent 'slumber'.

"I've changed my mind about tonight's viewing," I tell her. "It's your birthday," I say. "I'm not going to sit here and watch Number Six all night. Wonder at how she moves in that red dress. Not today."

Who am I kidding, believing that a day will make a difference? It's just that the disloyalty of spending the last eight hours of Trish's birthday empathising with – no, *envying* – how Gaius is repeatedly seduced by Tricia Helfer is just that bit too much, don't you think? Maybe tomorrow. *A token resistance, I know, but it can wait.*

I sit back, the whisky within easy reach, and start up the TV. *True Detective* it is. Now *this* is what we're talking about. I'm more alert than last night, despite recent lungfuls of moist air, and ready for all the Gothic brilliance. Episode One, opening scene: a body carried in darkness and laid beneath a burning tree; the rising discordance of the soundtrack.

It's good, but it's the following scene that gets me. Woody Harrelson leans back in an interview room, frames his unease on first meeting his partner. Gazes off into the middle distance and shakes his head. Flicks his nose with a finger. Lowers his hands to lie, palms down, on the table just out of shot. I'm in. So in.

We'd watched this show four times straight through since it aired four years ago. Each time during bad-weather weekends, the sort defined by rising river levels beyond The Schoolhouse's back wall, swollen with hill-water run-off released by the dam five miles upstream. Duvet days, hunkered against the weather in front of the TV.

Have *you* seen it? That show converted me from movies to TV drama as my number-one form. Until then, I'd happily and judgementally proclaimed that movies were the equivalent of novels, and TV shows more like inferior short stories. Four years on, I find it hard to achieve any kind of emotional resonance with anything that doesn't take eight to ten hours to develop. Not sure what that says about TV to that point. Or about me, at thirty… forty… fifty.

I marinate in the show for the next four hours. Thinking, breathing, imperfect men failing to make sense of their own bewildering and uncharted paths. Every aerial slo-mo, every darkly-lit wisp of cigarette smoke rising from an anguished or vacant face, brings the next sip of Glen Moray up from my lap, until the first bottle's gone.

It's possible I've annoyed Trish with all my unregulated outbursts. The "Jesus, did you see that?!"s, or "Wow – I'd forgotten that happened!"s. It's just so visceral. I try to tone it down, settling for half-strangled gasps or grunts, but each effort is short-lived.

(And just so you know, I know what I'm doing. I know she's not really there. I do. So please don't think I don't. But I like how these shows help me slip into neutral, take the brakes off, roll slowly down the hill

and let the hours have their way. They take me back to the two of us in adjacent armchairs, sharing something powerful. So to share all this art, all the emotions it conjures, with thin, empty air would be a complete fucking waste, wouldn't it?)

I still get breathless at the end of the stash-house battle. Push out the same bug eyes as Cohle. I need to come up for air, so I decide to head upstairs. I've got my second bottle, my glass inverted over the neck, and my iPad, onto which I've loaded a duplicate set of show files.

Don't laugh. I've no free hand. So what if it takes a while, climbing like a robot vacuum cleaner unaware that each step is only a foot deep? Things could turn wanky quick if I go any faster. I make it, though, which is something, right?

This bed's great. A bit soft, but who cares? I stack the pillows against the headboard and pour my first top-floor dram. Ambient light from my right (I've left the tweed curtains open) suggests a clearing sky. No stars, but then I've not invested any effort in adjusting my eyes to the celestial ambience.

I balance the iPad on the duvet. The battery is at 98%, and I've got my headphones. A different experience from downstairs. I can keep half an eye on the staircase. Why should that matter?

Ten seconds later I'm shaking. Shallow breathing like a boy knocking for the first time on a girl's front door. Give me a moment, if that's OK. Trish will have to stay down there tonight.

I choke down a mouthful of malt.

Air slowly penetrates lower.

Getting there.

To distract myself, I close down the video player, open Scrivener (my writing software), and pull up a small text file sitting at the bottom of a writing project called *Dalliances and Misadventures*.

After Trish's funeral, I redoubled my efforts to cut myself off. The initial difficulties of a secret, private cremation and the falsification of reasons for her inability to come to the phone or door morphed into deception on a grand scale. Presented me with enough problem-solving to keep me busy. *Insulate* me, even.

Yep. I've been doing more than my share of spurning, these past endless months. Friends. Parents. Sons. I looked it up, by the way. On Dictionary.Com. Spurn. One of the definitions? 'To kick and trample with the foot.' Except I took the pacifist route (legs not long enough, mood not aggressive enough).

In any case, I navigated the early steps of the cover-up to the point where I thought I could drop into a kind of 'run and maintain' mode. Gradual extension of periods between regular calls to parents and the boys. Lies about Trish's whereabouts – business trips to London and the Netherlands. Even a case of flu that had everyone convinced. For those locals put off by minor acts of rudeness, or claims of Trish's expanding work commitments, little more was needed than the occasional nod at the corner shop, or polite conversations at the front door. Anything that kept folk out of the house.

Trish's hatred and distrust of social media helped. Geraldine and Iain, the only friends local and tenacious enough to pursue things, to the point of my eventual capitulation, reluctantly agreed to silence. I'm not entirely sure why, to be honest, but they honoured their promise, for the most part. The main thing was, there were no new queues at my door.

I just needed to keep up the charade for family up and down the east coast.

Before the accident, I'd written two novels and was in the process of scoping out a third. My first, *The Quarant*, is set in late medieval Venice. It took me the best part of eighteen months to complete, and a further ten months to get it published myself. My second, inspired by a walking holiday with Trish on the

Aeolian Islands, tells of feuding brothers travelling as members of a Sicilian Puppet Theatre, falling out over a passionate love triangle, and the insistence of one of them upon sacrilegiously altering the established dramas drawn from *Orlando Furioso*. Publishers expressed no interest in either. Failing to secure an agent (should I have taken the hint?), I gave in and 'invested in myself'. Made materially less than I spent; a fact that hurts only when I think about it.

After Trish, the desire to continue writing fiction fell away. On good days, I composed small snapshots of our life together; a kind of fragmented 'in memoriam'. On less good days, I ducked out entirely to create short pieces describing life before we met. On bad days – which they all eventually became – even thinking about booting up the software was out. The snug, in which I'd spent half of every week writing over the preceding four years, became a place for my music, and then, not even that. By August the fight was lost, and the easy chair in the living room, with an obligatory bottle of malt, became my habitual domain.

My Skypes with Dennis dried up, too. We'd known each other for almost ten years. Work had brought us together, my boss sending him over from Houston to coach my London team in communication skills. It quickly became obvious, in the comfortable spaces between videotaped interviews and targeted feedback sessions, that we would become friends. A couple of meals after work in Covent Garden and a promise to meet up on my next trip to Houston was all it took.

His intellect scared me at first. One of our earliest conversational obsessions was around quantum physics. We tussled with what this might mean for how personality and character work. Interactions between people. 'Spooky action at a distance' began to play out for real. We sat at our desktops, three thousand miles apart, refining and developing our own personal connections.

He freaked out on his sixty-fourth birthday, scared to be the same age as the man in the Beatles song. I freaked out (more than once) after bad days at work. He smiled and celebrated with me over two promotions in five years for Norwich City. I applauded his Austin stand-up routines (he'd moved from Houston by then, glad to remove himself and Melissa from the increasingly conservative oil town) and his stepping back into broadcasting.

Eight or nine years in, he began to feed me opening paragraphs from which to work up short creative pieces. He called them WHNs ('what happens next's), and it was these, combined with his caring and enthusiastic reactions, that set me on my way.

I miss our conversations. But I couldn't share Trish's loss with him. So I cut us off. Took all that spooky action, and threw it away. It was a wanky thing to do, but I did it. Jack took the edge off that particular stream of guilt and (yes, I'll admit it) loneliness, but it changed nothing. Maybe he'll read this one day. Perhaps you might track him down and tell him why I did what I did (I wouldn't know where to start). Dennis Tardan, Austin, TX, communications and leadership coach, host of *Reasonably Spontaneous Conversations*, stand-up, and perhaps the most giving, thoughtful and reliable friend I ever had. Or ever will.

So all this, then, is by way of explaining the significance of the following prose poem. I birthed it, ironically, just as the early mornings were losing their late spring bite. With the exception of the short piece I wrote when returning home from the boys' a couple of months ago, and for reasons still unknown, it pretty much threw the last shovelful of earth onto the grave of Martin Rose, Author.

It's here on the iPad. Let me read it to you.

Lost

This is where we picked up the spilt, bruised berries.
Fingered the spoil of our hot afternoon endings in the fields into smiling, love-greedy mouths.
Laughed at the neck-glow sun, our crimsoned napes, gossamer skin peel.
Bestowed the cool flannel pressure of mutual care.
The care.

This is where you birthed me from my shirt.
Kissed my side. My breast.
Opened my heart and threw me into the bliss plunge.
Drowned me in lilac, crushed me in silk.
Pushed the brine from my lungs, renamed me as whole.
Breathed gentle breezes across my sheltering eyes.
Bathed me in trusted and tear-welcomed joy.

This is where we conjured our conjoined tomorrows, built our blessed and bronzed lives.
Dreams and stories.
Paired and passioned.
Promises offered, written, then hidden.
Read out loud with wide-eyed cries.
Spent souls recharged.
Buried again in smiling earth.

This is where you left me from.
Told of no more me. Of no more you.
Where openness slammed me shut, ribboned me down.
Down to a solitary ache, blasted pain to throw at the moon.
To cast out into ocean.
A volcano offering.

This is where tears scald and steam.
Where worlds blaze and I am scattered.
Thin on the wind.
Gone. And gone again.

This is where I sit.
In the dark.
The walls no longer loyal.
The air an absence to be breathed in.
Hosted as alien.
For now.

I'm surrounded by different walls today. But that last stanza has me reaching for the Glen Moray again.

A suicide note to my writer self. One bloody great stopper in life's bottle.

So, let's make one last toast to the past, then I'll fill the room with the opening bars of '*Far From Any Road*' and the opening credits of Episode Five.

It's gone two when the end credits roll for the final time.

I reach over and put the tablet on charge. Lie back in bed.

Still no bloody stars in the skylight.

DRIED UP
TUESDAY 8TH MAY 2018

He's been at his writing desk for four days after an exile into the kitchen, ordering supplies of Scotches and soups from Trish's laptop.

Word gets around. Geraldine and Iain have, in their usual respectful way, let the cat out of the bag. He cannot blame them. Trish had other friends, good friends, who have the right to know.

Few couples possess the courage to come to the house. Of those that do, it's the menfolk who look the most uneasy, beside tearful partners. The timings of next visits are not discussed. Non-return is a tacit, unspoken thing. They won't trouble him a second time; subject themselves to such lazy sullenness and anger. Grief dirties every surface, steals the oxygen from their commiserations.

A few days ago, he wrote a poem. Filled it with imagery that tore at his heart. Pushed down on his ribs until, one by one, he could hear them crack; feel them bend, then crumple. He tried to shit out all the bile and anguish. Purge it from his blood. He wrote of the absence of her breath, the silence of her empty chair and pillow. Of how he is scattered.

Afterwards, after its final words, he saw off two bottles of Laphroaig, then bruised his knees on the cold marble floor by the toilet, convulsed and blind.

Today, like each of the past few days, he sits in the snug. Faces the large, black-bezelled, crisply lit screen, framed in turn by slatted windows. Windows moulding and channelling sounds. Vans and logging lorries. Buses and bikes. Jets, always in pairs, the sound of ripped air never catching them. Leaves move to the left of his gaze, the creeper obedient to the demands of light breeze encircling the house.

On the screen, the blank white page stares back at him. Dares him, if he can, to respond.

He wants to write more about their lives together. To wander, however briefly, back to a world that can still be celebrated. Re-experience it. Shape it to bring out its beauty and wholeness.

But the words do not come.

He fears they never will.

CHAPTER 3

MONDAY 22ND OCTOBER 2018

In eternity, where there is no time, nothing can grow. Nothing can become. Nothing changes. So death created time to grow the things it would kill.

(Rust Cohle, True Detective)

NOT-SO-ABSENT FRIENDS

You need to know. I need to tell you. Before I get into the day proper.

He's back. Gallagher.

How did he find me so quickly? Blag his way onto the ferry without a ticket? Can gorillas swim? That far, I mean? The water's freezing at this time of year. But there's no doubt he's followed me.

My shoulder's bloody killing me, and that disturbed air hovers over me again. He's indulged in a couple of extra, point-making swings.

He's resentful. That's it. I didn't say goodbye. Or leave *him* a letter.

And the humiliation? That's worse still. How Gallagher stands by the bed, lowers my covers with a delicacy perfected through years of teasing leaves from branches or grooming any number of his troop, and turns me over onto my left side.

I'm bare-assed most nights.

It's a violation of the worst kind, don't you think? Not the sort of bedroom activity Trish and I had in mind when we sat and swooned at the photo of this room on my iMac this time a year ago.

No wonder they're endangered, going around doing *this* all over the bloody place. And that smell. Has he marked his new territory?

Oh no.

Hold on.

Sorry.

That's me.

WE'RE WORST, SO WE WIN!

I alluded earlier to the tedium of stories concerning other people's children. Unless you're half of a couple that considers mutual sharing of psychological mundanity to be the highest expression of love, listening to the retelling of dreams comes a very close second.

And yet. And yet.

Trish, ducking down under gunfire from a crazed drug dealer in a West Texas bathroom.

A young man holding Trish's urn, knocking it against an empty bottle of Jack, and saying, "Cheers."

Hinds gathering around a dead stag, wondering if they will be next.

An old man, skinny in his worn blue dressing gown.

The soft tear of an envelope being opened, amid the smell of rotting kelp.

At least I've not woken up crying. And I'm getting the hang of the spiral staircase too. Ten minutes on the pot, then a shower.

Feeling not too bad today, thanks. Good enough to tackle that food hamper, and sharp enough to stop off in the lounge to place ticks against *Justified* and *True Detective*.

What sort of breakfast do you normally have? I'm not one for deriving great insight from whether a person has eggs or cereal, or no breakfast at all. But repeated meals featuring fresh food do speak to one's ability to organise, don't you think?

Over the last few years, Trish and I moved to split catering for breakfast and lunch. I can't stand porridge (too many childhood memories of tepid, lumpy Ready Brek), but Trish loved it, claiming it kept her full until lunch. I didn't mind using the microwave to make her the quick stuff, but even then I was happy to walk away from that cloying smell of hot milk.

And at lunch, while Trish adhered to the calorific discipline of soup, I submitted to my lifelong love of the simple granary loaf sandwich. I can still see a standard cheese and tomato sandwich, complete with a layer of mayonnaise and freshly ground pepper, as my final meal of choice.

Except that I forgot to bring tomatoes. *Maybe I shouldn't have been so quick to dismiss the whole analytical thing.*

I can definitely manage some toast. I put a couple of slices on, then turn to take a look at the goodies in the hamper and the fridge. That salmon, smoked over beechwood at the smokehouse on North Uist, looks bloody lovely.

Five minutes later, I'm back up in the lounge with two slices of unbuttered toast covered in the deepest pink salmon at least one of us has ever seen. My senses of smell and taste are pretty much shot (have I mentioned that already?), but this takes me back. If Trish were here, we would have built the morning around this and the Bollinger. Instead, I raise the plate to her, and take a large mouthful, while unscrewing the top of the Jack.

Saltiness and butterscotch collide in my mouth.

Happy Monday, Trish.

I should probably make the most of this while it lasts. Feeling half human.

I nip across to the smaller side table, and bring back a heavy leather-bound folder of brochures and leaflets. I know broadly where I'm headed today, but I like flipping over each transparent pocket; the appearance, at least, of thoughtful discernment. These compilations are always a good indicator of an owner's attention to detail and (in a manner we often chortled about in the past) their sense of target clientele.

Depositing omega-3 oils over the plastic folders and flyers (*inquisitive but unhygienic guests, then*), Trish and I guess at their assumptions. High-end hunting, shooting, fishing experiences available by the day or week. Tweed outfitters. Art galleries screaming out for Home Counties money. Rosette-rated eateries. Traditional Scottish, Thai fusion. And, of course, fish. Plenty of fish. Not many C2s and below expected here, then.

For years, if we felt we needed or just fancied a treat, we'd book a beautiful Highland hotel, somewhere between Perthshire and the Far North. "*To hell with the money, let's just do it.*" These visits, in part, explain how we ended up living in the North-West Highlands.

Our challenge began with each arrival and subsequent return. Park up next to the smartest car present. Bentleys, or top-end Range Rovers. Take pride in owning the crappiest car in the car park, and upset the posh folk each time they leave the hotel for a drive.

At one point, it became a key criterion for selecting our destination. Do they have gorgeous food? Is the service wonderful? Are the rooms beautiful? Will our fellow guests be drawn exclusively from that social band that thinks nothing of wasting their money on overpriced luxury cars?

Imagine our warm glow each time we lowered the tone with our little Ford Ka, or (later on) our racing-green, eight-year-old Rover 2500 two-litre diesel. "Turbo!" we would declaim, as if this made any bloody difference – we were already bottom of the heap. In fact, not even part of the same heap.

We chose well once more, though, booking this place. There's no getting round it. Trish would have loved it here.

I'm not quite ready to move out yet, so I hook my phone up in the dock at the side of the TV, and play some Prefab Sprout. *The Gunman and Other Stories* is Trish's favourite album of theirs. Introducing my favourite albums to her, and standing by as she reacted favourably to at least some of them, was an early pleasure. Hall & Oates. Elvis Costello. Lloyd Cole. It worked both ways, of course. The Manics. Embrace. Geneva.

The merging of music collections also marked the year of our pre-divorce apocalypse, when we veered and swerved at high speed between joy, despair and guilt. As Paddy McAloon puts it so well (has he ever put anything in any other way?), it was the year when '*The Sound of Crying*' was "number one across the earth". Or at least in our small corner of Aberdeen.

If you don't know them yourself, you could do worse than pour yourself a nice glass of Rioja and stream *A Life Of Surprises: The Best of Prefab Sprout*. Consider Paddy Genius #2.

Distracted, I bring down my iPad and cue up a bunch of their brilliant '80s videos.

ON THE ROAD

Mind made up, an extra bottle of Jack in the bag just in case, I point the car back down the track to the main road. Trish is in her accustomed position beside me. I've no intention of bombing it, as I want her to savour the road trip.

Fifty miles and four-and-a-half thousand years to the standing stones, then. A trip from the Anthropocene to the Neolithic.

It'll feel different, that's for sure. 'Archaeological fun' over the past twenty years has had at its centre Trish's reactions to standing near, on, in or under stuff; and then each of us bouncing memories of our visits to and fro. Mexico, Peru, Rome, Athens. Places closer to home, yet no less mesmerising and confounding. The Orkneys, Avebury.

Her fascination with the pre-Christian world, not to mention the pre-human cosmos, was always at the root of her enthusiastic monologues. Tales recounted as though she alone knew their secrets. She'd often share her research months before reaching our destination, enabling us both to savour the countdown.

The skies have lifted. Curlews and other waders feast on the receding tide at Seilebost. Dropping into Tarbert, I skirt the harbour and follow the sign to Stornoway. The route from here, past the fire station and school, seems simple – just one junction to watch out for in the next forty miles.

Anathema, playing over the car stereo, complement the mood of the passing landscape.

I'm never more than thirty seconds from a sea view, or the fringes of some small freshwater lochan. Everything seems within reach. Small islands and outcrops. Tantalising glimpses of higher ground ahead. The perpetual sense of being on the edge of a continent.

The peaks take turns to loom in and out of view. Their outlines soften and sharpen with each gathering of cloud, harmless cottons and smudged greys, and it's possible, as I pass each old croft (weather-beaten), occasional new build (varying in imagination and build quality) and gallery (mostly closed) that flank the road, to establish each first impression of their character.

One more cattle grid, the road receding between two rising masses of rock, and there it is: my first uninterrupted view of the Harris highlands.

There's something magical about the way the coastline draws these slopes right down and into itself, as they scoff at any urge to colonise or tame their lower flanks. There's a dramatic rise to a high plateau on the right of the road and, to the left, the sprawling, multi-peaked hill of The Clisham, ascending almost eight hundred metres above the coast.

Let's you and I rise above the landscape, above that thin white scrape of a recent Atlantic flight. Higher still. Then look down and picture the whole island as Orion. See these hills as its Belt; the waistline dividing Lewis from Harris.

A mile or two on, at a high point on the pass, I turn onto a small ghosted section of the original road, its end proclaimed by two large boulders. To my left, beyond the passenger window, is one of the hill's wide shoulders.

I pause, then turn off the engine, the music suddenly gone.

Silence.

The main road links the island's two main ports, but there's pretty much nobody here. Heavily rusted Armco barriers add to the creeping isolation.

Nerves kick in. It's one thing having a plan, but this is serious shit. It's not quite up there with flipping the cover of the nuclear button, poised to enter the codes as enemy missiles arrive over home soil. But it's a close second.

The choice is simple. Get out, or drive on.

I could swing back onto the road, complete the remaining few miles to Callanish, and walk to the stones. But running from the first move in the week's endgame? Really? And let's not forget – I'd have to drive back this way later and face an ambush from my own worst, spineless self, blubbering and mewling by the phantom roadside.

I look across at Trish. She's holding her tongue on this one. This one's down to me.

I push open the door hard, fighting against the winds travelling south over the bealach, and step out of the car. Breathe in deep to purge the fear curled tight at the bottom of my lungs.

It's not as if I'm going all the way up today. Just sussing it out a bit.

I'll get my walking boots from the back of the car. How about you and I take a stroll?

DWELLING ON THE WAY THINGS AREN'T

I'm going to have to stop for a bit.

This flank, with no path, is tougher than I thought. And the salmon's swimming back up my throat for a return appearance.

I swing Trish and Jack down gently onto the grass, persuading the bottom hem of my coat beneath me. Name any time when a wet arse is helpful. *On second thoughts, let's not go there.*

There's probably only a couple more minutes' walk to reach the top of the hill's first small rise, but this is enough for now.

I'd love to lay out flat and invite more oxygen into my lungs, but I daren't do it. Too big a risk of shit. Deer. Sheep. Eurghh! (Grandad's pig shed, scene of childhood 'muckings out', remains the Ground Zero of my fear of and disgust at animal waste. My Commendation for Bravery from the Queen, acknowledging nappy duties for Kieron and Conor, stands as testament to my younger resilience.)

It's quite nice just sitting here, actually. Even the wind, gusting strongly down near the car, seems to have settled into a more relaxed, manageable flow. My mind shifts to neutral (which is also nice).

I should really offer you a little more of my background. It's not as if you'll get it from anyone else here. This might help. Something I produced on one of my writing courses: an autobiography in one hundred single-syllable words...

New life in the east, by the sea. Bike rides with Mum. Match days with Dad. Sis next door, then wed. Digs, not home. Brum is a drag, but done with. Love is found and grown. Two sons and work. Job runs my life, wife runs me down. Look for an out. Cry and shake, rage and shake. Find new joy, new guilt, rip and tear up home. Start again. Cut hair short. Oil Town, then Big Smoke. Tear down and shape new house from old. Love, love, more love. Pack in job, town and tie. Pick up a pen.

Have you ever tried to do this for yourself? Beats sudoku.

That said, I need to expand somewhat. I'm in no hurry right now – the sky remains high, some blue might be on its way, and the Jack is going down well now that I've caught my breath.

So let's break it down a little more. If it helps, imagine Ted Rogers (remember him from the '70s?) reading out each brief set of clues to the prizes on the quiz show *3-2-1*. (Where this comparison breaks down, of course, is that Rogers' explanations concerning the final reward usually possessed the simplicity of Fermat's Last Theorem. The makers of that show were off their bloody heads – did the average Saturday night viewer really have that capacity after a day at the pub or the bookies?)

New life in the east, by the sea. Bike rides with Mum. Match days with Dad. Sis next door, then wed.

I was born in early '60s Lowestoft, the once-above-average end-of-the-line coastal town on the Norfolk–Suffolk border. My mother, a shop assistant, met my father, a fireman, at their church. She was in the choir and he was choirmaster. Leaving work to bring myself and my younger sister up, Mum took on the full domestic responsibilities of parenthood. My recollections of Dad, due in part to additional jobs when off shift, are primarily of trips to watch the Canaries play at Carrow Road. My sister married at eighteen. She's still with the same man today, having devoted her life in equal part to being a hospital nursery nurse, and to finding increasingly impressive ways to keep herself fit.

Brum is a drag, but done with. Love is found and grown.

At eighteen, I became the first in Dad's family to go to university. Lacking any notable skills or interests (*high-school careers teacher: "What do you aim to do, Martin?" Me: "No idea. But I read a lot."*), I spent four years in Birmingham studying to become a librarian. I outgrew student life at least a year before the end of my course. Two weeks before the beginning of my final year, I plucked up the courage to ask out Carol, a primary-school teacher. That Christmas we were engaged, and married the following October. By then I'd graduated, and had my first job in the oil and gas business, setting up an industrial library, servicing workers in the Southern North Sea.

Two sons and work. Job runs my life, wife runs me down.

This, trust me, is the toughest to explain. Kieron and Conor were born in 1988 and 1992 respectively. The words above, on rereading them, feel particularly trite and shallow. Not every day as a husband was miserable, but looking back now, joy slowly leached from each subsequent year of our lives, replaced with something much less pleasant. I wanted to be a dad, and I loved my time with the boys, but everything just soured. By the time Conor turned eight, no number of control rods, dropped at increasingly brief intervals, could prevent meltdown. Arguments regularly concluded with the claim that I'd never have the guts to leave.

Look for an out. Cry and shake, rage and shake. Find new joy, new guilt, rip and tear up home. Start again. Cut hair short.

I found guts I didn't know I had, including those required to consign my marriage-long mullet to the barber's floor.

I'd got to know Trish a little in the years I'd spent travelling to Scotland on occasional business visits, and then during secondment to the Aberdeen office on project work. I'd heard that, in the aftermath of the Y2K debacle and during the act of falling for her, it was her relationship with her long-term partner, rather than the world's computers, that had rolled over to zero. For me, passive observation was no longer an option. Self-respect and the faintest whiff of happiness were both in play.

I alluded yesterday to our meal together at the *Shahbazz*. One less pint that night, and I'd have done nothing (except regret it for, well, how long would that be?). One more thimble of Kingfisher or Cobra, and Trish would have been wiping my vomit from her blouse, and walking out cursing her weakness in offering such naive and misjudged friendship.

Oil Town, then Big Smoke. Tear down and shape new house from old. Love, love, more love. Pack in job, town and tie. Pick up a pen.

I won't bore you with stories of the split here; of all the selfish thrashings around. I lost twenty pounds on a diet of anxiety and glorious self-fulfilment, my daily barometer veering wildly between 'Stormy' (the receipt of the latest ten-page letter describing the impact of my paternal dereliction) and 'Fair' (a most paralysingly love-filled afternoon with Trish). Suffice to say, I secured a permanent transfer north, and within eighteen months the divorce was finalised and Trish and I were married. We visited the boys every six or seven weeks from that point on; a bittersweet experience that injected additional guilt into dreams of my betrayal of them in the weeks between.

But we were happy, Trish and I. My sister declared at our wedding that she had got her brother back. I'd been reclaimed from the grasp of an inevitable depression.

After seven years together, in the year of Sam Brown, Amy MacDonald – a huge hit north of the border – and Glen Hansard, we transferred to London. Putting distance between us and the Scottish hills was tough. Trish was the first to vocalise our shared sense that we needed to come back north, and six months later we bought The Schoolhouse in Invermoriston. I secured promotion back to my old Aberdeen team, and Trish moved onto a homeworker contract.

Despite being apart each week, the move was an unquestionable success. Village life brought new friends, we finally felt that we were in the right place to put down roots, and when, three or four years later, the global oil price crashed, I took advantage of the chance to take early retirement. Thirty years in the oil business, of renting my head out to the company, was enough. Spending every night of every week with Trish, and attempting a novel that would not look out of place in the libraries of my youth, was hardly a tough change to pursue.

Hello? You still there? I hope I haven't gone on too long. I guess we all have our share of funny ha-ha and funny peculiar, and the deeply, downright unfunny. It's just the details that vary, I guess.

I'm quite enjoying it up here, though, this wander through the past. And the wind has dropped. I can even feel a faint warmth on the back of my hands.

There's a flash of brown further down the pass. There's supposed to be sea eagles up here, but I don't think that's one of them. A buzzard, perhaps, blissfully unaware that it's being watched from this small patch of sloping grass and heather. Most of us could benefit from a few moments of *that* feeling. A kind of unthreatened ease; a temporary dominance over forces that might otherwise seek our demise. If I ignore the terminus point of the mountain at my back, its small, obelisk-shaped trig point, I can feel just a little of that absence myself. Fresh air, Jack, and a friendly ear will do that to a boy.

Yet in five more days I'll be here again, resisting that same crying, raging and shaking from two decades ago, and the same kind of guilt that will weave in and out of that relief.

Enough of this for now. The buzzard's gone and I've some serious touristing to do.

The drive to Callanish is a quick one; dramatic at first on the winding descent to the South Lochs, but then the yellow snow poles morph into low wire fencing, occasional farm gates, and stray sheep. Unnatural forestry plantings, boasting jarringly straight-edged perimeters. Church buildings in every settlement.

After my sole turn-off, the road levels out into long straights reminiscent of American desert highways. Watery marshes, framed by mountains I only recently left, resist the incursion of power lines or telegraph poles seen elsewhere. Childe Roland could be deep in that marshland, wandering under massive skies on his sickly mount, eager for his mysterious dark tower.

Finally, I pass just a car-width from a low, stony beach, strewn with the autumn browns and yellows of tide-swept seaweed.

PROCESSING

I look it up later. The word. '*Farce*'. How it features buffoonery and horseplay. Ludicrously improbable situations, not to be taken seriously. I swear I *could* make up what follows, but I don't need to. Some of the details remain a little vague, for reasons you'll find quite plausible. But amongst all the *farce*, look for the weight of the thing. It's there.

I place Trish in the boot before leaving the car park, strapping her in with one of the luggage restraints. I'm not happy about that, but there are so many people here, and I don't want to share her. After my encounter with the young gillie, I'll risk nothing.

Let's call that decision – parting from her but retaining the Jack – my first significant misjudgement of the day.

The visitor centre's less busy than I expected. All the coach spaces are empty, and there's only a dozen vehicles in the car park. In summer, this place will be mobbed.

A few steps away, a traditional white cottage sits next to a beautiful low structure reminiscent of the traditional black houses scattered across the island. Its roof curves to enclose a cobbled courtyard. Textures and lines everywhere.

I pay my entrance fee at the main desk and walk into the exhibition room, drawn to the model of the stones rising from the tabletop at its centre. Each wall features Gaelic and

English text describing the history, confirmed or speculative, of the place. Some guesses at period offer a margin of error approaching three thousand years. I work my way round slowly, honouring as best I can Trish's demand that we learn of a place before experiencing it first-hand. *It's not just about respect. It's about curiosity and depth of feeling. Don't be so lazy. I'm not going to spoon-feed you.*

Despite her protests, it was easy to push her into being tour guide. I loved it, and I think she did too; the way her eyes lit up as she described construction methods, living habits, rituals.

I bypass the cafe (it's lunchtime for most, but I instinctively shy away) and the toilets. Let's call *that* decision the second mistake of the day.

I head back out onto a gravel path that winds around the back of the building and up onto the flat rise. There's a break in the stone wall, and I can see a scattering of folk where the first stones project from the ground.

I walk onto the site, and pause to take in the scene.

Over the years, walking processional pathways at the Ness of Brodgar or Avebury, approaching these monumental landscapes, we'd seek to place ourselves into the minds of the Iron Age men and women who would have done the same. Imagine what it must have been like for them, untouched by the millennia that shape us today. How they would experience these mysteries, unfiltered through the progress of the past one or two hundred generations. We'd try to find echoes of their feelings in ourselves, standing where they stood, seeing what they saw.

I look back through the gate, alerted by a jumbled flow of primary colours and laughter. Before they reach the gate themselves, I quickly step back through, stand to the side and let them pass. Scandinavians, I think. I'll wait until they've been and gone. I want the stones to myself.

I leave the path, head over a small rise and, for the second time today, drop down onto the relative quiet of uneven grass. Patterns from the breeze, and what might well be drizzle, lace the surface of the loch as I view it through the gap between my boots.

These few steps have stripped away most if not all signs of other visitors.

I reach for the Jack and toast the range of hills in the distance that might or might not include The Clisham. It doesn't matter either way. Any high place accepting of my appreciation will do.

I move on to the second bottle. It's really quite pleasant here.

A slight pressure in my bladder eventually brings me to my feet. Brushing myself down, I head back to the circle.

The Scandis have gone, but I'm still not alone. Two solitary women, their arms raised, are both framing snapshots. A couple stand close together in front of one of the megaliths, running their hands over its contoured surface. I'll leave them to it for a bit longer.

Beyond the circle, a trail moves back downhill in the direction of five or six other smaller circles. I join it, keeping my head down. I'll do my best to merge with the background.

ALIEN ABDUCTION?

The woman sporting the blue blazer, authoritative in her gentle Island accent, states her wish that I accompany her through the door marked '*Staff Only*'. "Please," she tells me, "take a seat."

Everything's turned decidedly wanky all of a sudden, without me paying much attention.

I recall several people looking at me while working reasonably hard to make it look like they weren't. One of them, a middle-aged woman in a cardigan that would make the Edinburgh Woollen Mill proud, gestured to a nearby companion with a small but noticeable nod of her head. "Tut," I think I saw on her lips. *Tut bloody tut.*

The woman seemingly in charge of the place turns to face me. "Sir, I'm afraid I have to ask you to wait here while a member of the constabulary arrives from Stornoway. They should be here shortly. If you wish, you can place your rucksack just there by the wall."

Two bottles emit a noticeable 'clink' as my bag hits the floor. *Note to self: I really need to do something about that.*

I politely ask what's going on. But she's unwilling to go beyond her initial explanation.

There's plenty to read on the walls while I wait. Staff rotas. Fire regulations. A small, glass-fronted bookshelf holds a number of coloured ring binders, and a photograph of a woman (not Blazer Woman) with a man and two small children. Relations, perhaps? A fellow worker, off shift right now? A general hum of activity enters the room from the main building but does little to reduce my sense of isolation.

The door finally opens and a uniformed policewoman enters. She smiles politely, hangs her jacket on the back of the chair opposite me, and lays her cap and small radio on the table. Her hair is mid-length, a reddish black, cut into a shape that means business.

"Good afternoon, sir. I'm PC Cathy Sinclair, and I'm attending in response to a request by the centre manager, Mrs Campbell. Can you tell me, in your own words, what you think this is all about?"

I spend a couple of minutes mumbling all manner of "I don't really know"s.

She eventually helps me out.

I was seen urinating, in full view of several groups of visitors, against the centre monolith of the main Callanish stone circle. It's not until PC Cathy shares this with me that I notice the pressure on my bladder is no longer there.

In response to her question, I confirm my personal details. Oh shit. *Kieron is a policeman down south. Will this reflect on him?*

In a flash of insanity or genius, I tell her that I've only just arrived on the island, and am staying at the main four-star hotel in Tarbert (I saw it as I drove off the ferry and remembered it from our internet searches a year earlier).

I offer no explanation for my actions. *How can I? I can't remember a bloody thing.* No extenuating circumstances. I speculate out loud that I may have been elsewhere when the offence occurred, but I sense PC Cathy knows my heart isn't really in it. I might have made it to any number of the other stone circles, but it doesn't really seem to matter now.

Bottom line? I have no idea what I've been doing since deciding to explore the whole site, or even how long I've been here.

Two folded sheets of paper appear on the desk between us.

"Sir, this is a standard Fixed Penalty Notice. I have no intention of arresting you, and you will not be prosecuted. However, the residents of the island have repeatedly insisted that we clamp down on all forms of antisocial behaviour. This includes public urination. I have little choice but to serve you. The tariff for this offence is £40. You have twenty-eight days to pay, after which, if you fail to do so, you will receive an additional fine."

She unfolds the papers, and passes them to me. I sign each of them without pausing to read.

Just as I think we're done, a copy of the form in each of our pockets, she reaches into her jacket a second time.

"So, now then, sir. One more thing. I have reason to believe, based on your behaviour and general demeanour, that you may be under the influence of alcohol. I need you to breathe into this for me. Will you do that?"

As if I have a choice. "Certainly, officer."

Her task complete, she moves to the door, and beckons to Blazer Woman. "We're all done here, Mary, thanks. But I need you to do a couple of things for me. This gentleman is in no fit state to take his vehicle onto the road. Could you call him a cab to take him back to Tarbert, please?"

She turns back to me, her hand outstretched. "And, sir, I'm going to need your car keys. Mrs Campbell here will hold on to them overnight. You're free to return here tomorrow to collect them and your vehicle. I trust you understand the consequences of returning in a similar condition?"

A brief fumble, and they're in the manager's hand.

"Right then, I'll be off." Her parting words emerge from beneath her repositioned cap. "I encourage you to pay your fine promptly, and to think twice about such behaviour in the future."

This is all too much. Best not to think about it.

I wonder who that man in the photograph is?

AND TO MAKE MATTERS WORSE...

The clock on the taxi's satnav shows 18.23.

We're back on the main road beneath moonlit hills, having just passed my parking place below The Clisham.

Then I realise what I've done, and it splits my head in two.

Not the peeing.

Not the fine.

Not the lying about where I'm staying.

The driver, a talkative young local who helps work his father's croft each morning, has been sharing how he saves up to go to the clubs on Ibiza every May and September. "You've got to be fucking mad to go in the middle of the season."

"No! Shit, no!"

He looks across at me. Do I object to his holiday venue, or disproportionately agree with his choice to avoid the peak summer months?

I tell him I have to go back. That I've forgotten something important. A couple of shrugs, a few more yards to the next passing place, and we head back north.

Two cars remain in the car park.

Only one of them is mine.

Damn.

I hide my panic as I pay the boy double and wave him on his way. I can't risk going in yet, but with the taxi gone, I've left myself little choice. The place looks shut, but there could still be someone in there. A cleaner, maybe. But I need my keys.

I walk to my car and rest a hand on the boot. I can't hear her call me – I've not lost it completely, *at least not yet* – but I need us back together.

I place my backpack beneath the driver's door (I'd love some Dutch courage, but the bottles remain clinkily empty). It's dark out here, and I can't put this off. Sooner started, sooner done.

I won't share with you the names I call myself as I complete a circuit of the whole building. The place is fitted out with low-energy night lights, casting what to my mind looks like an incriminating glow. Can't be helped. I doubt the local wildlife, down off the hills for the night, are known for their powers of description when sitting with police sketch artists. *(They always get the hands wrong – ha.)*

OK. Here goes nothing. I'll try all the doors first.

The front entrance won't budge, but the third or fourth one I try opens when I push down the handle. The door swings inwards to reveal faint strains of music. It's not the usual 'Celtic gift shop' fare. Sounds more like… Wait. Sounds like Muse.

I stifle a chortle. Will the intrusion of modernity leave a residue in the speakers that no amount of fiddle, flute or accordion can completely wipe clean? Ah, the persistent march of progress.

Right. Think.

The centre closes at six o'clock this time of year. The footfall through here must be lower than in peak months, but the worse the weather, the more dirt gets dragged in. I can't hear a hoover right now, but maybe someone's doing a bit of dusting or mopping? I consider a retreat. Maybe I should wait until whoever's here has finished and gone. But then the doorway I'm standing in like a prune could be locked until morning.

I don't need to tell you how ludicrous the idea of me smashing in and crawling through a window is. You'd need more than the *Mission: Impossible* theme for me to be up for that. For one thing, I've the upper body strength of Miss Daisy. No chance. No. I'm in now. I'll stay here and bide my time.

Five minutes of stealthy ninja moves – the kind made by drunk, uncoordinated white men of a certain age – and I'm hiding out in one of the gents' cubicles (I remembered their location, despite failing to use them this afternoon).

The music moves on. Foo Fighters; something that sounds like Psychedelic Furs but isn't; Soundgarden, I think. It finally stops and, straining my ears, I hear a door shutting.

My heart races for the next ten minutes (they feel more like sixty), and then I walk back into the corridor.

The place is silent. No one jumps out at me, or dramatically switches all the lights on. No "*Freeze, cocksucker!*"

I'm in, so I'm going to behave like I know what I'm doing.

I head to the room of my earlier incarceration. Desk drawers and the inside of that bookshelf yield nothing. One more office, back through near the restaurant, is equally uncooperative. One of its desk drawers is locked.

I know I shouldn't, but I do. Several blows from a nearby fire extinguisher confirm that I am still not even warm.

This is not going well.

I move back to the public reception desk. There's a camera mounted on the wall, pointed directly at the main counter.

Are you getting the sense that I'm in way over my head? Here's a list of criminal acts I've performed in my first fifty-five years on the planet (notwithstanding the spree I'm on right now) that might help you decide:

1. **Theft.** *(Shoplifted a paperback copy of The Phantom Tollbooth on a school trip to York. Age: fourteen.)*
2. **Drink-driving.** *(Once, in my dad's car, after dropping off my mates from the pub. I think I may have failed to wear a seat belt that night too. Age: nineteen.) (I'll happily ignore my more recent JD-accompanied jaunts in the old jalopy if you will.)*
3. **Illegal parking.** *(Arrived back late from various shops. Age: twenty-three, thirty-seven and, well, who cares?)*
4. **Adultery.** *(With Trish. Not sure if this really counts, but it's the only charge against me that's been read out in a court of law. Age: thirty-eight.)*
5. **Leaving the scene of an accident.** *(Driving and parking a company hire car in deep snow at Aberdeen Airport, while suffering from flu, to fly down south to spend a weekend with the boys. On returning, snow gone, reversing from my earlier parking space and driving home to my sick bed. Receiving a call from work explaining that the police had been trying to*

contact me for over a week. Was I deliberately refusing to do as they wished? Turns out, while I shivered uncontrollably with the kids on a freezing Norwich terrace, the snowmelt back north caused my car to roll down the hill of the car park (I'd left the handbrake off in my fuddled thinking) and into the side of a high-end two-seater. When the 'crash' was discovered, police were called, my car was rolled back into position, chocks placed under the front wheels to prevent a repeat, and a police notice placed under the windscreen wipers. Reversing meant I had no idea of the chocks, and I must have displaced the notice with the first swipe of windscreen wipers. I'm still not sure how I feel about causing an accident when not even being in the country. One flu I'll never forget. Age: forty.)

6. **Public urination** *(this afternoon. Age: Four or five hours younger than now, yet much less seasoned in life on the wrong side of the law)* and **making a false statement.**

Not much of a rap sheet. Even theft of my own keys won't add much to the mythos of this criminal genius.

Anyway, one courteous wave to the camera later, I walk round to the side of the reception area and clamber over the desk. Most of the drawers and cupboards are locked, but two are not. My keys are in one of the latter, and I punch the air. More footage to be proud of.

But thank Christ. Not even the raucous salute of the visitor centre alarm, activated as I return outside, can wipe the smile from my face.

Of course, all of this flippancy will not do. Even if the alarms aren't connected to the Stornoway police, the break-in will be discovered tomorrow, and a few pertinent words exchanged will see the efficient Ms Sinclair pursuing her inquiries at the hotel in Tarbert.

But my hope remains that, in the mere five days remaining, without knowledge of my real location, none of this will matter.

The car has the tarmac to itself. I quickly sort myself out. Rucksack in the footwell, Trish in the passenger seat. I can tell her all about my day once we're on our way.

The clock on the dash says 20.50. It's at least an hour back to Borve. I've still to complete The Ceremony, and I'm miles behind my schedule for shows.

I jump out of the car and, just far enough from the headlight beams, empty my bladder for the second time today in the assumed privacy of the Hebridean countryside. This time, in the dark, I'm certain no biped is there to dob me in.

WISELY AND SLOW; THEY STUMBLE THAT RUN FAST

I'm back.

The drive got a whole lot less worrying once I passed through the Tarbert megalopolis. From that point on, I had the road pretty much to myself.

I'm not sure what Trish thinks of all this. Where would she think it all went wrong? The blackout at the stones? Leaving her in the boot? Or further back, to the reason why she's in her urn in the first place?

Anyway, as I said, I'm back, the car parked behind The Broch and myself installed on the lounge sofa, set up for The Ceremony. It's almost eleven – I paced myself on the drive back for fear of being caught speeding, or driving off the road in the dark.

So. Three deep breaths again. Pour the first glass, and select the right packet from the tabletop: #22/10.

Tonight's malt was by far the toughest to source. I haggled with its owner, a chap called Angus. He'd obtained three bottles from the Scotch Malt Whisky Society in Edinburgh, drunk one himself and kept the remaining two "for a rainy day". The SMWS were initially reluctant to divulge Angus's contact details, but I think they could tell a connoisseur when they heard one. I delivered the rain he sought – £1,400 a bottle.

No. Don't. I know.

I linger over the uncorked neck of the bottle slightly longer than usual.

Here's what James has to say on the matter:

Glenmorangie Truffle Oak db *(***96***)*
n*24 a significant aroma: big, powering oak yet controlled with no sign of bitterness or tiredness. Some golden syrup on the barley is toned down by age. If you find a flaw or off-note, e-mail me;* ***t****24 bloody hell!!! Now the golden syrup comes out to play, but the intensity of that plus the barley fair takes the breath away. Something very breakfast-cereally about this experience. But for grown-ups...;* ***f****25 burning embers of honey-nut cereal last forever. Keeping them company are varying shades of golden to molassed sugar. One of the longest un-peated finishes you'll ever find;* ***b****23 the Glenmorangie of all Glenmorangies. I really have to work hard and deep into the night to find fault with it. If I am going to be hyper-critical, I'll dock it a mark for being so constantly sweet, though in its defence I have to say that the degree of sweetness alters with astonishing dexterity. Go on, it's Truffle oak: make a pig of yourself!!* ***60.5%***

My mouth is dry until I take my first taste and the sweetness hits. This is nothing like any northern malt, from Tain, Wick or anywhere else for that matter.

On a short trip to Mull to bag Ben More, a waitress at the local pub suggested I try a glass of Scapa, the honey-hued dram from the Kirkwall distillery just over the bay from its Highland Park rival. But this stuff is something else.

I leave a respectful few moments for Trish to settle, then I go downstairs and bring up some luxury salted caramel chocolates from the hamper. If I can't treat myself tonight, when can I? It's not every day you pull yourself out of the shit. That's not to say that I won't spend the next few days dreading the sound of car tyres coming up the track, or the ominous tread of service boots on the drawbridge. If I'm found, I doubt I'll be treated with such politeness a second time.

Oh, God, these are good. Whose idea was it to coat the exterior of choccies with salt? Wanky, but it really works. I take another couple and sink back into the sofa.

A thought hits me, out of nowhere. Will the police reach out to the boys? That's the last thing I want.

The next mouthful of whisky is a large one.

Think.

They'll put all the pieces together regarding the break-in, the security camera footage, and the lack of any sign of the English bloke at the hotel he stated. If they try to contact home, they'll get no reply.

How far will they go? The damage I caused is minor, and I stole nothing. They might put out some kind of alert to be on the lookout for my car, but the island roads are not exactly lined with CCTV or speed cameras. This part of the island has one of the lowest concentrations of al-Qaeda bomb factories in the whole of the Hebrides. And sheep tend to obey most of the speed limits around here. The fine for the Fixed Notice isn't due for almost a month, and the whole thing didn't amount to an arrest. Would they really reach out to known relatives?

Bugger. What's done is done, but this is not the kind of contact that I want for either of the boys. It'll be bad enough when their letters arrive. And what about Kieron, when they find out he's on the job?

You plan, and you plan, and then you do something stupid. You bust a gut, doing even stupider things to bring everything back together, only to realise that loose ends can screw up the whole thing.

My head's spinning. Have I missed anything else? What do you think? *Anything obvious that I'm just not getting?*

I lean forward and grab the TV show list. I look at it, but nothing's going in.

The decision takes itself. I need some light relief, and there's nothing like the destruction of a planet and its entire civilisation to put a smile back on your face. Frack, yes. And I think that Trish will forgive me if I enjoy those scenes with Gaius Baltar and Number Six now – she thought Gaius was one of the best parts ever written, and I didn't argue. James Callis is mesmerising throughout, and the moral mazes he navigates, stripped of all the humorous one-liners and visual gags, are as labyrinthine as those of any flawed hero. And of course, Mary McDonnell just rules (pun intended) as Madam President.

Apologies for veering into TV critic territory. It's a tough habit to break, and I'm not sure I want to, given its place in our shared lives.

I start with the two-part miniseries. I just love that opening scene. The colonial officer's shock when two robots enter the meeting room. The sound of approaching high heels, Number Six power-walking towards the man's desk and sitting provocatively in front of him. Her astonishment at meeting a living creature. Awesome.

I head upstairs with Trish and the iPad for the second night in a row, ready to watch the whole of Season One. As with last night's Speyside, I go back to bring the second bottle of Glenmorangie, and lay down on the bed. The urn lies next to me, lacquer pressing into my side; cool at first, then comfortingly warm. In today's wilder moments, I thought we might be separated forever.

The lights are off, and a pale glow comes though the voiles at the window. I turn to look up. And there it is.

The skylight, high above me, is framing stars. Three or four, then, as my eyes adjust and probe, hundreds. I raise the urn above my head. I hear Trish's astonished intake of breath as she takes in the view.

And now the tears.

SECRETS AND THEIR DEMISE
MONDAY 9TH APRIL 2018

The Skoda swings to a halt around the curve of the drive.

Iain normally arrives on his own, delivering eggs from his back-garden chickens, or chili-chicken-liver pâté from a morning spent in his kitchen, nine miles further west down the glen. But today, Geraldine accompanies him.

He sees them both stride the short distance to The Schoolhouse's door. Clap the bell.

The opened door finds the visitors stern-faced. Determined.

"Mr Rose, sir. How are we today?"

He steps back as they push over the step. Wipe their feet, but move past the customary removal of shoes.

"We've come to see her. May we?"

Their tone is friendly yet strident. Before he knows it, he is trailing them down the hall. Watching as they push open the door to Trish's office.

"We need to speak to you. This cannot continue."

They turn back into the corridor, through to the kitchen, the main room of the house.

"Coffee?" He struggles to keep his tone even.

"No, thank you." It's clear Iain is speaking for them both. "Sit here with us, and tell us what is going on."

Eleven weeks. Of managing phone and door. Of feigning Trish's presence in the office. Tales of long trips away, working in London or Houston. A two-week spell in Kraków.

"We know something's wrong, Martin. If she's not here to tell us herself, we need you to be honest." Geraldine's voice is heavy with dread.

He thinks for a long minute. A brief age, under their gaze. They do not know. Have not jumped to the most extreme answer.

He considers longer. His face reddens. Possibilities run through his mind. They've split up. She's left him and gone back to Aberdeen, or moved to work out of London. Or Trish has split from them; *wishes to have no more to do with them. With Geraldine, her best friend.*

They see him struggle. Geraldine puts her hand out. Gently holds his arm.

"Martin. It doesn't matter what it is. Just tell us. We're not leaving until we know."

It's over.

"She's gone."

"Gone?"

He looks up at Iain. Across to Geraldine. Confusion fixes them both in position.

"Gone where?"

He lets out the longest sigh. His shoulders drop a full three inches, and he reaches with his free hand, the hand furthest from Geraldine, to steady himself on the worktop.

"Just gone. Dead."

"What?"

"She's not here because she's dead. Died the day she came back from yours. That Saturday."

More long minutes pass. Flow into hours. Eyes become smudged and tear-grazed.

He stands in the door again as they leave. The rain is lighter, and the branches of the Irish yews at the gate hang their heads as their car passes beneath them.

CHAPTER 4

TUESDAY 23RD OCTOBER 2018

Let a complex system repeat itself long enough and eventually something surprising might occur.

(Number Six, Battlestar Galactica)

WHAT WOULD PETER DO?

A few years ago, we binge-watched *Fringe*. A quirky, stylish take on parallel universes, parsed through a light-hearted drama about a mad scientist, his heroic son (Peter), and a determined and curious FBI agent. It didn't quite make my list, yet what made it stand apart for us both was how, with little warning, shifts from humour to real pathos would arrive from nowhere.

Peter, the mad scientist's son with a questionable and complex past of his own – I won't spoil it for you – possesses an uncanny ability to figure out solutions that rescues his dad and Anna (the agent) from one life-threatening situation after another, *across multiple timelines and, – oh, check it out; I think it's safe to mention it – two universes.*

Trish coined a phrase that stuck with us both. If we couldn't make up our minds on what to eat for tea one night, which hill to head for in mixed weather conditions, or, on one occasion, whether to accept a job offer in London, we would spend a couple of minutes repeating the question 'What would Peter do?' in a series of increasingly ludicrous accents and emphases ("What *would* Peter do? What would *Peter* do? What would Peter *do*?").

I guess you had to be there to appreciate the collaborative nature of the joke; though, when it comes to couples, even being there won't work unless you're one of the two people involved. If you could pause one of those nature shows, where they follow pairs of birds or mammals that have mated for life, and listen in closely, you'd probably hear one of them say to the other, "The Horn!" or "Chinese, anyone?" It would be there on the tape, but you still wouldn't get it.

For the couple themselves, it's the sense of earned familiarity that feels so damned good. A bit like Donna's nob gag with Steve. Or my Skype sign-offs with Dennis; the synchronised crossing of arms across our chests in an 'X', and the chanted phrase "Big hugs", separated by a fifth of the earth's circumference. Shared rituals reduce distance to nothing at all.

Here's a question, then. Have you ever been having drinks with friends, and found yourself relegated to listening to your partner reminisce about an experience that you weren't there to create with them? How did that feel? You're occupying the same 'outside' as your friends, right?

Compare that to telling an anecdote of your own and, looking across at your partner, knowing that they're reliving that selfsame moment with you, *because they were there too*. Even more importantly, you can jointly anticipate what comes next. With each new embellishment, each small detail, you or your partner will actively assess whether to allow *that* detail to become *your* detail. Your newly modified *shared* story.

Death, at its cruellest and most cavalier, craps on all that mutual world-building. It turns our stories into arid, ossified things that have only a past. It took me a while, I confess, to stop interrupting Trish when she told stories if I heard a misremembered fact, or a misrepresented sequence of events. Several times, after leaving friends' homes or waving them off at our own front door, she'd turn on me with a rare venom. I was turning into my mother, she said; into someone who sabotaged stories to defend the canon from small, organic change. ("No, Tom, no – it was a *Tuesday*!" Mum might insist, sucking all the joy, flow and warmth from Dad's attempts to share the narrative of their lives.) What I should have done more of, more often, is just float in the warmth of our constantly evolving history. It's one of the things I miss most.

I wake three times during the night, Trish ripped from me, revisiting that jolt on realising, as if for the first time, that Trish was still back at the stones. One thing's for sure. I'm not intending to have more than a metre or so of unattached air between me and Trish for the rest of the week. With just five sachets left in the urn, it's even more important to safeguard them.

Do you think *I'm* safe here, holed up on the south-west of the island behind two metres of stone?

I guess if the police are really determined, they might follow up to see if I'm still on the island. A visit to CalMac might divulge the fact of my return ferry ticket to the mainland for Saturday. They won't find any record of my registration at the hotel, so short of a 'sighting', or a walk-in with my hands up, they'll only be able to find me through my connection to The Broch. They have my real name, which matches our original booking here from last November, but other than that, it's just the car registration. I didn't need to record that with the estate when I arrived. And it's parked, at least at the moment, well off the main road.

What do you think? Should I worry? Beyond an amount considered reasonable, I mean.

What concerns me at least as much is how I've slipped behind schedule. I'm being nagged by that voice that asks, knowing that *I* know I've left a listed action undone, *Were you pissing me about, writing all these things on me but secretly having no intention of doing them?* What makes it worse is that these promises weren't just made to myself. When Trish's voice joins the inner one, the prospect of failing starts to tap on my shoulder just that little bit more insistently.

Let's think this through.

One of the things to rub off on me from my last fifteen years in oil and gas, helping folk to solve, or at least understand, their business problems, is a tendency to break stuff down into bite-size issues. If I'm in the mood, or care enough about the consequences of not working things out properly, I'll reduce them down and see where that takes me. *Shall we?*

> **Fact/Problem 1:** I'm a bit at sixes and sevens. I'm not thinking straight, and likely to do more (and more stupid) things. I'd occasionally get to that place ('Twatland', Trish called it), where inaction was the only solution to serial error. If it was a clear night, Trish would drag me outside to defibrillate. She'd demand I look up into the night sky, and wait for the massed cosmos to reveal itself. By the end of her guided tour of the heavens ("Do you see that over there? It's Betelgeuse"), her insistence on the intelligence of mankind in general, and the need for her pillock of a husband in particular to man up and get a grip, I'd be close to the path out of Twatland

and ready to journey back to Sanity-by-the-Sea. We'd return inside for a quick debrief, during which she'd rationally talk me through what was on my mind and, more often than not, retire with me to the conjugal bed.

Fact/Problem 2: I've got six hours of *Battlestar* left to watch, but a whole new item on the list of shows to get through today already. I'm *behind*.

Fact 3: I don't necessarily feel happy to call this a problem, as, like *Battlestar*, the Glenmorangie is a joy. Yet it remains the case that most of last night's second bottle of prize malt remains unconsumed, and tonight's Bowmore beckons.

So that's the landscape. Solved, I think, by some serious bingeing on the TV this morning, while passing enough of this gorgeous malt over my tonsils to catch up. Substitute the daytime Jack, and we're sorted.

The first of them, though – the sixes and sevens – is the toughest nut to crack. Putting higher faculties on hold for a while might help, by immersing myself in Solutions #1 and #2. A state of general crappiness rarely dissipates naturally, but maybe I can just suspend any attempt to deal with it. Join the Fleet in their quest for earth, and their attempts to solve their own Cylon problem, until lunchtime. Other people's problems have been known to briefly overpower one's own.

I'll allow myself that one small anaesthetising thought.

So let's you and I get back on that horse.

IN THE ABSENCE OF AN EFFECTIVE CLOAKING DEVICE, JUST LENGTHEN YOUR STRIDE

The last six episodes of *Battlestar* are as great as I remember them. Cylon suicide bombers. Growing paranoia amongst the Fleet about who is human and who is not. Six tormenting Gaius, and Gaius tormenting himself. Hints of mysticism beginning to surround Starbuck. Above it all, the ongoing struggle of men and women, the last remaining members of their species, looking for a safe haven in which to begin again. I love how no one ever feels the need to state their feelings. Everything is implied. By words and actions. Glances and shrugs. But we get it.

I doubt if you've read it, based on its derisory sales on Amazon, but that's what I was aiming for in *The Quarant*. Let the external physical world of landscape and action and what characters *don't* say be the place where the real drama happens. The medieval setting doesn't matter. The individual concerns of a mere thirty generations ago are the same today: security, family, love, success. With each chapter, Trish sitting in her office at the other side of the house, I visualised those same glances, shrugs and silences threading their way through each scene. Imagined how their weight and significance might evolve with each fictional encounter. I still feel my goal in writing that story *that way* was an honourable one, and I, at least, got the chance to watch them trying to make sense of their lives and the roles they were destined to play. I think their behaviour even changed me a little as I observed them, my role as originator forgotten.

Anyway, I navigate my way through these six episodes, only once suffering a lapse that leaves my glass lying empty on my lap, a £200 stain across my groin (cue cheap jokes about high-class call girls and inexperienced but wealthy adolescents). The best way, I find, to prevent more spills is to get any remaining malt down my neck quickly. *Sláinte.*

So here we are. End of Season One. Six and Gaius witness a sublime vision of their future, and Lee Adama cradles the dying figure of his father, shot by Boomer. Alternate with me between the colour-saturated world of Kobol and the gritty, unnatural light of the *Galactica* bridge, to the strain of a beautiful choral soundtrack. Stunning. We did well, you and I, to feature this on our list.

The day outside is a third gone, but that's OK. In here, in *me*, the worry of being behind my viewing schedule is gone. I get up off the sofa, and stand at the window. Cloud is back, and the sea has turned a dark matt green. I return to the coffee table and reward my recent endeavours with a tick against *Battlestar.* Just four to go.

Another flashback. Our 'January 2nd' ritual. Recovered from our Hogmanay hangovers, Trish and I would sit with a glass of wine and the 'Things We Wish to Do and Achieve' list from the same day a year earlier, written by convention on a single yellow notelet. In a manner approaching the sacramental, we'd review the recurring first item: 'Remain happy together.' Jokes about whether we'd achieved it would be made (*"But what about when you bought the wrong dishwasher tablets, and didn't say sorry?"*), but it would always be checked off with a toast to ourselves.

We'd go through the body of the list, discussing in turn how worthwhile each task, if completed, had been. We rarely beat ourselves up; no point starting the New Year like that. Incompletions were either justified or relegated. Looking back, we were always able to tick off about 80% of the items as achieved, which I continue to feel good about, especially as we'd decided on them together. Before moving on to the current year, we would also invest time, and much of the next glass of Merlot, in reminiscing over any additional highlights of our recent past.

Spurred on, we'd then fill a second notelet to address the coming year. Holidays, hillwalking objectives, projects around the house. Money and the like. 'Garden' often made an appearance, mainly due to my own indolence or ability to kill stuff (two years ago, for example, I'd killed a lot of grass but very little willowherb). Literary objectives made their first appearance four years ago: 'Complete first draft of novel *The Quarant*', or 'Complete all research for *The Puppet Master.*' Even this we shared; I'd do the writing, but I'd need Trish to support the space required to do it.

What was on the lists, of course, was never *that* important, and we both knew it. It was just another way to keep the air in our little life raft in the North-West Highlands.

Back here in The Broch, having completed my annotations, I head back down to the hamper. Exercise is much overrated as a way of increasing appetite – just stand in front of some great food, and it'll do the trick just as well. You might not even smell so bad.

Raspberry shortbread. Rosemary oatcakes. Elderflower marmalade. It's working. And it'll probably help to have something to eat if I'm heading outside (*when did I decide that?*).

I raid the fridge for bread – the bubbly is still there – construct a feast of cheddar sandwiches, and plate up some shortbread covered in spoonfuls of elderflower marmalade. As I eat, I lean over the sink unit to get a view of the passenger side of the car. Still there, then. Not dragged away to Tarbert in an attempt to turn against its owner and his socially questionable behaviours.

Lost in further thoughts of PCs and assertive estate workers, a mouthful of seeded batch goes the wrong way. I thought autonomic functions were supposed to be, well, autonomic.

Maybe my nervous system is better able to transmit instructions through the medium of an exclusively whisky diet. Solids clearly remain a challenge. Yesterday's salmon and chocolate were a fluke. Fair enough.

I'm guessing that your own ratio of healthy carbs and proteins to rather less healthy ones is a little better balanced than my own, but does your body ever rebel against reasonable requests? It's not as if I'm trying to get raw oysters down me. One failed attempt at *that*, at a gourmet buffet on the shores of Loch Torridon, was more than enough to suggest that I stay well clear of *them*. How they count as an aphrodisiac, I don't know. The wrong kind of anatomical stirrings set in later that night, I can tell you.

Anyway, it's clear that this eating thing requires more concentration than I've given it, so I knuckle down. Small mouthfuls chewed well.

So, that thought I had earlier; the one about going outside. Fancy it?

A TOUCH OF THE VERBALS

Even now, two days on, I can't remember where the idea to take a walk along the coast came from. I know Trish would have suggested it, irrespective of the weather. Waterproofs, and a willingness to just get out there and get dry and warm later was her all over. She'd be kicking my arse out of the house about now.

I'm not going to travel far. But I've no desire to repeat any uncomfortable interactions with the estate. There's a beach just a couple of miles down the coast at Scarista. It looks pretty spectacular, if Google Maps is anything to go by, and it's off the main road along a secluded cul-de-sac. I should be fine, roadblocks, copters and well-briefed SWAT teams permitting.

Outside, the weather's uncannily similar to Sunday's, if a little breezier. Mild, moist air. No problem.

Trish and Jack are in their usual positions as the first few passes of the windscreen wipers spread a thin coating of overnight salt air. A few squirts of screenwash does the trick, allowing me to conduct last-minute surveillance for any signs of a stake-out.

The drive to the sands, stretching to fill the entire shallow bay and into a wide stretch of salt marsh, is a short one. I wind down the window, inhaling sea air as I head past a nine-hole golf course and the near-obligatory herd of cows grazing on the machair. The skies here remain enormous, despite lacking the slightest hint of blue.

I look across to Trish. Under other circumstances, the smile on my face would be considerably broader. We'd probably be punching the air at this point, Mr and Mrs Smug Bastard, congratulating ourselves on our choice of destination.

A narrow lane blocks the salt marsh from penetrating further inland, and leads me along the opposite side of the bay, heading towards the hill that dominates the horizon. I don't know its name, but its most northerly tip, where it runs down into the uninterrupted Atlantic, is called Gob an Tobha. 'Toe Head', to us Sassenachs. An elevated view of the entire isthmus might conjure up the inverted relief of one of those sauropod footprints found on Skye, just fifty miles from here. Perhaps 'Claw Head' would serve it better.

I park up at the turning circle where the road ends and assess the apparent steepness of the climb less than a mile away. Hillsides often seem more intimidating from a distance, and I've not read anything to suggest difficulty. On with the rucksack, and off we go.

The walk to the base of the climb is across an exposed and windswept strip of low grasses between two stretches of sea; grazing land for what look like stationary cattle.

To be honest, I've never really enjoyed coastal walks. Give me inland mountains, even those with names like Devil's Penis (or 'Point', as the Ordnance Survey now prudishly translates it), or Crap-Your-Keks Ridge, and I'll feel safer than when traversing a coastal path, cliff walk or otherwise.

The breeze stiffens (all that talk of penises?) as the narrowing track weaves towards the south side of the peninsula. A deep soup of mud and cow shit lies directly beyond a boundary gate, but I manage to tiptoe around it to join a series of fence posts that curves slowly up the nose of the hill. Darker skies seem to be gathering beyond the rise. Rain is on its way, but I'm here now, so I keep going.

I lose the trail every so often, but faint differences of shade in the grassy rise might indicate a route. It could be a sheep track, but even they have the ability to navigate around the boggiest ground. The dense heather, missing most if not all of its purple blooms this late in the year, provides a dry cushion to keep me out of the worst difficulties. I contour further on, my lungs closer to bursting than pride allows me to admit, to the point where the view to the north opens up.

You may already know this, but poor weather merely makes the Highland landscape even more outstanding. "Beautiful things," Trish would say, "don't suddenly become ugly just because you can't see them so well." When hill mists wreathe themselves around steep and craggy slopes, or one of any number of rainbows offers a sense of just how localised and confused our weather up here can be, it's magical.

Look with me. Just below us, the white Scarista sands and dunes stretch out under the waterline. In the middle distance, the outcrop of Taransay, separated from the mainland by a narrow sound of water, still fringed by further hints of bright yellow, serves as a boundary for this seven- or eight-mile stretch of coast. And further back still, the range of hills that runs west to east, culminating in The Clisham. Not many Brits are aware that such landscapes exist in their own country. And long may that continue. *It's mine, I tell you, all mine!* (Maniacal laughter follows.)

A few more minutes, and I reach a decent spot in the lee of the hill. The morning sun is long forgotten, and the dense cloud, while still well above the summit, is directly above me. My glasses are coated with raindrops and sweat, and I'm more than happy to stop here. I find a fairly level tuft of heather, and do the usual with the bottom of my coat. Aaah, that's good.

I remove Trish from the rucksack, rotating her slowly just above my head so she can take in the entire panorama. "What do you think of this?" Drizzle gives her an additional shine. "Not bad, eh?"

The wind drops noticeably, as if waiting on her reply.

"Can you see the car?" Another of our stock phrases, uttered by rote after long hill days, feet rebelling against the pounding they've had. "Can you see it?"

I place her carefully on the heather beside me, ensuring that her lid is secure. Out comes the Jack.

I sit back and the clouds put on a show. Squalls and pulses of rain steam in, front following front. Below me, the cows at the base of the hill are gathered together at the far end of their enclosure.

While I am not known for my resilience to the cold, the scenery beyond the hood of my jacket keeps me reasonably contented. There's at least an hour of decent daylight remaining. I consider this small, unpretentious hill my friend.

My mind drifts off to the days Trish and I spent together at home. No more weekly commutes to Aberdeen or evenings with my iPad in the King Street B&B. My eight-ounce hip flask, with its added inscription from Trish (*'Together forever, never apart, maybe in distance but never in heart'),* is as redundant as I am. But

I wish I had it with me now; that I could feel the run of those words under my thumb.

Sharing the house with Trish every working day proved, if proof were needed, that we fitted together well. Here's the template on which our new lives rested:

8.30: Breakfast together.
9.15: Take T. a cup of tea at her desk, then sit at Mac.
12.00: Mutual pause to make lunch and eat together.
13.00: T. return to office; M. chores or more writing.
17.00: Drinks o'clock. T. a dark red; M. a smooth Spey. Recap of day.
17.30: Tea made and eaten together.
18.30: Discuss evening viewing options.
18.40: Line up shows and share the evening.
Sometime between 22.00–23.00: Wake T. up from her snooze, and hold hands to bed.

What shape does your happiness take? What architecture contains and protects it?

In the centre of Machu Picchu, there's a structure called the 'Hitching Post of the Sun', carved from the bedrock of the mountain on which the settlement rests. It acted as both pivot around which ritual orbited, and as representation of the wider world.

What is the structure of your own life carved from? Routines? Relationships?

My father struggled with retirement, realising, after several months at home, how much he drew on the company and stimulation of workmates. On routine. He was never clinically depressed, but I think he came close. In our many conversations around that time (during a longer-than-average winter, which didn't help), he opened up to me just once, leaving me with a sense of sadness and privilege. All I could do was listen, but with the filter of parenthood temporarily removed, I saw what he saw. The changing shape of his life.

Have you seen those you love fail to make a transition that, on paper, should have been nothing but beneficial and welcome? Were you able to help them? And if so, what did it imply about your own abilities and wishes?

This new regime of ours, then, absent any radical change, still remoulded the contours of our happiness. Clarified our preconceived ideas about what we loved about being with each other. How, within a few months away from work, I dispensed with the need to maintain relationships with dozens, if not hundreds of colleagues.

Replacing the structure that held all *that* with something infinitely simpler, and assuming prime occupancy of the space between my ears for the first time in thirty years, felt great. I'd answered Michael's two questions – *Got enough? Had enough?* – and remain grateful that I was able to act on the answers.

As you can see, meeting you, having not spoken to anyone for the best part of a year, has opened the bloody floodgates. Sorry about that, but the drive to share is something else.

In any case, the rain here is getting heavier, and it'll be getting dark soon, so let's head back down to lower ground.

Over there, to the right, lie the small islands of Pabbay and Ensay. Celtic mythology is not my strong point, but I think the former is the God of Ironing, and the latter the Goddess of Bingo. (I may have got that last one wrong, as I often confuse her with Emvay, the Goddess of Mobility Scooters.) In the foreground of these two islands, tucked away on the southern coastline below and just a slight detour from the path back to the car, there's a really enticing inlet, lined by what appears to be, even by local standards, a stunning ribbon of sand.

I'll take a look on the way back.

The rain's here to stay, on a strengthening breeze, and the temperature's dropping with the light. I've sat too long – my hands struggle to screw the lid back on the bottle. Behind me, those black clouds are even lower. I reckon we're just minutes from them touching down on the hill.

It's good to get back to the fence posts. A small bird, white markings above and below his eyes, lifts from and drops onto each more distant post as I approach him. He leads me down, seemingly understanding that I'm not part of the local food chain.

Below us, looking inland in the worsening light, the hills of central Harris have closed in. I'm glad I resisted heading that way – navigation would be a real problem by now. At least here it's a straight up-and-down.

Feet nicely back on the track that will return me to the car, I concede defeat and zip my coat up until it grazes my chin, adjusting the peak of my hood to give it a little more sturdiness against the wind. My rucksack, lacking any protective cover, is soaked through, but Trish should remain dry beneath her ceramic lid.

I take the spur of the path that leads over the dunes to the beach, the wind whipping my trousers as I emerge onto the white sands. Low above the growing ocean swell, in one of the diminishing areas of clear sky, a full moon begins its ascent. I don't really understand the mechanics of tides, but it feels as though something or someone is doing its best to stir up things; provoke some kind of tantrum or spat with the land. Nothing is crashing or huge, but the amplitude of the waves chasing their way in suggests a restless, building disquiet.

Remember how I told you of my modest days of adolescent storm chasing? Those days come back to me now, and I lower my hood. It's still cold, but I'm back there, insulated by youthful angst and surging hormones. It's hard to explain, but something to be tolerated or endured has become something, well, to be savoured and enjoyed. Like a switch has been thrown. Does that make any sense?

I twist the lid off the Jack, and take a full mouthful (something my teenage self would never have done). I raise my head to the horizon, swallow, and walk down to the sea's edge.

You'll think me daft, but when the next gust of rain hits my face, I shout out. Cheer. A long, drawn-out "Yeees!" I raise my arms from my sides, inviting the next squall.

The sea stubbornly resists the apocalypse. No waves crash around my feet. Nothing swells to offer an answer. Pabbay and Ensay keep their thoughts to themselves, equally unwilling to acknowledge the existence of some crazed mortal on the Atlantic shore having himself 'a moment'. That's OK. I'm always happy to look stupid if no one is there to see me. To be fair, if only a fraction of my stupidities were witnessed, I probably wouldn't be allowed out on my own. But it feels good, you know? Standing here, giving the elements free rein. I'm in them. Part of them. Another slug of Jack, and for a moment, just a moment, yesterday's farce recedes to become just another disappointing day.

Another gust. The wind is really getting up, and I'm going to make the most of it. I turn and walk further along the sands, their light palette interrupted only by the darker flotsam of kelp marking the last high tide.

It's then that I see it. A large object, halfway along the bay, perhaps a couple of hundred yards from here. The late afternoon light plays on its surface, but I can't make out what it is. An upturned fibreglass boat?

I've no desire to interact with anyone, but I'm curious. This isn't exactly the Monaco Yacht Club. There's nothing resembling a wharf or jetty here, and I've seen no one. That said, that part of the sands is not that far from the end of the tarmac road. Maybe someone's planning to go out onto the water, or has just returned.

The thought that someone might need help crosses my mind. I outgrew any sense of civic responsibility years ago, a position accelerated in no small part by the Blair WMD fiasco and a growing sense that the world was fundamentally immune to any efforts I might consider could make a difference. But if someone, an individual rather than a community, was in trouble, could I just walk past?

The hull of the boat and what looks like its rudder are just a few shades lighter than the sand on which they rest. Towards the top (what is the word for the top of a boat?), where I imagine the deck to be, the craft offers darker colours; a kind of shiny charcoal grey.

I'm only about a hundred yards away now, but I can't see any mast or anything else that might offer further clues as to the type of boat or why it's lying there.

Another fifty yards, and I stop dead in my tracks.

Hold on.

Hold bloody well on.

The boat *flexes*; pushes light from it in ways fibreglass has yet to master, short of some kind of catastrophic adjustment. It resumes its original position. The whole thing lasts a second, maybe two. Less a flex, more a… More a *tremor*?

This is not the thing I expect. Not what I'm walking towards.

I close the distance down by half. And that's not a boat. *That's a fucking whale!* Oh Christ. Jesus!

Stop for a minute. Just stop. What to do? What to do?

Another shiver runs through the animal. A small part of its flank doesn't seem to move at the same time, in the same way. In fact, it remains static. Light doesn't bounce off it in the same way. A subordinate stillness in the foreground of a large, spasming mass.

I can't tear my eyes away. Five more steps, and the outline of the whale is fully resolved. Two more, and the shape lying in front of it offers up its meaning.

It's a woman. Lying on her side, her feet closest to the sea, hair soaked flat to her scalp.

I stop dead, ten feet from her.

A third tremor. The whale's tail fin lifts and then falls. Again, the woman doesn't move.

Her skin is mottled with patches of white and crimson. Her back is to the wind and rain, as it is to me. Woven in amongst the shades of chilled flesh is an unmistakable quilt of bruises, charcoal blacks and mustard yellows, distributed across her legs, buttocks and back.

Help.

Trish.

What would Peter do?

I need a minute. Hell, I could do with five.

One of the bruises resolves into a tattoo. Butterfly wings nestled in the small of her back. But the rest?

I can't help myself. I have to look around. Scan for any sign that she's not alone. I know I should be wholly concerned for the well-being of the woman just feet from me, but I'm a fully clad man standing, almost looming over, a naked young woman. *If anyone can see her, they can see me. Wonder what I'm doing here.*

Does that make me bad? Selfish? Either way, I'm not ready to close the last few steps to the prone figure. Instead, I move to my left, and take in more of the animal lying beyond. Scuffs and gouges on the whale's skin, one quite large and angry, thread their way across most of its length. Its tail fin continues to quiver, its lower portion dug a couple of inches into the sand. Another fin runs parallel to the woman, some three or four feet above her head. The sheer mass of its body seems to generate its own gravity.

I draw level with the plane of the woman's body. She looks tiny against the bulk of the animal lying just two or three feet from her. I see her arm now, falling easy in front of her chest. Her hand lies flat on the sand, palm raised upwards. If she has any awareness of her surroundings – and I'm not sure she does – she's going to notice me very soon. I don't want to startle her. She could fall into the side of the whale. Or scream and disturb the bloody thing.

She's trembling. She must be freezing. How long has she been here?

That's it, then. I take the remaining steps to her side, crouch down, reach out and touch her wrist. Her eyes appear open, but fixed on a point at the front of the creature.

I do what I can to remove any harshness or threat from my voice. "Hello? Hello? Can you hear me?"

Nothing.

"Hello. My name's Martin. Are you all right?"

I move my hand up from her wrist to her elbow. Her skin is cold and wet.

At the edge of my vision, a movement. The whale's fin briefly lifts and drops back. When I turn back to the woman, her head has turned. She looks directly at me.

"Whoa!" I lose my balance, and fall to my left. I put out my hand to steady myself, *on the side of the bloody whale.* I hold my breath. Nothing happens, and I struggle back up.

I repeat my name. "I just saw you here."

This isn't going well. You'd never guess I once spent two days on a St John's Ambulance course. So much for the half-life of an unused skill.

I might have missed it, but I've yet to see her blink. Her eyes are glazed. Vacant. She turns her head slowly back to its original position.

I walk round behind her and look across to the animal, following her gaze.

The front half of the whale is all mouth and, cutting through the breeze, a cloying stink of rot. Instead of teeth, there's a long curtain, thousands of bristles, each up to a foot in length, the same light grey as the animal's skin. At the point where its jaws meet, sunk into thick rolls of skin, is the black, shiny pool of the whale's eye.

So that's it. Her head's directly opposite the midpoint of the whale's body. She's been staring straight into its eye.

I read somewhere that if you stare into another person's eyes for ten minutes – a harder task than it sounds – there's a material weakening in your connection to the reality around you; a loss of colour perception, maybe even a sense of suspended time. The cheapest of intimate highs. How long has this woman been out here? It's been raining for a couple of hours, and the wind, while less strong beneath the lip of the dunes, brings with it some serious cooling.

I shrug off my rucksack and unzip my coat, ready to put it around her. Crouching down behind her, I place my hand on her shoulder. "Come on. Please. I don't think it's good for you to stay here."

Her attention remains elsewhere, but I feel her submit to my request. As she rises, I bring both my hands up, reluctant to touch her. Instead, standing between her and the wind, I position my palms on a harmless, unthreatening cushion of air a couple of inches above her bare skin. When her knees weaken, I instinctively reach out, bracing for her scream as I grip the cold flesh at the top of her arms. But her silence remains unbroken. She's shivering all over, but keeps her feet.

The whale seems oblivious to the new level of movement around it.

"So, then. Do you have any clothes?"

There's clearly nothing lying nearby. What the hell has she done with them?

"Here. This will have to do." I keep one hand on her at all times now. "Come on. Put this on."

She's still fixed on the whale. When my coat nudges her shoulder, she brings her arm back and I guide it into the sleeve. Her wet skin causes her arm to stick before it's even halfway in. The second arm is no easier. She's doing nothing to help me.

I don't feel happy reaching around her to do the zip up. I might frighten her. There's nothing for it. I turn her round to face me, severing her connection to the animal. My own hands are really cold now, and it takes a couple of minutes of fumbling with the zip to complete the action. I do my best to ignore the tight purple buttons of her nipples and the dark hue at the top of her legs. I secure the coat around her, and pull up the hood around her face. The coat is way too big, but the upside is that it falls to within an inch of her knees. She looks straight at me for the first time, her eyes a placid bluey-grey. But she's still not really seeing me. Her face is washed of all colour.

"Come on. Let's get you off the beach. Out of this rain."

I pick up my rucksack, clench my teeth as we turn side-on to the wind, and slowly walk the twenty yards to where the land tilts sharply upwards onto the dune. I'm way too anxious to put my arm around her, but instead push it through hers. That'll work.

She puts on the brakes when we reach the back of the beach, raising what is becoming a daily 'clink' from my rucksack. Joined, we turn slowly to the right. A pile of clothes and a small leather bag sit just a few inches into the short grass adjoining the beach. We shuffle across, and I pick everything up. The clothes are totally sodden, so there's no point in offering them to her. Another couple of shrugs, and they're in my rucksack (the Jack and Trish seem fine). Her shoes won't fit, so I carry them in my free hand. She reaches out for the bag. If she wants to carry it, that's up to her. I'll just focus on getting us back to tarmac.

We look quite something, don't you think? Stumbling up the dunes, like some couple awaiting early elimination from *Strictly*, or survivors walking from the shattered remains of some terrorist's handiwork. All that's missing is a partially severed limb, or ripped clothing. The smouldering ruins of a crashed jet. Quite a sight.

We complete our walk to the parking area in silence, but inside, I'm the opposite of quiet, with several *What the fuck?!*s exploding with almost every step. The route back is rough in places, but the woman seems happy, if that's the right word (*it isn't*), to continue on bare feet. They must be numb.

Or maybe I'm not quite remembering this clearly. Maybe the screaming in my head only really starts when we get back to the parking circle, when she tells me, quietly and calmly, that no, she doesn't have a car, and no, she has no one to call, and (you guessed it) no, she most definitely has nowhere to stay.

A NECESSARY IF BRIEF BEGINNING

Her name is Caitlin. And she likes tea. That's all I've got from her to date.

She's upstairs, having a shower. I helped her up there, worried she might struggle with the stairs. Showed her how to work things. All her clothes are in the washing machine. I put her shoes in, too – they were filthy. Her laces are soaking in the sink. Three notes and a few coins from her jeans pocket are on the utility-room worktop. I don't think she has a phone. That's unusual nowadays, isn't it? What's more unusual still is the absence of a proper coat, beyond a thick fleece. I'll go up there later and recover my Páramo; bring it downstairs to dry.

I've put her black tea (I've no milk) on the cabinet beside the bed. Unless she calls, I've no intention of going back up.

Put mildly, I can't settle. Put honestly, I'm bricking it.

Two minutes on the sofa, and I'm up at the window again. I'm still pretty cold myself, but the underfloor heating here is slowly doing the trick. I need to calm down a bit before I can even start to think about tonight's Ceremony.

What the fuck was I thinking?

This morning, my concerns were for the car. But this afternoon, a whale's decision to beach itself and a young woman's choice to join it have pushed that issue well down the pecking order.

I'm unsure if there's anything in the T&Cs here that objects to guests. But the estate would probably find my current circumstances a little out of the ordinary. I've done nothing wrong. I really haven't. If I'd left her there, I'm not sure she'd have made it through the rest of the day. Look at it out there now. The weather's really set in. She's not quite skin and bone, but she was heading for some serious hypothermia.

And what about the bloody whale? I've seen the odd news item in the past; mass beachings and the like. It's usually sonar failure or what have you, or sad cases involving fishing tackle or pollution, or some kind of collision. This one did have those couple of gashes in its side, but they didn't look too deep.

I'm not sure what to do about it. If I report it, I'll probably have to give my name. Overlooking the fact that I have absolutely no idea who I should tell – Robert at the estate house would be as good a start as any, I guess – I don't want to get involved in anything that means my name might get around. PC Cathy might latch on to the unexpected windfall, and the next thing you know I'll be re-enacting the closing scene from *Butch Cassidy and the Sundance Kid*, or its Hebridean equivalent.

And of course, there's Caitlin. A full-on, off-its-head mystery, pulled back from whatever abyss she jumped into earlier. And I was the one doing the pulling, so, like it or not, I've got some kind of duty of care. She's an adult, of course; free to make her own choices. But I'm not sure she was in any fit state, with the cold and the rain and the freak-out hold that whale's eye seemed to have on her, to do much other than follow my lead.

But this really fucks things up.

The shower upstairs goes off. The house drops further into a silence that I thought was already complete. My arms tighten across my chest. This is ridiculous. Yoga breaths. Nope. Not working. *Still ridiculous*.

Ten minutes and a lifetime later, Caitlin walks barefoot down the staircase and loiters at the edge of the room, her face almost crimson with recirculating blood. She's double her earlier size. Spare T-shirt and jumper from my case, tracksuit bottoms and, above them, the white, fluffed-up luxury of one of The Broch's complementary dressing gowns. My Páramo drips from her hand.

"Hi. I've left the towel hanging up. And this is cosy." She pinches the collar of the heavy towelling to her clavicle (few parts of the body have been more beautifully named), and holds out the coat. "Do you want this back?"

Happy to have something to do, I jump up from the sofa and take it from her. When I get back upstairs, she's still standing there.

"Is it OK if I go lay down? I'm knackered."

"Absolutely. I'll stay down here tonight. That's fine."

I'm thinking of what else to say to her long after she's wound her way back up to the bedroom.

I get my first full lungful of air since leaving the beach, and take a couple more circuits of the room. I'm not happy, but I'm just about ready to settle down to The Ceremony.

I lift the urn from the side of the sofa, where it's been hidden from view. *See. I'm already changing things because she's here.*

Anyway. Tonight's selection is my first Islay of the week.

Norske Cask Selection Bowmore 1993 Aged 11 Years *(***96***)*

n*24 a picnic by the sea: plenty of ozone and salt, the most beautiful peat-reek with clear iodine from rock pools. Man, this is soooo Islay…!!!* ***t****24 a meal in itself: thick, intense layering of 90% cocoa chocolate with sludgy peat and gorgeously sweet barley, all sprinkled with a little sea salt; the degree of oiliness just about hits perfection;* ***f****24 long and sweetens as the gristiness of the barley comes through, shuddering layers of more cocoa and peat that go on ad-infinitum.* ***b****24 why do we so rarely see casks of this distillery's malt exactly the way I remember it some 25-years ago? This is a true classic destined to be one of the talked-about all-lifetime greats. Sod the sample: I'm off to find a bottle…!!* ***65.5%***

I'd be lying if I said that I didn't rush things. No sooner is #23/10 empty than Trish is hidden back away on the blind side of the room.

What *is* that?

I need that piercing warmth to hit me fast. Two swallows and my first full dram is gone. So much for picking up on the iodine and salt.

This is stupid. I've spent months building and obsessively checking my defences. Inspecting every vulnerable corner for any potential weakness against attack. Or (and it's hard to admit this) any distractions that might lead to thoughts of my escape from all this. These few minutes every evening are my most – possibly my *only* – valued moments, briefly closing the distance between Trish and my memories of her, and here I sit, compromising them. *Embarrassed* by them?

I pour another glass. Move the rim until it gently presses on the cartilage where nose joins philtrum (another brilliant body-part name). If you try this, be sure to take care. A moderate miscalculation in pressure will have your eyes filling up and the whole experience spoiled. Mr Murray should be a little clearer on this point.

I empty my lungs, tip the glass forward a little, and take a long, slow breath in through my nose. That's *so* much better.

Now. Reach over and restore Trish to her rightful place on the coffee table. *There. Now. Settle back into the routine. Where's the list?*

Four more shows to choose from. It's another sad indictment on the day that, to cheer myself up tonight, I'll plump for the story of a Jersey-based community of Italian-American psychopathic misogynists experiencing their own unique brand of familial loyalty, questionable levels of self-awareness, and platefuls of ziti, macaroni with gravy, and (my personal favourite, even though I've no idea what it looks or tastes like) *gabagool*. I've the appetite of a hibernating tardigrade, but it's still fun to watch Tony and the boys do their dance around food after a particularly harrowing mob execution.

The light has gone outside, the sky impervious to moon or stars. Rain still paradiddles across the huge glass panes to my right. To the south, a whale, alone now unless found by others, slowly suffocates under its own weight.

And here I sit, with absolutely no idea about what tomorrow might bring, sinking into chocolatey, peaty sweetness.

CORRESPONDENCE
TUESDAY 6TH MARCH 2018

Scottish Fatalities Investigation Unit (North)
Great Glen House
Leachkin Road
Inverness
Telephone: 0844 5612925

REF: 18/037/GM
DATE: Tuesday 6th March 2018
STRICTLY PRIVATE & CONFIDENTIAL

Dear Mr Rose,

I am writing in reference to our investigation into the circumstances of the road traffic accident occurring on the A887 on the 20th January of this year, in which your wife Tricia lost her life.

Having reviewed the initial evidence provided by the Road Policing Unit and the two pathologists attending the post-mortem, and subsequent post-incident interviews, we have confirmed the cause of death as accidental, arising from multiple injuries at the time of the accident.

We have forwarded a report to the Crown Office and it has been decided that no criminal proceedings will arise from this incident. Therefore, our investigation is now concluded.

Should you have any further questions regarding the above, please do not hesitate to contact us.

Yours sincerely,
James Finlay
Principal Procurator Fiscal Depute (North)

CHAPTER 5

WEDNESDAY 24TH OCTOBER 2018

It was an idea. I don't know. Who knows where they fuckin' come from. Isaac Newton invented gravity 'cause some asshole hit 'im with an apple.

(Christopher Moltisanti, The Sopranos)

COASTAL EXPLORATIONS

Some nights possess a reset button. Allow you to wipe previous settings and trajectories based on an acceptance that the past is best left there.

My slate isn't completely wiped this morning, but its details are reassuringly blurred. Unresolved. I wake into a kind of weightless neutral, shaped only by two laws: Trish gone, and me going.

Early mornings at home were different. My first ninety minutes or so involved little more than my latest e-book, the odd unplanned doze, and feeling the ambient warmth emanating from Trish's side of the bed. At eight, we'd be bombarded by the crackling, staccato flex of radiators and pipes enjoying their sixty-second chorus. Think Edinburgh Tattoo with drummers straight out of the pub, or a John Bonham drum solo. If that didn't wake her? "Trish. Trish. It's eight o'clock. Time to get up."

I didn't need a reset button back then. Didn't want one. That firebreak – of sitting in the dark, Trish's breathing marking time, my head sunk in worlds so much like our own, yet so different; the worlds of Atwood, Banks, Block – was enough. Happy to bring any unresolved issues across with me into the new day, confident in our shared ability to work through them. Quite something.

Last night, Carmela kicked out the priest, and Tony lied to his best friend at gunpoint before confronting Livia on a gurney as she was wheeled out to St Vincent's following her stroke. Tony's incandescent rage and confusion at the culmination of his mother's dislike for him are astonishing. And then the scene at Artie's in the storm. Tony's toast to the need for his children to remember the good family times.

That can do it too. Just like the best words of a Faulks or a McEwan or a Mitchell, the things that gifted actors and actresses do, the words they say, the emotions they choreograph and show. They reset *our* world, even as they fail to put the brakes on their own.

I can't read. I can't write. The week hangs by a thread. That's what dumb chance mixed up with a dumb man can do to any plan.

But this morning, I'll wear a smile for Caitlin when she comes down the stairs.

Oh, and this is the right time to clear one thing up. Caitlin is the proud owner of a full-on, no-holds-barred Glaswegian accent, all sing-song rhythms and take-no-prisoner currents that will wash you off your feet and dump the full weight of the Clyde on your head with every utterance.

I, on the other hand, despite a real love of this extraordinary dialect, have neither the skill nor the time to make an even passing attempt at capturing its richness and inherent, rib-threatening humour. So please accept this apology – Caitlin will speak to us both, for the purposes of my tale, in the pale vanilla of my own tongue. But trust me, she's all Weegie, and then some.

"Can I get you any breakfast?" she asks, from the square foot of floor nearest the bottom step. No eye contact. It's a good way to postpone any serious conversation, but she's no idea what the food situation is downstairs.

I'm not hungry, but I go with the beginning of a flow. "Sure, let's see what we've got." What we've got, as you know, is pretty much hamper, bread and banana.

The washing machine goes on tumble-dry (she's got no other clothes – thank God for the dressing gown and my spares), and we return upstairs with coffees and two plates of toast and Prosecco marmalade. Caitlin heads to the furthest chair from where I sit, on the sofa.

A shared or joint experience is often the basis for dialogue. Like adventurers who agree that each of them is up to their arse in crocodiles, and there's a hole in their canoe. ('You bail, I'll paddle.') I'm older, this is my home (at least temporarily), and I'm the rescuer, so to speak. But I bottle it. Wait for her to start.

She clears her throat. "This is quite the place."

I offer the appropriate humble acknowledgements.

"So how long have you lived here?" She's dodged the fact that she probably can't remember my name.

"Oh, not long, Caitlin." That's a cheap bit of cruelty, I know. But this place is for me and Trish, isn't it?

Anyway, it works. "I'm sorry, but I don't know your name. You may have told me yesterday. Down at the beach?"

"So I'm Martin, and I'm just here for the week. I live back on the mainland. Near Loch Ness." I'm doing my best not to sound too spiky – I really don't need any of this.

"And you looked at this place on the map and thought, *Just the place to go to get away from water*?"

It's a start, I suppose. I've not spoken more than twenty words with anyone new for six months, if you discount Robert, the gillie, and the folks at the visitor centre. This, right here, feels like a home invasion.

"I suppose you'll be wondering what I was doing down there yesterday."

Right. This is an easier one. "Well, only if you want to tell me. But first just tell me how you're feeling. Have you warmed up?"

I put bruises and naked bodies out of my mind before she can see what I'm thinking. I've always been pretty easy to read, apparently; it's testament to her state of mind that she even agreed to get in the car yesterday. Any sane woman would have run a mile at the sight of me.

"I'm actually much better, thanks. This place is well cosy. It's the warmest I've been since I left."

"Left?"

Her smile disappears, the crumbs on her plate demanding her attention. "Yes. I'm not from here either. Although I'm not technically on my holidays. If I was, I'd do better to pick a nicer time of year. Or a place with more sun."

"You up from Glasgow?"

"Good spot. Well, I suppose so, although I've been out of the place for a few years now. I think we grew out of love with each other about the same time, so I did the honourable thing and got the fuck out. It was the right thing to do then, and I don't miss it."

"So where's home now?"

That glance across to the window again. "I belong to Skye, as they say. Well, me and my 'significant other'. Are you going to finish that?"

We swap plates (still no eye contact) and she descends on my leftovers.

I clear my throat, sidestepping the obvious follow-up with a less intrusive one. "So when did you come across? I'm guessing you came into Tarbert?'

"Well, no, actually. Ullapool, on the mainland. So I came into Stornoway, further up."

"So maybe this is an extension to your holiday? Or were you working in Ullapool?"

I've gone just that little bit too far.

"More coffee?" And she's off.

It's my turn to look out at the bay. *Shit.*

She comes back with her clothes from the dryer. "I won't be long. Thanks for getting them clean."

She's forgotten the coffee. I'll wait until she's back, then offer a refill.

We tiptoe around each other most of the morning, between bursts of mindless daytime TV. Sketch out the shape of our boundaries. Despite her continuing nervousness, there's a kind of strength underneath the obvious signs of crisis. As she speaks, I sense vulnerability is not Caitlin's natural state. Have I messed things up for her? Should I have left her where she lay? *Brought the whale instead?*

Trish was quite clear about interventions. "Do them all you like at work. Knock your socks off. But out there?" She'd point to the Aberdeen street below our bedroom. "Out there, you're dealing with people who don't give a shit about company safety rules, or contractual requirements. Some people just can't be approached. They don't care about you. They don't *know* you. And some of them don't even know what *they're* going to do next." It was simple. "If you care more about helping a stranger who might stick you with a knife or beat the crap out of you, than you do about leaving me looking down on this street on my own, *then go right ahead*."

No wriggle room there, then.

I got involved just once after that. In a bank queue, of all places, challenging a woman behind me as she repeatedly slapped her small son around the head in rhythm with her demands for silence, pulling violently down on his arm to emphasise every other word. ("*Do* you *hear* what I'm *saying*?") I escaped unharmed, with merely a blue-aired earful, but then Trish weighed in on *me*! Hadn't *I* listened to *anything* she had *said*?

Since then, I've been what can be accurately termed the Indifferent Samaritan.

Yet here we sit, Caitlin and I.

She's of average height. Her hair, out of the rain, is a mixture of light straw and brunette. Mid-length, swept back around her ears. A slight overbite, with a small chip out of one of her front teeth. A mouth that suggests she's ready for any next surprise. Her eyes remain their bluey-grey, but they're much more alert now. Like someone's back in residence, but unsure if her stay will be a long one. Her clothes: a pair of jeans and an '80s-style blue-and-white striped sweat top. She's channelling (or is it me?) a sort of fresh-faced Patsy Kensit vibe, circa Jim Kerr or that arse from Oasis.

I'm aware I've not described myself in too much detail, so I guess this is my chance. Let's get it out of the way.

I've mentioned the goatee-cum-biker's-beard, right? (*That* appeared after seven series of *Sons of Anarchy* – I claimed it made me look like Jax, but Trish rightly compared me to Chibs, a man at least twenty years the hero's senior, complete with lived-in face and Glaswegian smile.) Add to that about five days of stubble, which always emphasises rather than hides some small but distinctly jowly bulges. Hair swept back off my forehead, long enough to match the length at the back. Mostly a dirty white and grey, but darker when I've not washed it or left it damp. Specs we've covered, I think. My mother's nose; in fact, her *family's* nose. Let's call it muscular (the only part of my body that is). I'm a tad under six feet and, if it helps any, a Virgo.

Caitlin might also offer mention of the slight yellowing of my eyes where you would prefer to find white. The ruddy hue of my face. My mostly uncertain smile. But don't trust anyone describing me from close up; they'll be too distracted by a need to establish the origin of that musty, chemical smell of sweated alcohol to get it right. Not when at least one of their senses is being mugged.

And that's another reason why I don't mix these days, although a lifetime's introversion has given me a head start.

Every Friday teatime, at drinks o' clock, Trish and I would take turns to say, "Let's tell everyone to… what do we tell them? Oh yes… to *piss off!*" As in, simply go away and leave us alone. Together. We functioned in the outside world, remarkably well on occasion, but we often felt that we swam in alien waters, and yearned to hop out and close the door behind us.

Outside, the day is opening up a little, but here, in the space holding the three of us, things are closing in. I'm scared to misstep, but at the same time, getting tired from wrestling my curiosity to the ground.

Just as I'm wondering if I can be bothered with all this, Caitlin settles back into her chair and launches into her story.

"We were in a B&B just outside Ullapool. Up on the north road. Sean said it was easiest for the river. I didn't care one way or the other, as long as he dropped me by The Ceilidh Place in town before they headed off, rods tied on the top of the Golf. Clapped-out thing. He'd give me money for some food and a book if I asked. He was glad to dump me off. Put him in the holiday spirit, no mistaking. But there was always that look. The one that said, *Behave*.

"The car stunk of maggots. *Poacher*, by Paco Rabanne, right? That kind of earthy, mouldy reek? Sean was never one for flies, or to chance buying bait when he got where he was going. The back of the car was a midden. Three hours to get there, and the empty crisp packets and tinnies were already building up.

"Anyway, from the first morning onwards, Sean and Callum would come back late afternoon. Before tea tables were set. Callum would stand us all a pint just down the road at *The Seaforth* – 'To cover the petrol,' he said – then it would be back to the guest house and more tinnies. Sean didn't want me sitting in places where there were other blokes drinking."

Our conversations follow no real chronological or thematic order. Stuff just bounces around the lounge, lands, gets caught and examined, then maybe relaunched.

As a kid, I loved playing catch with Dad, with a tennis ball. We'd start off just a few feet from each other, and alternate our throwing hands. Every two or three exchanges, Dad would take a few steps back, and we'd go again. Different styles of throw. My arms would slowly catch on fire, and the game would be on in earnest. I didn't want to let him down. My left arm always gave out before my right, but we'd end up separated by half the length of the street. We only stopped when it was obvious I couldn't bridge the gap. And then came the day when Dad introduced a cricket ball. Its weight, its lack of forgiveness on either hand if you mistimed its arrival, still feels like the first suggestions of adulthood.

Our first game of catch, the one between Caitlin and myself, fills the morning. I tread carefully. Too much probing, and our volleys will cease. Too little, and it's hot air. Random words to fill awkward silences. This, I realise, is a cricket-ball day.

My first high throw is a simple one. I go down to the kitchen and bring back one of the last remaining bottles of Jack. The question remains unasked. *Do you mind if I drink?* What the hell is the etiquette for such situations, anyway? Caitlin watches on, unfazed, as if expecting it. I offer her some, but she declines.

"Maybe later. Tea's fine." Give her credit. She didn't blink an eye.

It might be that this one gesture and exchange offers us both the confidence that we will both commit to this. Lets the light into that space between us, so we can find our way around each other without harm. Avoids chafed elbows or scraped knees. Builds trust.

This might seem a little melodramatic. A little too deep or heavy a reflection to be truly felt. Insight with the benefit of hindsight? But *I feel it*. And I think she feels it too.

I stink of whisky. Probably *Poacher*, too. When I take this first mouthful of the new bottle, Caitlin will be in no doubt as to my physical condition, or its immediate reason or cause. My openness seems to invite a mutual letting go.

And while I'm on the subject of openness and mutual trust, I want to make one more thing clear. This will not be the tale of a lonely, heartbroken man falling in love with a young, virile woman who somehow falls from the sky in some modern miracle of divine compensation. You might wonder if the tension I feel, this anxiety, is somehow a function of sexual attraction. I won't be so naive as to suggest this could never be the case. But it is not. My caution, my wish to proceed slowly and with care, is borne only from a desire to not frighten her. It's fine if she wants to leave, but I don't want her running from here feeling scared of the bogeyman. We experienced it together, didn't we, you and I, that whole scene on the beach yesterday? Didn't we? Her lying there, utterly vulnerable. Those bruises, the base layer to her blue-red, soaked-through skin. You felt her violent trembling, the second I helped her to her feet?

My confession, if confession is required, is this. I want to know her story; understand more about what has led her here. But I also want to remain faithful to the reason *I* am here.

So, then, back to our game of throw and catch.

I share some of the basic facts of my life with Trish, and her death in January. Caitlin weaves tales of post-school years in Glasgow, and her trudges through the privately run, hourly paid end of the social care system. Of the impossibility of moving out from her family home, and her father. The tightening coil of *his* resentment at her mother, run off a decade or more earlier with "some bawbag" he never knew or met.

Not every declaration demands a response. No one's keeping score. One of us might sit silent for minutes at a time, quietly seeking to make sense of each revelation. We pause several times, for pee breaks and then oatcakes and cheese. *Homes Under the Hammer* and *Bargain Hunt* provide words from the other side of the coffee table when we occasionally tap out. Each resumption feels easier than the last, though. By the one o'clock news, we've covered pretty much all the 'what's, 'when's, 'where's and 'how's.

She doesn't give me everything. No explanation of those bruises. But then, I've let on nothing about The Ceremony, or my real reason for being here this week. So let's not be too harsh.

Here's the gist of Caitlin's story.

INDEPENDENCE, AND THEN...

Caitlin had decided to make changes. She doesn't really tell me what it was that finally made her decide to get out. One big thing, lots of small things, or maybe some of both.

"I jacked in the shifts at the care homes. When you're wiping the shite off someone's arse five times a week, in various places around Govanhill or Castlemilk, you at least want to feel like they'd miss you if you left. Knowing that would never happen loosened things up a lot for me. The money was OK when I got the hours, but sitting around waiting for the agency to call was crap. I'd never earned enough to buy a car, even though Dad bought me lessons so I could pass my test. That was a bloody waste. I couldn't even go into town on the bus, unless I bought a mobile; the calls could come any time. So I just stayed in. I always had a book on the go. Helped fill my days off, and worked like pepper spray in the staffrooms. No bloke would come anywhere near if he saw I had a book bent back with my coffee. Must send out some warning sign. Who knows?" She shrugs, takes another bite of banana, and glances across at her reflection in the TV.

Maybe the books worked too well?

"Only times I left the house, other than getting the messages in for me and Da, was when I did the rounds of the charity shops on Sauchiehall Street. There's bloody loads of them, although half their stock is always the same. A tenner gets you four, maybe five books? Anyway, I'd hoist them home, keep one in my bag for work, and hand the old ones back in. At least they could be sold again. Help someone who might need a couple of quid.

"Da didn't like me sitting upstairs in my room reading, but he was glad to have the TV to himself. And there's no way *he* would ever swap places. Freeze *his* arse off upstairs through the winter. It was nice to sit there by the fire when he was off down the pub, though, right enough. He could afford his lager and fags, but never heated the bloody house properly."

Three summers ago, she took out the £450 in her current account, filled three small Bags for Life with her gear and headed to Buchanan Street. She stepped off the 915 in Somerled Square seven hours later, and claimed her room at the nearby Portree Hostel.

Why Portree?

"Well, why not? It felt like the furthest I could get in a day, and I wanted to get away from crowds, not head further south into them. And there'd be summer work."

It was a pretty good call. Skye was already creaking under the strain of more tourists than the island could handle, and there was no shortage of cafes, eateries or what I used to call 'tat shops'; purveyors of cheap and tacky fridge magnets, decorated mugs and commemorative key fobs. Harris tweed handbags made in Thai sweatshops.

On her second day she landed a summer waitressing job at The Portree Hotel, just on the square. No one knew her, and that was how she preferred it. Those who did show any curiosity (there were a few of both genders) seemed satisfied with a brief description of how she'd outgrown the city of her birth, the noise and dirt. The truth of it, albeit the only part she could put into words.

When the summer peak fell away, sensing her days were numbered, Caitlin shifted jobs, moving just a couple of streets further from her digs. The Takeaway was nothing special, but Bryan, who'd taken over the place from his mother, was grateful for her customer savvy and her stated wish to stay on over the winter.

It was Bryan, with assistance from Gumtree and a couple of friends, who helped her find and furnish a small flat above one of the shops on Wentworth Street, just a couple of minutes' walk away. She envied him. He had roots. A cottage out on the Dunvegan road, his father still working on the boats, and his mother working with him at The Takeaway for ten months of the year.

"I've never had a real place of my own. It's different when every square foot is yours, whatever the size. Bryan brought me a bookcase as a moving-in present. I put it up by the side of the bed. I kept hold of the books I bought from then on. The charity shops in Portree are crap for books. Good for tea towels and old ladies' cardigans. A couple of the churches sell bric-a-brac, but you know what they're like. Fine for your Joanne Harrises, or your Harlan bloody Cobens. Always a bit funny to see one of those pish *Shades of Grey* books being sold to raise money for the church roof appeal or new trousers for the priest, though. Ill-gotten gains, eh?"

She looks across at me. It's the first time we make eye contact.

"So Bryan showed me how to use Amazon Marketplace on his laptop at the shop. I was careful to ration myself. Money was a bit tight, even though my hours were good. First book I bought to keep was *The Virgin Suicides*. I loved that movie, but the book's even better. I've still got it at home." She goes quiet. "I hid it in the lean-to at the end of the cottage, after Sean missed it in his round-up. If I'd known how things would play out last week, I'd have brought it with me."

She jumps ahead a bit, but not before another prolonged silence.

"It was quite nice to sit in The Ceilidh Place last week. Slow coffees while I read. I'd saved up a bit without telling Sean. I'd missed being able to do that, like when I was back in the flat."

"So why did you stop?" I hope the question is unloaded enough.

Caitlin ducks an answer. "Can I have one of those beers in the fridge?"

By the spring she had two full shelves of books, sourced from shortlists and less recent winners of the Booker and the Pulitzer. After letting it slip that her birthday fell late in January she found herself, halfway through a shift, opening brand-new copies of *Paddy Clarke Ha Ha Ha* and *Never Let Me Go*. A friend of Bryan's mum's worked at the community library up by the high school, and these were two of her favourite books. "But don't read them if you're feeling a bit sad, love. Mum said they were likely to see you bawling by the end."

She met Sean later that year. He was working on road repairs just to the south, having shifted down from working on the car park at Kilt Rock. His run of nine consecutive days of curry and chips seemed less driven by the intrinsic quality of the food than by who was serving. A suspicion that proved true when, over his tenth helping, he asked her out.

"*Out*. That was a laugh. There's only really The Isles and The Merchant, and even they're a rip-off. Everywhere else is just for day trippers and their cash. At least he didn't suggest The Portree Hotel. *That* would've been just plain embarrassing."

She agreed to go, if only to get him away from Bryan's piss-takes. But it felt good to be noticed. In *that* way, especially. To sit back and let someone else do all the chasing.

"I went along, anyway. He looked a bit different with a proper shirt on. One of those grey-and-purple paisley jobs, right enough – he didn't say (well, he wouldn't), but I found out later it was his best and only one. His 'Saturday night special'. Quite flattering, a man dressing up for me. I let him buy me a couple of halves of Black, and he seemed interested enough. Ran through the usual questions. Every so often, he'd raise his head in the direction of new arrivals – blokes in small groups, or one or two solos making their way to the bar. Later on, a couple of them came over. They'd already been down the harbour, having a few while checking out the incomers. Pickings must have been thin to downright anorexic. Anyway, although one of them splashed me with lager, his mates seemed all right."

Caitlin pauses, taking a swig from the bottle. Maybe all that talk of drink has honed her thirst.

"At the end of the night, I let him walk me home. I was only the other end of the street. After he left, I went upstairs, and caught the back of him heading round The Chippy corner. Probably off to the pier to see what he was missing. I sunk my head in *Atonement*, I think it was, and felt pretty good about things."

Summer became early autumn. Tourists thinned out. Ditto the midges. Caitlin's predecessor at The Takeaway confirmed she'd be staying at home with her new baby. By September, Caitlin and Sean were an item. Saturday nights together expanded to all weekends and most evenings. Carry-outs in Caitlin's flat saved money for them both. When they were apart, she thought of him constantly, pushing down the persistent sense of vertigo in her chest. She would often wander down to the harbour wall and look out over the inner loch, beyond the rise of The Lump and its mirror spit of land opposite across the sound to Raasay. "It's weird, I know. But it was like, if I looked hard enough, just through that gap, I'd be able to see what the rest of my life could be. Even more clearly when I shut my eyes."

She was in love, and it felt great. Sean didn't share his feelings much, even in those moments after they'd made love in her creaking single bed, lying close and looking through the net curtains to the flats opposite. But he seemed happy to be with her.

By Halloween, without them ever discussing it, he'd pretty much moved in. They visited his parents once a week or so. His mum let Caitlin use her washing machine and, much to her surprise, appeared uninterested in her family, or her reasons for leaving Glasgow.

Sean stayed in work the whole winter. In the spring, he announced that he'd found somewhere bigger for them; a cottage out along the Skeabost road, overlooking the River Snizort and the broader estuary to the west. "The place needed a bit of TLC, but the landlord had just put in central heating and was planning to replace all the windows. We could move in for just a few quid a month above mate's rates."

It seemed perfect, and the landlord was as good as his word. Sean dropped her off in Portree for her shifts, collecting her on the way back from one of his road-repair sites. "I used to love the fact that I'd have time to stick my head in a book before or after work, before Sean picked me up. So if I ever got a bit fed up, I could visit all these other places, just by turning the pages. Places I'd never been. Nice places, like Pemberley or Howards End. Places where people didn't have to work for a living. Had 'domestics' for all that. The routine was good, though; backwards and forwards to Skeabost with Sean. That sounds like I wanted away. I didn't. I was with a man who loved me. Our new home put distance between us and everyone else that wasn't us."

I share with her how Trish and I used to tell everyone to bugger off. She laughs, but the laugh is not quite as long or as hearty as I imagine it could be. But there's something there. You'll have sensed it too. A coolness; an off-key note.

They worked to make the cottage theirs. Weekend drives around the island to pick up additional pieces of furniture. Sean changed agencies, and picked up a job on a big two-year construction job funded by EU money.

Two more things about this time are worth saying. First, I think Caitlin believed that her life was taking on a shape that fitted her; one to which she felt matched. Second, she felt that this new life of self-constructed happiness could be trusted.

The TV's on mute now. But the room is in meltdown.

Yesterday, on the beach, Caitlin's body shook with cold, but these new convulsions, ripping and twisting through every inch of her, originate from a far more violent, tortured place. A place of anger. Perhaps even rage. She bites down on her sobs. Her arms cross tightly, the sinews of her neck sculpting an almost feral intensity.

I'm worried, I admit it. Where is this heading? Is she going to trash the place? Attack *me*? It's hard not to react selfishly when confronted with such a transition. I watch, silent, as she fights to regain control. My own jaw tightens.

"Caitlin?" I'm lost for the next thing to say. I can't be this far away and still feel helpful. But I don't want to make things worse. Cautiously, I tip forward from the sofa and move to kneel on the floor in front of her. "Caitlin. What would you like me to do?"

She takes a long, forced breath in through her nose, her mouth clenched tight. She reaches out a hand and then, as if all her energy just leaves her, she falls back into the chair, eyes closed. "I'm sorry, Martin. I… I don't know where that came from." Her eyes open. She seeks me out. "And that's a fucking lie." She laughs. "Just think. If Da could see me now, he'd either skelp me and tell me to toughen up, or wimp out and go for a pint."

"Lucky for us both I don't like beer any more."

The truth, that part she's prepared to share, comes out in dribs and drabs. It's easy to see she's unused to telling it. What she's been through. Maybe it evolves as she relates it, even for her. New connections made, small nuances of thought remoulded by the telling it out loud. To a stranger.

"It's so obvious, looking back. Do you think that's always true? Two hundred miles away from Da, and I pick a bloke that turns into him more every day. But I didn't see it. *Feel* it. Not then, at the beginning. The first few times Sean told me he couldn't take me into town, he said it was because he was heading out to work in completely the opposite direction, up past Dunvegan. It made sense. And the back step was as good a place as any to sit and read with a coffee. I think it was just after Easter. It was nippy, but so peaceful at the back, away from the road. A few tourists, the postie. The fish van on Thursdays. No. Missing work, it actually made a nice change.

"It was two weeks before I saw he was heading out the wrong way. East, back to Portree. When I tried to make a joke of it, he said he'd just gone on autopilot. That they were still lifting and resurfacing over and around the coast, trying to get done before the Whitsun build-up. *Fair enough*, I thought. *Easily done*. That weekend we went into Portree, visited his parents and did our usual shop. Eventually, I told him I missed the routine of going into town. Even the crap charity shops might have had different books after the Easter tourists."

She reaches over to hold the top of her left arm, above the elbow. "He was quiet. That's what got me the most. And the bruises were like a ring – you know, like those Polynesian tattoos?" She makes a claw of her hand, holds and twists it over her bicep. "All the way round. Used to see them on Sauchiehall Street; girls in black cap-sleeved T-shirts and DMs. Flashing their piercings. 'You'll be fine here,' he said. 'Send off for some more of your books. I'll bring back some takeout.' It was like the grip on my arm cut off the blood to my brain. I couldn't think of anything to say. And then he was gone."

That was the first time, she says, that Sean gave any kind of clue about just how much he wanted her to himself. Sure, time with his friends in the pub had dropped off, but that was about saving money, and how they loved their own company, right?

But when he came back, that first night after gripping her, trays on their laps in front of the TV, he said he'd decided to make some changes.

"He'd seen me give the come-on to one of his mates, apparently. Heard that one of them had told another that he fancied me, and that he thought he had a chance. 'That's not going to happen,' he said to me. Those were going to be my words, more or less.

"But somehow, I knew he didn't want me to disagree. Like it would lead to him, I don't know, losing it. My arm was still sore, just sitting there eating the Chinky. I suppose I didn't want him to do it again. From where he sat, I could almost feel the heat coming off his body and pressing down on that arm. Like he was already thinking about doing it again. In the same place, I mean. Then he told me he'd been in to speak to Bryan at the chipper. Told him I didn't want to work there any more. That I was too embarrassed and worried to tell him myself. I'd decided to make a new start, and he shouldn't call. It would upset me too much to speak to him."

Caitlin looks up at me. "That hurt more than my arm."

It was another week before he hit her. In the stomach. For saying she needed to get her hair cut. By the end of the summer, he'd stopped apologising, and by the arrival of the first dawn frosts, he was blaming *her* for the new daily ritual. *Look what you make me do.* Maybe a spilt morning coffee, or one too many drinks after work. Usually fists. But not always. The belt on his jeans (mainly the end without the buckle). But fists were his weapon of choice. She stopped going out. His parents were sorry that they'd somehow offended her. They would love to see her again.

That Christmas, Sean knocked back Caitlin *and* the beers. At Hogmanay, Jools Holland on the box, she caught a glimpse of herself sat there next to him, flinching at her first swollen black eye whenever the screen went dark. "'My mistake, love,' he'd said. 'Don't want it to show, do we?' Weird thing is, I think doing that frightened him a bit. That he'd lost control."

Caitlin's chuckle sends shivers down me.

She did go out, though. Just never on her own. Stolen pleasures on the back step weren't worth the risk. "He could come back at any time. But he took me places with Callum, lochans for the fishing, even though I reckon it was him that lied to Sean about me. I don't know. I never knew how to feel when we were out. Still don't. Escaping the house should have been like a holiday, right? Hills and stuff. Fresh air. But I worried that maybe Sean would hit me, and Callum, well, Callum would just watch. Do nothing. Or maybe even have a turn."

She's starting to tremble again.

"Do you want another beer? I need to get more JD anyway."

She takes a long glug when I get back. "I'm sorry. It's just… well, let's just say I'm used to giving myself grief for the most recent beating, for doing whatever it is I do that brings it on. I'm not used to seeing the whole stupid bloody mess. Or showing my patheticness. Is that a word? Almost two years. What the fuck?"

I don't mind admitting that I'm at a bit of a loss too. The bruises make total sense now, though. "I'd like to help you, Caitlin. Really. But I'm the last person to talk about how to stand up against stuff that feels so unfair. Your man sounds like a right psycho, though."

Am I hitting the right tone here? I've never been sure when it comes to the plight of women. Not sure if men ever really are, or if it's just me. Or whether, in extreme circumstances, we even have the right to try and comment on such things. Whenever I sat with Trish and watched stuff depicting some abomination visited on women (rape, trafficking, violence) or inequalities (gender pay gaps, abortion rights), I always struggled to find the right words of support, for her personally or her fellow sisters. Not because of any lack of sympathy, you understand. Far from it. It's just that I always felt like an imposter. That I should apologise for being born with a cock.

Maybe even mentioning this now already labels me? Maybe throwbacks like me should wait until there are officially more genders than people. Maybe then the risks of causing offence will become so diluted or pointless that I can relax.

I spent the last ten years with Trish keeping shtum, running from these two simple premises:

Premise 1:	Men treat women badly.
Premise 2:	Martin is a man.
Ergo:	Martin (*fill in the blanks yourself – I don't even want to say it out loud*).

And here I am again. Inadequate but caring. Caring, in fact, about something or some*one* other than myself for the first time in a long time.

Anyway, my smile and comments are enough to allow Caitlin to continue.

"Psycho? Maybe. He never got bored with finding another part of me to hit. He even offered *me* the chance to pick somewhere. Where I wasn't still feeling sore from the last time. That's the thing. Just because bruises aren't showing, doesn't mean that whatever was underneath them isn't still bloody sore. So that's how I coped. Went along. On my birthday he took all my books out into the garden. Had a bonfire and made me watch, standing in the smoke until I could barely breathe. Read the title of each one out loud before it went in, like it was one of those sacrifices on the top of an Aztec temple. He knew I loved them. Like friends. So yeah, maybe psycho's not too far off the mark.

"Two months ago he said he'd booked a week in Ullapool, to go fishing with Callum, and that I was coming. That was when I started thinking about how I could get out. Get away, I mean. From then on, I risked a few minutes every day out in the lean-to, reading random pages of my only remaining book, the one I hid, and counting and recounting the cash I'd been filching from Sean's pocket change over the past year."

I suggest that she must have been thinking about leaving for a long while, given the cash.

"I guess so. But it never felt like that; like getting out was a real option. The money was just my way of winning a little bit. Crappy little victories that Sean wasn't even aware of. A couple of coins from a pile of pocket smush left on the kitchen worktop when he got home from work. Sometimes even a fiver, when he came back from drinks in town." She laughs. "Hanging on to the tips I told Sean I'd given the mobile hairdresser he allowed me to have. I wonder if he's worked it out yet?

"What do you think he's doing right now, Martin? Do you think he's still in Ullapool, trying to find me? By rights, he should be back at work by now. We were due to check out on Sunday. Where do you think he is? Do you think he worked out that I got on the ferry?"

She's exhausted, and she looks anxious again, her eyes flickering backwards and forwards across mine. I want to reassure her, but how can I, knowing so little about how well she made her move?

Here's how it happened.

She'd been as careful and logical as anyone could be, living in daily fear for her safety. Last Friday, she walked from The Ceilidh Place to the harbour to find out about timetables and fares. The morning of her escape, relieved beyond words that the sailing was on, she went into the cafe toilets as soon as she was dropped off, unpicked part of the inner lining of her shoulder bag, withdrew two fivers, and returned to the ticket office. Standing in line with the other foot passengers was nerve-racking, but nothing happened. She just refused to turn and look around her.

She landed in Stornoway within an hour of my own boarding of the Uig ferry. Three hours before Sean and his friend would arrive back in Ullapool to find her gone.

The three days that followed were like something from a Bear Grylls show. Armed with little more than a couple of small bottles of water and two Scotch eggs from the supermarket opposite the ferry terminal, she headed out of Stornoway.

"I wanted to get as far away as I could from where we landed. There's more of the island south than north from there, so I went south, down to Harris, and then I'd begin to think things through. I got a lift from a transit just on the outskirts, and he dropped me off in Tarbert about an hour after dark. I asked around at the pub and found The Backpackers Stop. Twenty quid for a hiding place with a bed, a shower, and porridge for breakfast. I didn't sleep too well. My head was all over the place. And my bag was real uncomfortable under my pillow. But then it was a new day. Without a new bruise."

Stornoway and Tarbert were by far the riskiest places to loiter if Sean's suspicions were anywhere near accurate. Her chances of buying provisions on a Sunday were zero, but the hostel proprietor sold her a few items from her own weekend stash. "People still need to eat pretty much every day." She bought more water, two cans of Coke, another two Scotch eggs and a Mars bar. When she let slip that she would probably be moving around the island all day, the woman put a couple of additional ham rolls into her bag. "These'll keep the wolf from the door."

She'd aim to put some distance between her and the east side of the island, to reduce the chance of discovery if Sean decided to come across in his Golf. Two miles further down the road on which I'd left the town the day before, with the weather overcast but dry, her paranoia got the better of her. At the next break in the thin wire fencing, she took her first few steps on the short-grassed hillside. Never losing sight of the tarmac, she began to yomp across open country. 'Slow going' didn't even start to cover it. Every so often, usually realising her dilemma one step too late, there'd be some boggy ground to avoid.

"I don't know what any of those plants are called. Never have, even with all the fishing in the hills, but there was loads of different types. I got the hang of which sort lived in the boggy bits, and navigated by shades of green, as much as anything. It slowed me down a hell of a lot, and to be honest, my shoes were already pretty much soaked through, but I really couldn't face getting in any deeper. Some of the stuff felt like I was on some weird waterbed."

We share our ignorance of flora names. I tell her how impressed I used to be at the writing school when several friends, all women in this case, listed off plant after plant, describing their characteristics with immense confidence, as if their knowledge was commonplace. *Pill sedge. Bog-myrtle.* We come up with our own, equally credible names. *Arsewipe sponge crud. Lavender sphincter. Poxbucket.*

When she continues, her words come a little freer. "Anyway, the rain came in and out, and I got pretty cold. Cars had their headlights on each time the cloud dropped. It would have been so easy to move back down and thumb a ride. But, well, I'd got this far doing it right. I didn't want to throw that away, I guess. So I kept on, until the real dusk came in and I couldn't see where the hell I was going. I mean, one set of headlights and my night vision was shot.

"Eventually, I dropped down behind this ruined crofthouse. There was still a bit of the old roof up one end, and some of the ground below it didn't look too bad as far as prickly stuff went. I treated myself to a ham roll and a Coke. I should have been starving, but I didn't have much of an appetite.

"That was a long bloody night, I can tell you. I thought my knees were going to seize when I got up to pee. I probably slept about ten minutes, two or three times, but not much more. I'd never spent a night outside. Not once." She gets up and walks past me. Stands by the window. "It was all right, though. I was on my own. And that made up for it all."

The next two days followed much the same pattern. *Two days!* Her appetite remained strangely muted, but the food ran out anyway. She walked a bit higher up the hill every so often, until she could find a burn that she trusted enough to refill her bottles. "I'm probably riddled with bloody parasites now, but that water tasted good, actually." All the while, she headed west and then south. "Some of the places you find these fences, you know, you just wonder why the hell they're there. And the walls, too. Can you imagine lugging the stones out there to get them built?

"By yesterday morning, I think I'd pretty much had enough. I hadn't really *got* anywhere. I was just wandering through the same day, every day. Fine, there were the beaches, but the land was just one big mass of rock and grass. The occasional hill track, and varying amounts of sheep shit. My legs were pretty much shot, and I'd got one of those cricks in my neck from lying back on my bag. I'd still got money, for all the good it would do me out there. I didn't have any food, but I still wasn't that hungry. Like I'd moved past it. But I couldn't do it any more. So I walked down to the coast, passed a few houses just off the main road." She turns from the window to face me. "To where you found me."

The whale, already beached, drew her down to its side. *Just as I was?*

"I could smell it. And every so often, when it moved, it was like it was being, I don't know, being jabbed by the wind. Like it was one of those boxers, knocked to the floor, trying to get up. It was so sad. And its *eyes*. Martin, its eyes. Like they'd seen everything there was to see, but none of it made any sense any more. Like all it knew now was sadness and pain. I can't describe it. Not really. But I wanted to share it. Be part of what it was feeling. Stop walking and just sit and feel."

She can't remember taking off her clothes. Or laying down, resting her head on the sand.

Her own eyes well up, and her gaze drops to the floor. My mind conjures, not for the first time, the moment when I helped her to her feet, unclothed and fragile. The submissiveness with which she obeyed my requests.

Caitlin raises her eyes. *Can she see my renewed distraction?* "I'm sorry. I can't really explain what I was doing there. I *do* know I didn't want it to be on its own. The whale. Just lying there. It was dying, wasn't it? When they die like that, the weight of the entire world pushes down on their ribs, you know. It's horrible." A look of panic. "I should have gone and told someone. We still can, can't we? We should tell someone. Now, I mean."

I call the estate. Describe as best I can the stretch of sand where the whale lay, but make no mention of Caitlin. I lie, in fact. Tell them I'm only just back. *Will that make any difference to what they or others do next?* The part about not knowing what to do is true, though. They thank me for the call – they'll contact the coastguard. These things happen, apparently.

This seems to calm Caitlin down, but I continue to tiptoe around her. She solves this immediate problem for us both, to a degree. To a degree, that is, because she changes the subject. Wants to know about *me*. This is a different kind of difficulty. How much should I reveal? The easiest part, I decide, is the writing part. I tell her of my reinvention as a writer.

"So what have you written?"

I tell her. Two novels, and a bunch of short stories, several of which grew from my initial writing exercises. The story of Rick and his self-imposed exile from his band members under Queen Mary's Peak on Tristan da Cunha. My imagined tale of my dad's departure from his parents' smallholding to begin his national service. I show her a couple, on my website.

"But have you written anything that I know?"

Burying a sneer at the question, I tell her about *The Quarant* and *The Puppet Master*. What it felt like to research them, to track down people who knew the things I needed to know. The double meaning of the word 'submission' when it came to the task of gaining publishers' interest. How each book finally made it onto Amazon. *Why not?* I think. "Wait here a second." I come back down from the bedroom with the copy of each I brought with me, hand them to her, and sit back.

"Oh my God!" Caitlin's words, her excitement, hover and float above me. Why not, indeed.

I watch her flick through each paperback, scanning the back-cover blurbs. Running her thumb over the raised print of my name. Over each title. I confess, I feel a brief shiver run down my spine as she does so. She wants to read them. Which one should she read first? I shrug. Feign an impossible nonchalance.

Then, the million-dollar question. "And what are you writing now?"

It's *my* turn to feel the weight of the planet on my ribs, remembering the years I swam in warm, distant oceans lost to me now. I consider lying.

But the day. Her story. Her willingness to get through it with me. I can't do that to her. Or to myself.

So I take a breath, and out it floods, filling the room with painful stories of my own. Of bruises of a different kind; some self-inflicted, others not.

I almost lose it when I describe The Ceremony. I show her the urn. Run my own thumb over the raised enamelled surface, and gently remove the four remaining sachets, placing each one in order along the front edge of the coffee table.

It's late afternoon. The room has long since begun to dim. I stand up and switch on the stairwell lighting.

As Caitlin looks on, I perform The Ceremony, turning to face her only when it is done.

WHEN THE LEVEE BREAKS

She hasn't left.

She's still here.

And we've moved on to my second first of the evening: sharing a glass of my very special malt.

BenRiach 1984 Limited Release Cask Bottling (96) cask 594, bott June 06 db

n**25 mainland Scottish peat gets no more delicate or sublime than this; a truly faultless aroma, this is a nose that repays 20 to 30 minutes' study. The shift in shape and form of the peat-reek is beguiling yet for all its hypnotic power it seems fragile enough to collapse into peat dust at any minute. A world-great aroma; **t**24 as the nose suggests, the malt dissolves in the mouth; the peaty deposits offer varying depth and intensity, from a sweet cough lozenge to kippers. The bitter-sweet balance is beyond reproach; **f**23 long, seductively layered and excellent oaky strands to soak up the lingering smoke; remains chewable and lip-smacking for many, many minutes dying* *out to strains of medium roast Old Brown Java coffee;* ***b*24 it is malts like this that turn whisky into an art form. An unforgettable and very rare experience: easily one of the whiskies of the year.* ***54% nc ncf.*** *240 bottles*

Caitlin has just a couple of mouthfuls, to be fair, but maintains a smile even as the liquid penetrates succeeding layers of her throat lining. She's happy to exchange the glass for the water I've put in front of her. "Da used to drink Bell's, and even now the smell of it, from the glass in the morning sink; actually, worse, from his kiss when I left for school... It put me off it for life, really. But," she adds hurriedly, "I can see how it could be your thing."

Telling her about my drinking probably qualifies as the least needed words of the day.

We settle down to watch *Sons of Anarchy*. Caitlin's never seen it (not that many have, which I consider criminal). School for her meant *Macbeth* rather than *Hamlet*, but I explain the basis of the relationships between Jax, the VP of SAMCRO, the Sons of Anarchy Motorcycle Club, Redwood Original; his overbearing, manipulative tramp of a mother, Gemma; and his stepfather, Clay, played by the extraordinary Ron Perlman.

The last scene, at Donna's funeral – in fact the last twenty seconds, in which Jax rises from the gravestone of his baby brother Thomas to stand over that of his father – is so powerful. Delta blues on the soundtrack; we know exactly what each mourner is thinking. Opie's own father, Piney, hands Jax a clean copy of his father's memoirs, replacing the copy Jax pulled earlier from the flames. The final shot of Jax, his back to the camera, is so laden. The camera backs away, low to the ground, Jax standing at the end of an avenue of stones, each marked by an American flag. Fade to black. Cue Mr Mayhem, the club symbol, grasping a rifle that terminates in a scythe dripping blood. So well done.

It's been a long, intense day. I tell Caitlin I'll clear up the empty beers and coffee cups in the morning. She smiles, and heads up to bed. I turn off the TV, and sit back.

So, then. I realise I've not asked *you* much for a wee while. Probably too caught up. I apologise. My commitment to you remains. Caitlin's presence changes nothing in this regard.

My reaction to seeing the boys' letters on Saturday morning was really all about me. I realise that now. It wasn't about how I'll upset them, but how they'll think even less of *me*. Of how, in my absence, they'll spend the rest of their lives cursing their twice-absent father; shaping their stories of me to others with shrugs of indifference and lingering dislike. And I see that now. It's not their hurt I feel. It's their disdain. Those letters have served to dig me in. A 'no way back' mechanism.

That last five minutes tonight was heavy as hell. John Thomas Teller left all his thoughts on the page for his son. Me? I sent two short letters and two large cheques; the money from Trish's Death in Service award, of all things.

They have every right to think the worst of me. But there's still time, perhaps. Not to justify myself to them, but maybe to offer a little more; at least a sense of how I really feel. About them. About myself. About the things I've done and why I've done them. It's worth a try, even this late on, don't you think? I'll still be sharing with you, but the boys'll get to hear from their wanky dad too. About how he really feels and thinks. *God help them, but maybe I should do this.*

That tingle is back. It's been some day.

So let's summarise.

Sean is Caitlin's partner. They live on the outskirts of Portree. Callum is Sean's friend. Sean regularly beats the shit out of Caitlin, and she's on the run, with no idea where she's headed or what she's going to do when she gets there. Or where and when Sean might catch up with her and take her back.

Trish was *my* partner. She and I lived in our forever home. Our actual one, not some phantom up on the Mam. What friends I have, I've burnt. I regularly, *daily*, beat the shit out of myself, and I'm on the most final of runs. I've known where I'm headed for months, and what I'm going to have to do when I get there. But now? Between this moment and then? Everything's changed.

I need this. I need to explain things to the boys. To make up for so many months of silence.

All right, then. I reach out to the coffee table for my iPad and open the case. Type in the four-digit code and open Scrivener. I pour another BenRiach. Feel the air around me lapse into peaty seascape.

Jesus. Three nights and two days to make this right.

CEREMONY ORIGINS
THURSDAY 22ND FEBRUARY 2018

He has made a mess of it.

His heart pounds. His breath, and the air above him, are redolent of his curses.

The new urn gleamed at its recent welcome, breathing easy of its box and protective coverings. Glistened with lustred seahorses and deep-sea blues.

Now it sits dimmed, its flank a powdered grey. Dust hovers in the silence. The original ceramic container, similarly coated, shares the veined-marble kitchen surface.

He didn't think. Tipped instead of ladled. Failed to consider what might happen. Wanting it done; to offer Trish her new home, replace old, anonymous grave goods with new.

The same pale grey paints the creases and wrinkles on the backs of his hands. Dulls the thin cotton ends of his sleeves.

He raises a hand to his face. Bends slightly. Inhales. He hesitates, then the point of his tongue flicks the surface. Retreats, leaving a small, darkened spot just below his knuckle. Neck muscles shift and tense, tongue travelling the inside of his teeth. Each tooth retains a residue.

He looks down to the smooth lip of the urn. A wetted fingertip runs along its surface, withdraws and yields to inspection. Raised, and with closed eyes, it enters his mouth. Lips tighten around it as it withdraws, wet but purged. Gritty chalk crackles and grates in his mouth.

He turns and walks to the cabinet near the dining table. Pulls the Glenmorangie forward from the second rank of bottles. Unsummoned saliva pushes the first grains of her to the back of his throat. His tongue moves down and forward, blocking the top of his throat. He reaches for a crystal tumbler. Places it on the dining table, twists the cork. The bottle raised and tipped, he splashes the sides of the glass in unrepentant haste.

His eyes fill.

Pushing down a sob, hoping not to choke, he lifts the glass to his mouth. Slides the lower rim between his lips, opening a fraction further to allow the inflow of spicy, fumy whisky. Spirits invade and permeate the grainy solution. He returns bottle and glass to the table. Pauses a moment while the burn builds on his tongue, inside his cheeks.

He closes his eyes and swallows. Moisture falls from an eye. Rolls into his beard. His legs tremor. He leans forward. Presses the front of his thighs into the chair back, braced against the table edge.

He looks back across to the urn. Down at his hands.

Thoughts begin to form.

Will not let him go.

CHAPTER 6

THURSDAY 25TH OCTOBER 2018

Some days you're the Beamer,
some days you're the goddamn deer.
(Jax Teller, Sons of Anarchy)

PREVIOUSLY, ON THE BROCH...

I promised earlier that I'd tell you about *American Psycho*. Hardly the pinnacle of romantic fiction, it's nonetheless a foundation stone of our relationship.

Nineteen ninety-seven. *Teletubbies*, Swampy, and Tony Blair. Kieron had just moved up to middle school, and Conor was following in his footsteps in primary.

We sat opposite each other in the company dining hall, just in from the airport from the private ten-seater service I used for my quarterly-or-so business trips north.

Trish switched the conversation from, I don't know, movies or something. "So what are you reading at the moment?" I'd stated at some earlier point that I was 'into books'.

"Bret Easton Ellis. I'm not sure if you'd like it, but it's called

American Psycho. It's selling by the ton in the States. I saw an article about it in *The Guardian*."

"Is it good?"

"Brilliant. It's all about a bloke on Wall Street, obsessed with how he looks and what people think of him, going around killing people before, during or after having sex with them."

Trish told me years later that this conversation stayed with her for the rest of the day, and the following weekend she bought a copy from Waterstones on Union Street.

Several years later, during the fortnight in which we decided whether we were going to see each other seriously, we exchanged a series of brief emails. Rather than ask questions about each other, we agreed instead to compose lists volunteering ten things that we thought we should share with each other to help us make the right choice. Forgetting about our earlier conversation, one of my unsolicited offers was that I used to thumb through *American Psycho* and get a kick from revisiting the sex bits. Looking back, I'm amazed she wanted anything to do with me. (My sixth fact stated that I ran towards lightning, while my seventh confessed that I ran away from bees.)

So here I sit, knackered but buzzed (pun not intended). Like I've just completed an Ironman and drunk three cups of Americano at the finish line.

I might have got two hours' sleep last night; maybe a little less. And most of *that* time involved me sitting on the floor with my back to the sofa, dictating on Scrivener a rough skeleton of the events and reflections I could recall since my departure from home on Saturday.

I panicked when, just after one, the power ran out. Absorbed, I'd paid no attention to the drain symbol. Worried I'd lost everything, I raced around – *another Ironman?* – to finally get the tablet on charge.

I mentioned that I'd not opened Scrivener for months, didn't I? Seeing each of my projects listed again – the novels, my short stories, fragments that might or might not have led to something important (*they hadn't*) – felt like a visit to old friends.

The option to 'Create Project' had my palms itching. I hit the '+', and typed in the new title.

The Broch.

I can't stop thinking about the boys. About the future arc of their lives. They are both adults; one (Conor) with a child of his own. Their lives ceased to orbit around my own twenty-five years ago, but their phantom gravity still pulls me out of shape.

They'll receive those envelopes today or tomorrow. The ones I posted on Saturday.

I'm not sure I can really explain to you what I think I'm doing. Or even – *and don't laugh* – how I'll know if I'm doing it. It just feels like I should try. I should have thought of this earlier; made it the bedrock of my plan.

I told you last night that I'd try 'to make this right'. That was stupid. Nothing can make any of this 'right'. But a tale is a tale, and always preferable to the void of unknowing.

Anyway, last night, *this morning*, I've written a kind of introduction, seeking any future reader's indulgence and patience, and a skeleton outline of the past five days. The least believable episodes within it will – ironically, given the shit that's happened – be the most true.

Ho-hum.

PUTTIN' ON THE RITZ...

Caitlin comes down a few minutes after I put down the phone.

She's carrying some scrunched-up clothing and the copy of *The Quarant* from last night. She waves it at me with a broad smile; a school sports day prize displayed to a proud parent. "Look how far I've got!"

I pass on the phone call I received earlier from the estate house. Not a great way to start the day, but she deserves to know. "The coastguard have had some whale and dolphin rescue team out, and a vet from Stornoway. Apparently, your friend's a common minke whale. They're still there, but it's looking pretty bad. Robert says that whenever it gets to calling out the vet, it usually means they're going to have to put it down."

"That's horrible. Just horrible." She pauses. "Do they know how it got up there?"

"Not really. There's a few standard explanations, apparently. Radar malfunction, or whatever the word is. Rogue wave or swell. Collision or damage from boats or nets. They don't really know which one applies. I didn't notice any major injuries, did you?"

Caitlin shakes her head. "Do you think they've already killed it?"

"Maybe. It partly depends on how long it's been there, he was saying. Whether any other wildlife have started to peck at it, or take mouthfuls. I don't know how long it takes, you know, to end things. Do you really want to know?"

She grimaces, thinks it through. Perhaps, although this is a guess on my part, reliving how she sunk into that large, unblinking eye. Examining what it might have opened up or closed off *in her*.

Shaking it off, she walks into the room and sits down next to me. "It was just so alone. I know nature's cruel. A big machine. But it should prepare us better. You know, warn us? I thought all that evolution stuff would have sorted that by now. Made us all a bit more… more *able* to cope with all the surprises. Good or bad."

Tell me about it.

Time to change the subject. "Anyway, while I was on the phone, I thought it would be a good idea to order some more of that luxury hamper food. I've asked them to throw in a few extras. Cuts of meat. Beers. We'll not reach Saturday on half a packet of oatcakes and a few spoonfuls of poncy jam. It'll be here by lunchtime."

I've told her about my scrape with Ms Sinclair, and 'lying low'. But we've not discussed how long she wants to stay, or anything about my plans for check-out day (pun very much intended – sorry).

Conversation goes on hold while Caitlin continues her journey downstairs and washes out her dirties. She comes back with two coffees and the last of the cheese and ham.

"I guess we need to talk some more. Talk through what we need to do."

She's got no plan, beyond keeping clear of any place that Sean might be. "Wherever he is, he'll be all stoked up and ready for a doin'."

"That's OK. I get it. There's no rush, if you can manage with the clothes you've got."

We drop it. No requests. No offers. Just a relaxed absence of anything definitive. She can stay as long as she wants (as long as what she wants doesn't run past Saturday, of course). And she knows, I think, that she can leave as soon as she wants too.

"Can I ask you something?"

"Sure. Fire away."

"OK." She picks up and brandishes *The Quarant*. "I want to know where this thing came from. I mean, where you got the idea."

Safe ground, then. No landmines. No lurking traps for the stumbling into.

I'd become fascinated with Venice after seeing a programme that laid bare some of the city's hidden structure and explored how most of the buildings we know and understand today replaced equally impressive timber predecessors. The transformation occurred over a relatively brief period of time, in parallel with Venice's growing wealth and population. It evoked images of places like modern Dubai; a city swarming with cranes.

Further revelations, such as the existence of a secret 'half-floor' in the Doge's Palace (echoes of *Being John Malkovich*?), the preserve of the secret police's interrogation and torture facility, offered a tantalising glimpse into medieval thought and power.

I tell her about how, in 1348, just as the Doge's Palace was being rebuilt and on its way to being the building we see today, the city was hit by an earthquake and a tsunami. And that, a mere three months later, the Black Death arrived, killing six in every ten. (It was these facts, more than any other, that boosted sales at local book signings from three to perhaps, *oooh,* five.)

I don't see it coming, but she's got me. Seen my enthusiasm for what I've done.

"You told me why you stopped writing. But I can see how much you loved doing it. So what will it take for you to start again?"

I take a deep breath. "Well, actually, whatever it is, it's already happened." I lean across and open the iPad. "Last night. Talking to you. Watching that show. I've always been a softie for movies or books that feature kids separated from their dads. *Field of Dreams*. The last time I watched that, I rang up my dad and told him that I loved him. I'm not sure, to this day, who was the most surprised. But I felt better once I'd done it. There's something about that bond; the one between dads and sons, or maybe just more generally between parents and kids. Any harms you do to it come back and eat your fucking guts out. It's not your usual guilt thing, either. That I can handle. Lying to a friend. Thoughtlessly making your wife cry. They're all bad, don't get me wrong, but it feels somehow more equitable, more between peers. But the whole father–son thing? I had nightmares for years, you know. They never really stopped; all the years after I left them. Dreamt they were in some kind of danger; crazy stuff. Train crashes, bullies. Lost. I'd work entire nights, over and over, to save them."

Does this make sense? To you or to Caitlin? She'd asked me some harmless question about writing, and now I'm rambling.

"But then, picking you up off that beach. Walking away from that thing. And watching Jax last night..." I can feel tears welling, but I'm not going to let them fall. To compensate, my diction tends towards that of Peter Boyle, tapping his cane onstage to tunelessly pacify the locals in *Young Frankenstein*, but I manage to pull back.

"I need to help them understand why I made the choices I made. How I know I shat on them when I made them. Making a go of things with Trish was the bravest thing I ever did, the most wonderful thing I ever did, but probably the most cowardly too. For them to have to live through that. They woke up every day, knowing just the cowardly part."

I pull back again, but it's a close-run thing. I can't look at Caitlin until I've calmed down. "So I've decided I'm going to try to get as much of my story down as I can. Here. On this. It might not help them, but it might help me." I look at her, and then the room. "Help me make sense of all this."

When Caitlin breaks her silence, it's a relief to sense that none of this seems to have freaked her out. Her voice is calm. "Sounds like you've been on the run just as much as me. But at least you've worked out what to do. Found some answers for yourself. That's good, isn't it?"

She reaches out and pats my thigh. Puts on a comic, matronly tone, reminiscent of Lady Bracknell. A young Glaswegian going decidedly House of Windsor. "So why don't you go upstairs and get a couple of hours' sleep, young man, and then you'll be in better shape to write for the rest of the day? I'll keep an eye out for the hamper."

...WHILE DINING AT THE SAVOY

Two hours upstairs leaves me not so much refreshed as with an enormous appetite to get back to where I left off. Expand on my journey over here on Saturday, and crack the lid off my final Jack.

More good news – Gallagher has thought better of a daylight visit. A welcome by-product of a sleepless night.

Caitlin's where I left her, her thumb slotted into the spine of the book almost at its midpoint. "Ah, here he is." Her tone is warm, noticeably lighter than earlier. I wouldn't blame her for a little nervousness around the resident middle-aged emotional wreck.

"You enjoying that thing?"

She flicks over the cover, light catching the raised decal of the lion of St Mark. "Of course. And what's funny is that, last night, when I saw that list of characters in the book, I wasn't sure how I'd get on. But you take it easy on anyone having a go, don't you? Just a few new people to meet at a time. I like that."

"Well, how about you read some more, until the hamper comes, and I'll get a couple of hours' writing done? Tell me then if you still like it."

When the bell rings, I'm already at the door, having seen the car come up the track from the main road. It's the young man from Sunday, with a couple of large boxes.

Everything's polite and to the point. "There you go, sir. We'll have an additional invoice ready for you when you check out on Saturday. Enjoy your food, sir, and be sure to let us know if you need anything else." All this accomplished with the briefest of eye contact, the boy is back behind the wheel of his small Peugeot and out of sight.

Caitlin barely contains her enthusiasm. "It's funny, isn't it; I've had no appetite for days, but one look at that venison and I'm bloody ravenous. Do you want me to have a go at these? It'll probably take a couple of hours to suss out the oven, and another twenty minutes to actually cook."

An hour or so later (the oven *was* a little tricky, as it turns out), we're at the dining table in the kitchen. Caitlin's poured her beer into a glass, and I'm on the last third of Jack with my favourite glass. It goes surprisingly well with both the oatcakes and liver pâté, and then the succulent venison, covered in some gorgeous red wine gravy and accompanied by fried shiitake mushrooms sourced from Croft 36, a deli along the coast.

I decide to eat slowly, like a baby weaned onto solids, knowing instinctively not to rush it.

Conversation seems to have stalled.

"So, tell me more about your life in Glasgow. How long were you working in those care homes?"

Hearing anyone speak of their past, especially when they're given the freedom to focus on whatever aspects they wish, always feels like one of life's greatest rewards. Even those unaccustomed to such requests will slowly rise to the occasion, chiselling and refining those aspects they share until they recognise themselves. The best stories, in my opinion, always concern 'how I met my long-term partner'. I collected them. Never wrote them down, but basked in what are, without fail, positive, joyful retellings.

But with Caitlin's recent history with Sean already known, and wholly unsuited to joy, I hope that she'll take this chance to construct a comfortable and familiar structure within which to feel safe.

"Och, well, I guess I was a bit like you when I was at school. Didn't really have a clue what I wanted to do, but knew what I definitely wasn't up for. Office jobs. Christ, how boring. Stuff needing a degree or anything like that was out. I bloody hated school. The idea of spending another four years with tossers that liked it was just *pish.* Trouble was, after Ma left, Da was pretty much stuck in a rut in the council. He was what they called a 'property technician'." (She does that speech-mark thing with curled fingers.) "He'd pretty much drifted from firm to firm before then, but never held anything down. Never found a way to get on with people, if you know what I mean. Picked arguments. So he went around in a gang, fixing council houses. Painting and decorating, mending windows. Stuff like that. He only just had enough money to keep the two of us going, what with the beers and the bookies, so I needed to find something that didn't take years to get qualified for.

"I got a job at Fopp on Union Street, right near the station. I must have caught them right the day I went in, because I didn't really have any shop experience. The money was rubbish to start, but I stuck it." She pauses, tackling another mouthful of venison. "Long to short, it didn't last. The supervisor was a bit of a twat, and couldn't handle even the slightest bit of banter that made him look daft. He started to cut my hours. It was obvious where things were going. I jacked it in before he got the chance to kick me out.

"After that, it took bloody ages to get anything else, apart from a few hours a week as a shelf-filler in Morrisons, and washing up in the kitchens of a local pub. That was pretty shite, I can tell you.

"Then I got a job stacking shelves at a Chinese food place, over near the School of Art. I quite liked it, actually. They wanted someone local to give them a bit more of a chance at interpreting some of the more – what shall I say? – thicker-accented visitors to the store. The guy that ran it had two sons and a daughter working there too, and he gave me some real help to learn what all the ingredients were called. What they were for. And I got to take quite a bit home. Da wasn't that keen to start with, but I got to the point where I could hold my own against any wee bastard with a wok and a bamboo steamer. Everything was going OK, really, but then some nephew joined the staff. He had all the patter, so all of a sudden I wasn't needed any more. First time I'd been pushed rather than jumped. I didn't know how much that bloody job meant to me until it was taken away."

It was her dad who told her about the jobs going in social care. A friend of his had a wife working in some place in Burnside. "He said the hours were good once you got in, and the turnover rate was pretty high, so there were always chances to apply. If I could stick that for a couple of years, I might be able to get a full-time job with one of those agencies that did the home visit stuff. Anyway, I gave it a go, and got in. I worked across three places within five miles of the house, and pretty much dug myself a nice little rut of my own."

"So what happened? Why didn't you stay, or move on to the home visits?"

She hesitates. I might be reading her all wrong, but why take the chance?

"No, don't answer that. It's OK. You told me that you were fed up with wiping arses. There are worse reasons for leaving anywhere."

"Well, yes. Although…"

I'm right. She's struggling with something.

She reaches forward and drains her glass. "So, I haven't really told anyone this. Not Da. Not Sean. Definitely not Sean. But I went to find my ma. Turns out, she lived just an hour away. Up near Falkirk. I found her. Didn't take that much asking around, to be honest. Several of Da's mates knew. Hadn't really stayed in touch, but knew a couple of her old friends. I found her. Headed up the M80. I called her first. She said she'd be in. She sounded a bit off, to be honest. But then, it was ten years since last, you know, we'd spoken. I suppose that was to be expected.

"But it wasn't that. Well, not only that. She'd got a son. Four years old. Ethan. Picked him up from school every day after her early shift at one of the locals. Ethan Stewart. She'd gone back to her maiden name. Lived with him in a flat out towards Stenhousemuir. I recognised her, but didn't really feel what I thought I would." She pushes her last piece of venison around the plate. Sticks a couple of fork tines into the edge of it, and drags it through the last drops of gravy. "Just as bloody well, anyway. I don't think she was too keen to see me.

"I went back home, feeling like a right twat. Anyway, I got into a bit of a hole after that. Couldn't really get that excited about anything. Not that it was all that brilliant before but, you know. So I decided to get out. Just get away and see what might happen. Didn't expect any of this, though."

I nod, sage and compassionate (*I wish!*), and then bring her another beer. "Do you fancy some tablet? It's way too sweet for me now, but it'll pep you up a bit, maybe."

CAVEATS

The afternoon still haunts me. Drops doubt into what I think I know. What I think I'm doing, or have done. How can I be sure of my story for you when I can feel my own grip on it loosen? And my plea for you to hang in there with me? I'm not sure I can even expect that any more.

Not after this afternoon. Turns out I'm not a very nice person.

I made promises to you earlier. Talked about glass skulls, and ribs pulled back in a commitment to share all with you. But what if that skull is full of some kind of self-deceiving blancmange? If *I* don't know truth from fiction, how can you?

My promise still holds. But I might lose you here, just as I might be losing myself. I've had a day or so to get things straight enough in my head, but even now, telling it the best I can, part of me, the part that chose to feel it necessary to cover my own tracks, is still there, waiting for its next outing. And it scares me.

Just one knock at the door, and the universe tilts on its axis.

Give me peeing up a stone any day.

Anyway, let's do this.

A TRUE MAN OF ACTION

After lunch, Caitlin asks to borrow my coat. She wants to check out what's happening at the beach. It's quite a walk, but she can get there and back by dusk if she leaves now. Any other day, I'd be tempted to go with her. But I desperately need to get back to the iPad. I make a half-hearted offer to accompany her.

"Thanks, Martin, but I'm getting the hang of this… what did you call it? The 'yomping thing'? See you later."

I stand at the window and wave her off. I think The Broch breathes a sigh of relief. At how I've not upset her too much, or dragged her back to confront her fear of Sean. I sympathise with her, but now she's gone, my own breath comes a little easier too.

Seems I still don't want her here. If I spent another hour wondering why that might be, I could nail it. But that's an hour I don't have.

I'll ask her more about how she's feeling when she gets back.

The afternoon goes too fast. My fault, of course, for starting too late.

I discovered the benefits of Scrivener's dictation software early on. Great for first drafts, for just getting everything out, or with dialogue, where you want to stay in rhythm. It doubled and tripled my output, even allowing for the need to educate it in, or accept its defiant resistance to, the finer points of the East Anglian accent.

So if you're reading this after someone's pored over the ugliness of uncorrected dictation, here's my apology, spoken sincerely into my tablet, but bereft of human intervention:

I'm sorry if a lot of these doesn't make sense. I don't think I've got a enough time to polish this I spend too much time giving every sentence right on the get through.

See what I mean?

Anyway, enough of this frivolity. The lounge is warm without being hot, and 'the final Jack' (*why didn't this ring an alarm bell?*) keeps me in that zone where words come easy, where everything is permitted and nothing is scorned.

I review the skeleton I've created since I left Jax in the graveyard, add in Uig haddock and Glen Shiel summer snow, and then bring the whole file up to date with today's events and the outline of Caitlin's history.

I need to tell her, I know, that she'll feature in the second half of this record. Make sure she's OK with it. And no – *I sense your question, naturally* – no, I don't know if I'll change anything if she objects. She's coped with bruises and beatings and serial Scotch eggs and whales and absent mothers and the like, so this latest revelation should be reasonably low on the trauma scale. But you never know. I once wrote a short story as a gift to some friends in appreciation of a cracking evening of drinks and conversation, only to find that my homage to one of their anecdotes touched on a real nerve. End of promising friendship, and a lesson learned.

Dictation enabled, I go back upstairs and flesh out the rest of my journey here. Cover the closing episode of *Justified*, and share my sense that I've done one of the two hardest things that must be done this week by getting here intact.

Forty-eight hours to The Clisham, give or take.

So, then. While Caitlin's out, allow me to shade in the outline I gave you, back on Monday, about Trish and I getting together. How we sparked the first pulses of a new, fused heart.

As my Aberdeen secondment entered the final autumn of the millennium, I found myself alert to Trish's every office appearance. I remember the day of that first telltale flutter in my stomach, as she stood at a colleague's desk, outlined against the view over the city behind her, laughing at something one of them was saying. That evening, sitting in the taxi taking me back to my accommodation, I first admitted to myself that I was becoming – no, *was* – possessed. A feeling with sharp edges, but a warm, soft centre. A weight that grew with each flight home, and the dread of another few days there. Days with Carol.

Trish had split up with her long-term boyfriend. Word was that she was understandably upset, and socialising more with her work friends. Is it unforgivable to admit that I felt I could exploit her recent single status? She was probably pretty vulnerable.

I didn't know which way to turn. I'd been married for fourteen years. We had been happy, I knew we had. But that was years ago. The house was now a battle zone. Minefields, tripwire, with no safe way through. Any clumsy or misspoken word would see one of us pull a pin. Shrapnel is no respecter of flesh, innocent or otherwise. Rare occasions of reconciliation through sex were soulless, lonely affairs. Ceasefires that reduced rather than extended any shared territory that remained.

Our descent should have been easy to predict. The signs were there from the outset. A row on the drive to the airport departure for our honeymoon (WTF?). The unreasonably jealous vendetta against any offer of help to a college friend – female – to settle in in our home town (a betrayal of mine that haunts me to this day). There are many other waymarks I could offer, but I'll withhold them, for fear you'll think me an idiot for not acting earlier. We just let the waters drain out, to then be surprised at the advancing tidal wave.

And the boys were there. Breathing the same air. Like passive smoking, damaging them in ways that might not be known for decades.

It's really hard to share this. Possibly because, deep down, my actions may to this day seem, even *be*, disproportionate. But I come back to the same old issue. Our marriage was pulling us down, and I had absolutely no idea what to do about it.

Were we both on the rebound, Trish and I? Does it matter?

I heard that she was taking part in a fun five-a-side night at the company venue I was staying at. I signed up too. Predatory again? Is any courtship entirely exempt from that accusation?

I walked to the pitch determined to talk to her. My delight at seeing our names on the same team list was short-lived; my first pass to her knocked her to the floor, doubled over by a ball arriving into her midriff with unintended force. *Fuck. Nice one, Martin.* Lady skills as remarkable as ever.

Things looked up after the game. I gave myself a good talking-to. Told myself to grow a spine. I noted where she sat, who she was with. When the opportunity arose, I took the empty chair next to her. We discovered a shared love of curry. She offered, the next time I was in Aberdeen, to take me to her favourite curry house.

I barely slept a wink that night. And poorly for the next two weeks, until my return to Aberdeen, excitement trading blows with guilt like Ali and Foreman. And beneath it all: would I have the courage to see this through?

We spoke just the once before my return, confirming that we were still on. *Jesus*. We met at the top of Union Street, on Holburn Junction.

"Do you need any cash? Let's nip to the hole in the wall, and then go to Rose Street."

With a visitor's topography of the city in my head, and a growing sense of transgression in my chest, I nodded and followed her across at the next lights, my bearings completely lost, and on to the restaurant.

The place, and the food, were as good as she'd said. The meal was over by nine, but we continued talking well after the removal of dishes and the arrival of hot flannels. I suggested two more Kingfishers, and when the conversation finally turned to Trish's newly single status, I teetered briefly on the brink before eventually, finally, *screaming at myself to do it*, I plunged head first into a declaration of love.

None of this, I feel obliged to say now, is a matter of memory. It's simply part of who I am; how I see myself. *The man who did that*. Stated out loud the single most honest and vital feeling I'd ever felt. End of.

And the letters? At the back of one of our wardrobes in The Schoolhouse, Trish kept printed copies of most, but not all of my emails to her in the weeks that followed. A few – though, frustratingly, not all of them – include her own correspondences. I transposed and filed them, driven by some sense of nostalgic curatorship for their swoops and dives; their moments of magic and, occasionally, profound sadness that are hinted at just below the surface.

The truths they contain aren't mine alone. We read them

together each time we moved house. Acknowledged them as emotionally true, and capable of taking each of us back to those weeks.

AN EPISTOLARY TALE

Martin, 9th November, 2000 17.02

Where to start?!

If you're still interested in having another social evening, of whatever kind (but preferably just us two), let me know, and we'll arrange something. Despite, or possibly because of, the way our evening went last night, I would really not blame you for wanting to do this. I had a roller-coaster time last night (did you?), but I for one am not put off – I really hope I haven't upset you or come over as anything other than someone who respects your feelings, but I'm afraid I'm currently hooked – I can't yet believe, given the few hours I've spent in your company, how many things I'm impressed with. I also can't believe how quickly the time went. Sorry, Barbara Cartland over and out.

Could you drop me a quick line tomorrow?

Trish, 10th November, 14.02

Hello.

Hope you're well and have recovered from your hangover – I had one too.

Where do *I* start? I am going to be completely truthful here.

I also really enjoyed our night out on Wednesday. I think we get on really well together; I think you're brilliant company. You're also a very, very lovely and interesting person, and lots more too.

I must admit, I did not expect the night to go the way it did. Am I naive? I was a bit taken aback, and when I got home on Wednesday night I was somewhat confused. I was thinking, *We've known each other for years, so what's this?*

I would like to see you again. And I don't know if this is right, or why, or what I'm expecting. I can only offer you a friendship.

I hope I haven't waffled. I hope I'm understandable.

Speak to you soon.

Martin, 14th November, 22.40

Hope the title is innocuous enough – matters of library and archive budgeting would certainly blend in in my inbox.

So then, one very wet bike ride home, the house alarm going off because I wasn't thinking when I put my bike in the garage. Boys are now showered, chicken soup (eurgh! I can still taste it) has been eaten, and I've got a few minutes before reading Kieron his four to five pages of *The Lord of the Rings*.

I can't tell you what a relief it was to hear how you feel, as it's been so difficult to tell, through all the 'friends' stuff. When I get to Aberdeen next Thursday, you and everyone will hear me say things like "Hi again, how's it hanging?", "How are we all?" and "Hideous flight/crap taxi driver" to the gang, but what I'll be communicating telepathically, in a manner that only gorgeous Scots can pick up, is how much my soul smiles at my renewed ability to see rather than remember you. A prize to the one of us who keeps the straightest face.

I'm spending most of the evening doing what I can to subtly keep a distance from Carol – same tactics as the weekend, really – until I get to take Conor to school tomorrow morning before work.

All my love.

Martin, 16th November, 15.51

Let's speed things up in the getting-to-know-you stakes, given that we are living under different parliaments!

Things about me you don't currently know:

1. I used to be a drummer in a band called Underground Movement (sounds like a laxative now, doesn't it?).
2. I lost my virginity at the age of seventeen to a girl who had three nipples.
3. My favourite soul singer is Bobby Womack.
4. Myself and my wife both highlight our hair.
5. I once broke my best friend's knuckles in a fight.
6. I love thunderstorms.
7. I hate spiders and bees.
8. I love gory crime thrillers if they are consummately written.
9. I do not want to make love with my wife again, because I want to make love with you.

Trish, 16th November, 16.25

M.,

Do you know what you're doing to me?! I'm now feeling the physical effects of seriously wanting to be with *you*. I hate it and love it at the same time.

Things about me:

1. My middle name is Sophia.
2. Height: five foot five. Weight: dropping drastically as keep thinking of you (which is a good thing). Hair: brown. Eyes: green.
3. I love to sing – it's my favourite thing.
4. I broke a toe once pretending to be Bruce Lee.
5. I've made up my mind that I don't want Aaron in my life, and I'm going to take the consequences.
6. I wish you were here in Aberdeen currently. I wish I could talk to you when I need you, which is just about twenty-four hours a day at the mo.

Speak to you soon.

Martin, 16th November, 18.44

I hate the first two seconds after the receiver goes down, but not as much as the next four, six, eight, etc. I think the meal just outside Portlethen is a great idea, as I'll probably still have my passport with me. (!) Is there an English Embassy nearby offering language lessons to converse with the chuckters, or whatever you call the locals?

It's overused, and intimidating, and corny, and lots of other things besides, and I'm starting to worry that after all this phone/email traffic I'm going to be a little bit of a let-down in the flesh, but nonetheless I'll use the word in the sense it was always intended to be used, by saying…

Love.

Martin, 19th November, 18.15

Hi, Trish.

It's 5.15 Sunday afternoon, and I'm *really* hoping you're OK – what's happened?

I'm guessing that when I rang you back at 12.30, Aaron was still round yours. I can't believe how protective, jealous and powerless I've felt since then. I know you can look after yourself, but it's just that that little bit of uncertainty has really got under my skin. God, I hope you're OK, and not upset at all. Trust me, if anything is being said to make you doubt our feelings for each other, you must talk to me about it when we next speak.

I'll try to ring you at your home 6pm your time – I may not hit the exact time but I'll do my best.

Anyway, better get off now. Up at 3.45am, and still got the kids to sort out and my bag to pack. Give yourself a huge hug from me; I'll pay you back on Thursday (with interest).

Martin, 26th November, 13.18

Trish,

Just to keep you in the picture, I sent this after we spoke.

———Original Message———

Subject: A proposition

Charles, Sandy,

Apologies for resorting to print but the likelihood of being able to talk to you separately or together over the next few days is probably low. The reason I am writing (and I accept this is rather unconventional) is to make a proposition regarding my involvement in the above programme.

It is a simple one, although I confess I have no idea of the practicalities or mechanics of it. I propose my full-time Aberdeen-based secondment to the project as soon as possible. I have no idea of the overall cost to the company of something like this, although I obviously know how much going up and down to Aberdeen each week costs, WRT money, opportunity cost, and wasted personal energy better channelled to customers rather than flight attendants!

Could we discuss this further, to see what if anything can be done?

Kind regards,
Martin

Martin, 26th November, 20.36

How are you? It was great to speak to you again, after all that went on here yesterday – I really do miss you like crazy, and have your face about nine inches from my view everywhere I look. I'm not kidding; when I saw you walk into the OS centre last Thursday morning for the first time, you were *glowing*. I josh you not – it was unbelievable. If I had anything to do with that, I burst with pride.

That walk along the beach, and then just sitting with you at the airport, for me was as sensual and as important as Thursday night. Last week *had* to happen, to help us lay early foundations – I know you were nervous (so was I), but I would have been really disappointed if you hadn't been. Going to bed on Thursday night could so easily seem a mistake in hindsight – I for one took it as a token of trust and closeness, and although I found it difficult to resist the obvious temptation, I'm really pleased I did. Especially after you explained how you felt. I hope you don't think any less of me for being so attracted to you physically – as far as I'm concerned, I would enjoy two hours of conversation with you just as much as two hours making love, although honesty impels me to admit that doing both simultaneously would be far, far better (oh yes!).

By the time you read this, I should only be a matter of minutes from Aberdeen – I may even be there already. I really can't wait to see and touch you again, and talk with you. I'm getting the third degree here at the moment as you can imagine, and seeing you tomorrow is the only thing keeping me going today. I hope the plane is not late – the frustration would be too much.

I'll of course abide by any rules, behavioural or emotional, you feel you wish to set, but please don't hold it against me if I sometimes stray beyond them – when you start to live this intensely, a couple of degrees out can make quite a difference. I hope the note I forwarded to you earlier today, outlining the case for full-time secondment, hasn't intimidated you – I guess it must look as if I'm totally obsessed with being near you. This is, of course, true, but there is nothing sinister or frightening about this, I think – tell me if you feel there is, and I'll try to tone it down.

I miss you... Until I see you, take care.

Martin, 29th November, 19.48

Trish,

My work login seems to be knackered tonight – forgive me for using my Hotmail account. If you want to write something, still use the normal work one, though – I'll sort it out tomorrow.

Anyway... I was stunned to hear about Aaron coming round – how are you after all that? You must be exhausted and confused, what with me pulling you one way and him pulling the other.

I've been really worried about you all afternoon, wondering how you're coping. Did you mention the solicitor or the house? How did you get him to leave? Again, I'm feeling incredibly protective and helpless in equal but huge measure. I know you are strong, but even so, who needs it?!

My day's been crap as well, for what it's worth. Had two hours of the clergy this morning, invitation of Carol, and then this afternoon I had the honour of my in-laws. The phrase 'beneath contempt' was used on more than one occasion, and I'm starting to think that they might have meant me!

I'll let you into a secret, though – don't tell anyone... All the way through I had you in my mind's eye. This gave me strength, both to get through this and to find refuge in your arms on Tuesday.

I repeat what you said yesterday morning – there's going to be a lot of crap, but at the end of it, I get you.

Have to run – tea on table, after watching *Gladiators* with the kids.

Love you tender.

Martin, 29th November, 22.22

Dear, dear Trish,

I just got into the system, and read your note (twice). It was wonderful and most welcome. I've just about had enough today, having been summoned round to my parents' for the past hour or so. They appear to have rung my sister to tell her of the woe, which must kind of make it official. So don't worry yourself one iota about me going back to Carol – it simply will not happen.

My parents have offered to have me back in the spare room if I want it. I'm not sure about that (I'm thirty-seven, Goddammit!). Being away from Carol when in Lowestoft has its attractions, but I still wonder about the boys, and how I can tie this in with work.

I think I've just missed *The X-Files* again, and strangely, I no longer care, given that I'm fundamentally obsessed with thoughts and memories of you and our time together this week. I have never been so close to fainting from pleasure (while wearing clothes) as I was on Monday night at the seafront. That night could have lasted forever as far as I'm concerned. Mixed feelings seeing you at the airport before I boarded – I absolutely detest leaving you, especially now that I know that Aaron hit the house later that evening.

Better go – Carol is gearing up for Recrimination #18: The Rematch (she's back, and this time it's serious!).

Trish, 30th November, 15.36

Hello,

This is a quick one; I'll write something better around 4.30 when there are less people about.

You know, it's incredible how often your name comes up in conversation here. I even had to *say it* at this morning's meeting, trying to sound like it meant absolutely nothing to me! A near impossibility.

Must go, and will speak later.

Martin, 30th November, 15.38

So then, what to say... I got really defensive with my parents yesterday, as it appeared that my dad and father-in-law were sharing information that I only wanted to tell my parents about, such as wondering if I should request the short-term transfer to Aberdeen – he hadn't said anything, as it happens, but I must have sounded really bloody awful when I accused him of betraying a confidence (see, I *can* be a bastard). I'm still lying to everyone about us, which, as far as my parents are concerned, I find really difficult, but there is no way I'm risking a repeat of Carol ringing you again.

Anyway... some more of my list:

41. My best mate Colin and myself were so paranoid when the AIDS scare first happened, we used to go out on Friday and Saturday nights with our own pint mugs.
42. I'm worried that when we make love, I'm going to come in less time than it takes to say, "Leave the light on, Martin."

43. My ego is really massive at the moment, knowing that someone like you cares for me.

I can't stand not knowing who you're with, or where you are. Every time I put the phone down, or press the 'send' button, it's like someone's nipped in, nicked my soul, and hidden it somewhere between here and Aberdeen. Christ, I miss you, Trish – you've no idea. In the words of Prefab Sprout, '*Absence makes the heart lose weight*' – I'm getting emotionally anorexic, and can't accept any substitutes for the depth of feeling I have for you.

So take care, my demon soul.

Martin, 3rd December, 20.59

Dearest Trish,

I guess you'll be reading this Monday morning, after one of the longest weekends I've ever had, being away from you. It's no good; I just can't get used to it. The stress of it is far greater, and harder to cope with, than all the other crap I've been inflicting on everyone (including myself) over the past few days here.

I hope you had a chilled-out day yesterday, after your shopping and viewing exploits on Saturday. I expect you wondered what had happened when you got the final answerphone message that night – sorry, I just needed to hear your voice. Don't be the slightest harsh on Ellie for warning you – if I wasn't so damned biased, I would be doing the exact same thing. I *am* still using my head, and not just my heart (although the former hardly gets a word in edgeways), but you need to do the same.

I've endured attacks of various kinds through the day,

ranging from sobbing hysteria to cloying affection. It looks like I'm moving out on Friday night, after I finish the week in the office. Isn't it incredible that we only went out for that first meal about four weeks ago? I had real worries those first two or three weeks that you wouldn't feel for me the way I did for you – I guess it took a while to catch up, as I had been thinking about you for several weeks before we actually went out. Christ, I don't know – who's counting?

Look after yourself – you're needed.

Martin, 15th December, 19.49

Dear Trish,

Here I am again, hundreds of miles from the nearest Scottish soil. I guess the weekend's over for you to be reading this. Spoke to you an hour ago in town, before you went for your drinks with Annie and Pam – hope you had a passable time, and that I can get you on the phone later. I really don't want to use my parents' phone, or they'll suss out what's going on – how incredibly frustrating all this creeping about is.

Dad offered to lend me cash for the estate agent on Tuesday, so I've got to get a cheque drawn from the Rose bank account to be able to pay him back – that should get over any issues around the lease when I come up. Just got to make sure I don't get mugged on Tuesday, with all the dosh in my pocket. Getting the flat sorted out will be brilliant – will you help me on Tuesday night? Can't wait (as long as the answer's yes).

I'm going now, on my pedal bike from work – I'll go the long way and pop into the Kentucky for a chicken sandwich before going back to Mum's. I'm going to ring Carol tonight, and arrange to go round to get more stuff at some point over the weekend – I'll probably have to bring two suitcases on the plane anyway, so I might as well fill them up properly.

Martin, 17th December, 14.28

Hi, babe – at the office with the heating off. I froze my cobs off about two hours ago, but I'm starting to lose the function of other bits now. *Must… keep… going… must… try… to… find… shelter.*

Sundry parents are now walking past my office window with their toddlers for the age-nought-to-five kiddies' party in the staff restaurant – it must start at 2.30 or something. My two are too old for it; even Conor only just sneaked into the older kids' party this year.

You're right; Tuesday's effectively when I move up to Aberdeen to be with *you* – there'll just be the odd weekend when I 'visit' Lowestoft. I'll be able to tell you all weekend, every weekend to your face how I feel, and then watch your reaction. Most excellent!

And I've just remembered – we're going to have the works' Christmas dinner together in Aberdeen on Tuesday. Is this still OK? Leave that to you, sweetmeats; it'll be a midday prandial laff.

I'm going to send this to you now, try and have a quick conversation with you on your mobile, then get my huskies and salted meat rations ready for the trek home. Mush!

Martin, 18th December, 17.55

T,

Sorry about earlier; the 'orifice' was heaving with people.

Good news – I had a session with Rich, and told him of my plans; he's comfortable with what I've done but wants to speak to HR about how it's all paid for, to make sure that I don't fill the books with flats, cars, etc. I'll have to trust him to come up with something that doesn't jeopardise the existing arrangements.

Just think – you're reading this now, and I've just got off the plane at Aberdeen airport. Not long now, eh?

All the *very* best, darling. No more nights to go!

Revisiting that time still feels strange. I'm glad she kept these emails. All the triggers they contain can still dial my emotions up to eleven.

And Trish was right about the weight – we both dropped pounds. After our first week in the flat in Aberdeen, guilt or no guilt, I slept for a straight fifteen hours.

I don't remember why I claimed to have severed connection with Trish after Carol discovered her mobile number in my wallet (a direct consequence of my reluctance to put Trish's number into my phone, thinking it might be more easily discovered there than on the scrap of paper I used to compensate for my inability to memorise an eleven-digit number). She could have continued to call her, put pressure on her to back off, but by then I was pretty sure we were solid. It meant prolonging the fabrication of my lonely weeks in Aberdeen.

I returned to Lowestoft to be with the boys on Christmas Day. We spent it at the home of my in-laws; the same people who, only a month earlier, had expressed their disgust at me. One of my worst days. Ever.

Every day, from that day on, I've told Trish that I love her. On the rare days she beat me to it, I told her I loved her more, and therefore I was the winner. Now, of course, my daily ritual is shaped by no such affectionate rivalry, light-hearted or otherwise. I simply take the next mouthful of her, and her smiles are all imagined ones.

I'm lost in the intensity of that time. In our correspondence, the preserved artefacts of a trembling, tumultuous time. Without her to read them with me, I'm rudderless; adrift. I hear Trish's voice; my heart sheds twenty years, and then drops through a trapdoor onto burning coals. I'm dizzy with it all.

How we explored each other. Learned and solved our newly shared geometries. The unique particulars of interlaced limbs. Angles of joining and separation. Different sounds, conveying unpracticed and different meanings. The extension of neck or arm to place our mouths on each other, cradle or grasp. In still moments, we marvelled at the stretch and crack in our DNA, unravelling and re-forming to better match our re-partnered selves. As weeks and months passed, we found ways to comfort each other under the shadow of each assault invited by our reimagined existence together.

Melodramatic? Yes, but this is all way more powerful than I anticipated.

I sink into the sofa, and look across at the urn for help. The seahorses peer back at me, offering little but their blissful cartoon innocence.

And then, that knock at the door.

Words don't come at first.

Caitlin stands just this side of the drawbridge. She's trembling, but something tells me it's not from the cold. The Páramo is unzipped, and the colour in her face is high. Her lips are thin and tight, sucked in between teeth mounted in a determined, jutting jaw. She looks up at me. There's defiance there, but her eyes betray something else too. Something less easy to label.

"Can I come in?"

I'm not wrong – there's a challenge in there, but a hint of uncertainty, too; something I thought we'd moved past yesterday.

I step back to let her through to the utility room. She removes my coat and her trainers, then stands with her back to me, as if waiting for something to happen.

I'm about to take a step towards her, ask her if she's OK, when she spins round. The air between us crackles, and I can't help taking a step back. Caitlin's eyes are piercing. Fierce. But her silence continues.

So I begin. "Where have you been?"

I've struck a nerve. She storms through to the kitchen. Cupboards slam; then comes the sound of a fast-running tap. A glass filled and overtopped, then the water supply wrenched off again. Silence returns.

I walk through. She's standing next to the worktop, her hands placed flat either side of a tumbler, small spills of water around its base. Her head's bowed, and she shows no sign of looking up.

"Caitlin?" My thoughts race. Is Sean nearby? "What's wrong?"

"Wrong? You're bloody joking, aren't you?" She grips the glass, then raises her head. That same look; this time with her eyes wide, disbelieving. "Are you just going to stand there? Like nothing's happened?" She raises the glass. It's shaking as she takes a large gulp. A second.

She looks away. "I wasn't sure if you'd let me back in. Or if I even wanted to stay and do this again."

I'm lost. "Do what?"

"All this. All this housey stuff."

"I'm sorry, Caitlin, I don't understand. What's happened? Where have you been?"

The next look I get is enough to make me consider taking a step back again.

"Are you serious? Really?" She looks across at the table. The two bottles of Jack on it. "Don't tell me you don't remember. That's just ridiculous."

But I don't, even though it probably is.

"You finished your last bottle over lunch. Where do you think these came from?"

That had me, for a while. Until, flustered, I deny running out of Jack.

"Jesus, Martin. Really?"

So here's the rub. I really don't remember. I thought I'd been here all afternoon, writing. But if Caitlin is to be believed, and I've no reason to think she's lying, that's not true at all. Not by a long shot.

In her version of the past two-and-a-half hours, I drove us to the Leverburgh community shop, to look for more drink. And I found it. Except that the two elderly women behind the counter seemed none too happy to sell three bottles to me. Caitlin stood and watched while they discussed it between themselves in Gaelic. I then joined in – in Gaelic too, I'd like to think, with a series of generous and mildly offensive hand signals; the sort left on Jim Carrey's cutting-room floor for being 'just too much'. When they failed to be convinced, I got louder and more flamboyant and, well, obnoxious. Gaelic – it was no such thing – turned to ripe Anglo-Saxon, and several shelves of crisps and (bizarrely) peat spades ended up across the floor. *No one deprives a writer of his tools*, and the like. I climbed over the counter to claim my whiskies, and shuffled out to the car park with my basket, Caitlin running a few seconds behind me.

Apparently (and that's the last and only time I'll say that – I'm not questioning her veracity), I then drove off, loud and confident in my barely intelligible claims that I'd done my best to respect local traditions, but that no one had seemed prepared to reciprocate. Or words to that effect. I'd considerately left the empty basket by my vacated parking space.

Meanwhile, Caitlin urged me to go back and apologise, and pay for the drink. But I started to rage at her. *Jesus.* Said some mean stuff. Looked and sounded angry. When we approached Northton, she told me to pull over, withdrew the Páramo from the back seat, and walked off.

I don't remember a thing about how I got back. But those bottles of Jack, one of them almost empty, sit there as my accusers, and their gaze is imperious.

Caitlin's had it. Apparently (*oh, what the hell*), I told her to piss off and not come back. But here she is. Jack and Caitlin, witnesses for the prosecution.

And the toughest thing of all? Somewhere deep down, I think I meant it. I think she scares me. A woman beaten from pillar to post, pretty much imprisoned by her bastard of a partner, desperate for shelter, even at the cost of sharing it with a miserable old scrote, and yes, it scares me. That my plans will not survive intact.

She heads upstairs. I stand there, listening for any signs that she's getting her bag together. After ten minutes of silence and no-shows, I sit back down.

Can seahorses frown? I think they can.

It's dark again before she comes back down.

It's possible we're back to where we started yesterday morning. I can only hope that's the case. I've returned to my writing, but behind it all, I've been trying to think of a way to recover ground.

I muster a "Hi", in a voice that travels mere inches from where I sit. Stripped of threat.

She's settling into the lounge (a good sign), but takes the furthest chair again (less good).

I'll try pretending that nothing's happened. See how that goes. "How did you get on? At the beach, I mean."

I can see her deciding things; or putting off deciding. Her voice mirrors my own. In some circles, that's considered a good sign.

"Fine, I suppose. Well, actually, I'm not sure."

When she got there, the beach above the high-water mark was churned up, deep tyre tracks running its length. No debris, no litter, and no whale.

"I guess it died. Or they, you know, put it out of its misery? I don't know how they got it off the beach."

"I guess they did their best. The right thing."

I'll do my share of thinning out the silence if I can. I want to ask her if being there again brought back any memories of why she lay down next to it, or took her clothes off. But I've already pushed any new disclosure back into the shadows.

I conjure what I hope will be the right kind of light tone. "So if you'd still been there when whoever arrived at the beach checked out the whale, do you think you'd have been hauled off on the back of a trailer too? In one of those thick plastic bags with a zip down the middle?"

That didn't come out right.

She bows her head, but not so far that I can't see her eyes looking across to one side, thoughtful. Picturing the scene, perhaps. She has no answer, but that's OK, isn't it? Would *you* press further? I've asked this young woman to imagine standing over her own mottled, bruised, phantom corpse.

I shelve it. She can take all the time she wants.

So we reach a kind of unspoken stillness, both of us stepping up to the high glass panes and looking across to the lights of the estate house, and beyond to the equally silent Atlantic and the dark mass of Toe Head.

We might be OK.

SURVIVAL RATIONS

I need to get back to the writing, but it's time for The Ceremony.

Even Mr Murray seems to be affected by the quiet, offering merely the following on his highest-ranking Ardmore:

> **Scotch Malt Whisky Society Cask No. 66.16 Aged 20 Years (96)**
> ***n**25 **t**24 **f**23 **b**24 Best whisky not to win an award in 2006 Bible.* ***54.8%***

I've had a love-hate relationship with Ardmore in recent years. Their newer peated bottles taste great one week; bland Islay parody the next. But this one, from ten years ago, has all the richness you'd expect from a smooth, mellow Speyside. I wish these places wouldn't tamper with the very thing that has allowed them such longevity.

The Ceremony completed, only two sachets remain: #26 and #27. And one of them is for the hill.

I've been pretty open with Caitlin about what I'm doing here. But I've said nothing of what happens on Saturday. And before you say it, I know, OK? I get the irony – asking her to face up to her actions on the beach. I know I'm applying different standards to myself. But I allowed her silence to stand, didn't I? I'm simply doing the same, right? Evading questions of a similar kind, by evading the subject.

Downstairs, Caitlin grills venison sausages and opens a bottle of Rioja while I expand on Monday's visit to Callanish, recalling how it felt sitting on the lower slopes of The Clisham with Trish, three spoonfuls more present than now.

I eat the sausages with a generous smear of Colman's. Caitlin tells me how she brazened out the walk to and from the beach this afternoon, staying on the road the whole way.

I'm getting agitated away from my tablet, and bloated from the food. Cancel my appearance at next spring's competitive eating heats. I'll not be defending my title.

LOST IN TRANSLATION

You may recall how, in one of my emails, I suggested the equivalence of a failed marriage and a missed *X-Files* episode. An incongruous, possibly even insensitive complaint, given the turbulent nature of the time.

In my defence (and, sounding like a complete tosser, I'm pretty sure I need one), I'd caught 163 first-to-air episodes of the adventures of Mulder and Scully without missing any. *Not one*. A seven-year unbroken run, itself a small distraction from things closer to home, was cast aside for the following two months, another piece of debris in a growing pile of rubble around my feet.

I'm still a collector, a completist. *As if you couldn't tell, right?* So here I sit, with an important dilemma. Biting down on the discomfort of dishonouring the TV listing, or risking the incompletion of my writing.

I ask my new companion to be my proxy. Caitlin's never seen *The Wire*, but agrees to give it a go. I explain to her the entire pan-series arc, the genius of its coverage of policing, politics, education and the press, and how all four strands are pulled together in a fifth, heartbreaking run.

I set up the hard drive, she settles down to give it a go, and I head upstairs with the Ardmore. Earphones on, Harold Budd cued, and I'm back where I was, reliving the visitor centre heist and the paranoia of the drive back.

I'm deep into Tuesday morning when I see movement from the corner of my eye. Caitlin coming up the stairs. I pull out my earphones, and feel an empathetic blush climb, or rather surge, up my neck onto my cheeks. My teeth throb.

Bedroom. A man. A woman. *A shared awkwardness, then.*

"Hi, Caitlin. Everything all right?"

"Sorry, Martin. Aye, well, it's just that I needed to tell you. This *Wire* show. It's OK, but the accents? I can't work out what the hell most of those guys are saying. It's fine when the police are on, but see, when those druggies and gangsters start to speak, I've no idea what they're saying."

If I point out the occasional impenetrability of her own accent, things might go south fast, but I still can't help smiling. Trish felt the same, watching it the first time back in Weybridge. *"What was that? What? Speak up. What did he just say?"* Anyone wanting to find out why the show has been Top Three Ever for years submits to the same rite.

"That's OK. I should have warned you. Sorry. But it's worth it if you can hang in there. It's like watching Shakespeare. You get the general drift initially, but then your brain adjusts, you get into the rhythms, and bingo – everything makes sense."

She's unconvinced, but nods and goes back downstairs.

That was shitty. I want space, and I've pushed her away. Pressured her into something she might not want to do. *Bloody hell.*

I go down after her, and sit with her through Episode Four. Cops plot their own medical pensions; fix up cons with high prison sentences to get leverage. Bodie's in juvie with a bunch of boys from DC; Omar hooks up a young mother carrying her six-month-old baby. Lester chisels miniature furniture, his detective mind outpacing all around him. The infamous scene where Bunk and McNulty investigate the location of an old shooting, trying to reconstruct how it all went down, remains stunning. The entire dialogue, as they measure distances between bullet holes, assess injuries from morgue photos, search for shell casings, repeating variations on just a single Anglo-Saxon expletive. My favourite remains the "Ah, fuck" when McNulty nips his finger in his retractable metal measuring tape.

By the end of the scene, we're belly-laughing at each outburst. Rewind it, watch it through again. Applaud when Bunk holds up the overlooked casing, silent in his moment of triumph. Genius #3.

The episode's light on the patois, but Caitlin is happy to continue and see how she goes. "I can always stop and read more of your book. Although those Italian phrases are every bit as bad as this stuff."

"Very fuckety-fuck-fuck funny."

Back upstairs, I pour the last of the Ardmore, and clink the side of the glass onto the nose of a seahorse.

It's near twelve when I come back down again. The screen's blank, and Caitlin's asleep on the sofa. We need to swap. She needs the bed, while all I need is a room where I can keep writing.

"Hey. Hey, Caitlin." *Don't frighten her.*

She comes round, and swings her legs down. I explain how we should swap.

"Are you sure? I don't mind staying down here."

"It's fine, Caitlin. Really. I'm going to see how much further I can get with this tonight. And that bed's more comfortable than the sofa. If I go up there, the next thing you know I'll be asleep. I've only got until Saturday."

She looks at me, as if weighing her next words. "So… the checkout on Saturday. What's the deal?"

"The deal? Well, I've got to get the keys back to Robert."

"But do you have to get your writing finished by then? Can't you do the rest when you get home?"

I make the choice, and go for it. "Well, yeah, I could. But I'd like to get the bulk of it done here. It feels right, soaking up the atmosphere of this place while I can. It's worked so far. I've never written so much in twenty-four hours. Feels good, and I need to stay in the groove." *That's it. Blend the unspoken lie with unquestionable truth, and give her no chance to cross-examine.* "I don't want to pry, Caitlin, but what do you think you'll do? You know, at the weekend?"

She straightens; pushes into the back cushion of the sofa. One hand grips the fingers of the other. "Well, I don't think I can stay on Harris forever. Nearly everywhere's shut, and my money will run out soon. And it's still too close to home. I need more distance, from Sean. It's the weekend, so he might be looking for me again; maybe even with Callum. I don't know. Well, the one thing I *do* know is that I can't stay here, so…"

"Are there any friends you could go to? Stay with them a bit while you work out what to do?"

"There's only really Bryan, and I haven't seen him for well over a year. In fact, I don't even know if he's still down at *The Takeaway*, or in Portree at all."

"You could call him?"

"I could." She looks down to her lap, her hands still tightly entwined. "But I won't. Too close to home again."

She won't cry, but she's close to it. We both sit there, trying to think where she could go.

"What about your dad's?"

It's hard to interpret the look that races across Caitlin's face. Did *you* catch it? Something between surprise and, well, a small pinch of fear?

"Well, yeah. I suppose I could. Although that might be one of the first places The Arsehole thinks to look."

"So he knows where your dad lives, then?"

"We went down there once. In the days when, you know, I wanted to show him off. But we've not been in touch in ages."

"Maybe you could call him. Find out if Sean's contacted him. See if it would be OK to stay there while you work out what to do?"

Her lips tighten.

"Why not think about it overnight. I can help you out with a bit of cash, if you need that to get down there. But it's up to you." I lie a little on this last bit. Yes, it's up to her. But I want to get involved. Help her form a plan. Keep her away from Bastard and Bastard's Mate.

My brain's banging away fifteen to the dozen. Twelve hours after telling her to piss off, I'm buzzed at the prospect of helping her on her way to an unblemished, healed body and healthier prospects.

Caitlin finally upstairs, I lay my palm on the top of the urn, then plug in the iPad charger. The second bottle of Ardmore, all ninety-six gorgeous points of it, will act as both tonic and hammock for the night.

Now then, where was I?

CREMATION
FRIDAY 26TH JANUARY 2018

The container is not heavy. A couple of bags of sugar, perhaps. Buffed, cylindrical cream, in a tasteful grey box.

He repeats that he won't leave without it. Insists. A private room is arranged so he can wait.

Other services flow around him. Tides of voices and footsteps ebb and flow every hour. Hymns. Robbie Williams. James Blunt. On one occasion, Postman Pat. He screws his heart down hard for that one. Two men talk about the previous night's Burns Supper.

Frasers have delivered. Nothing in the papers. No polite but firm 'Cremation private at own request'. No name on the crematorium's web page of the day's programme. A taxi for him, to and from The Schoolhouse.

They suggested a humanist. He went along with the idea, then rang back to say no. Thank you, but no. He could not stand there, hearing his memories repeated back to him. His stories, their *stories, were their own. He will hoard their shared mythos.*

So he curates a private collection. Gathers in each grain from the beach of their past, each anecdote or recollection, and places them carefully in their preordained places. No one else may touch them, lean their weight on them. Press them into false shape.

His withdrawal to the private room disrupts nothing. No gathering. No handshakes from consoling men and women. No parade of black suits, waistbands strained, or tightened around thinned-out age with new belt notches.

He's *changed shape. He can feel it. Attached to the earth in a different way. Grief etches and carves into clavicle and hip, elbow and scapula.*

He imagines her telling him to straighten up, to lift his head. "Tits to the sky, Martin."

Four billion more people walk the earth now, since the day of Trish's birth. One hundred billion human deaths and counting. Fourteen ghosts for each of us who are still here.

But his most recent one hides well. He told her to stay away from here. And she has.

He leaves with her. Past the tended, low-lawned gardens that spread to fill the foot of the slight rise above the town.

Protocol Five of Travelers states, 'In the absence of direction, maintain your host's life.'

He'll do his best.

CHAPTER 7

FRIDAY 26TH OCTOBER 2018

Ain't no shame in holdin' on to grief,
as long as you make room for other things too.
(Bubbles, The Wire)

A HELL OF A RIDE, BUT A JOURNEY TO DUST

It should be clear by now that I'm offering you no new or striking insights into the nature of love, or the carnage that ensues when it is gone.

Rather, I'd like to hear such things from *you*. Any thoughts about how to navigate a life to the point where *'my last day'* is uttered only after ten years in sheltered housing, or just as a parachute's deliberately left unopened while mentally assigning the last 'tick' to a bucket list.

I've thought about it a lot, of course. It's just that I've not yet found a way – and this is the heart of the problem, I guess – to take Trish's loss, *my* loss, and move it from the particular to the general. If it was Grief and Loss and Loneliness and Guilt, I might be better at this thing. It's like that with Caitlin, even.

I won't presume to draw any conclusions about the workings of the cosmos from that poor girl's plight, or my own tentative rescue efforts. Things happen. People do what they do. There's no grand pattern. Everything comes down to what you do, what you think. How you feel. Uncapitalised particularities. Period. *My* wife. *Her* death. *My* sorry responses.

There. That's just about as much philosophising as you'll get out of me. I'll leave you to source the other stuff from Boyd and Brontë and Brookner, from Faulks and Updike and Roth.

I admit it. I'm having a few wobbly moments; thoughts drifting forward to 'events of the morrow'. And while we're on the subject of admissions, I should come clean about what you've seen me do every evening since we met.

It's true that, for me, grief squares with distance. Even before, I felt less at ease when we were apart. But I know, for sure, that Trish is long separated from any physical remnants of calcium phosphate; of sodium or potassium. I don't pull her closer to me in any *real* sense with each small spoonful, I know that. I'm not claiming any transubstantiation miracle here. But it's the best I can do. Each mouthful pulls me back. To those moments, good or bad. To mark the passing of that other, earlier version of myself.

I'm rambling again. Sorry.

Half the problem is that I've had practically no sleep for two days. Although to be fair, Shagged-Out Martin is not that different from his rested self. Except when it comes to his tendency to self-importantly refer to himself in the third person (ha).

Yep. Definitely drifting.

But while we're talking, there's another thing I'd like to get off my chest. I worry that you might be feeling a little marginalised by my suggesting that I'm writing this as a final gift for the boys. It's true, this ambition will inevitably put a certain skew on what I choose to share, but this doesn't stop me from appreciating your company. Our friendship still matters to me too; more than you might think. Without you, I wouldn't have got even this far. In fact, without you there, I'm unsure if I'd have intervened with Caitlin on the beach on Tuesday. As I told you before, almost all my betrayals take place when no one is looking.

So please know that I still have you in my mind's eye, even though I'm going to try and get this testament south of the border somehow. Stay with me, and I know I'll see this through. We both will.

PONDERINGS

I'm glad I've got all that off my chest. I've got a lot of thinking to do right now. Being Departure Day Minus One is not helping.

Last night and earlier this morning were little short of amazing. I honestly don't know how the words hit the page so quickly. I've had periods like this at home, but never for more than a couple of hours at a time. After that, I drift, or smugly award myself the rest of the day off. Anyway, despite the dictation software continuing to surprise me with its decisions on which words to get wrong, I'm blasting through. It's the roughest of rough drafts, but at least I'm getting the basics down.

But this past hour or so? Not so much. The tone of my inner voice has changed. No longer the soothing tones of Mariella Frostrup or, occasionally, Nanette Newman (remember her?), I'm barracked now by a voice reminiscent of *Il Duce* inciting seas of blackshirts from his balcony; or perhaps, worse still, the drawn-out nasal sneer of Kenneth Williams. Either way, it's the voice that tells me what MUST BE DONE and CAN NO

LONGER BE PUT OFF, unless I want to think EVEN LESS OF MYSELF THAN I ALREADY DO.

And, of course, what makes it so much harder to ignore is that it's right. I've been bent over my iPad like some Dickensian grotesque while a growing number of serious impediments to the week's success have snuck up on me unaddressed. I'm desperate to continue my writing, but some important problems need to be solved. And there's only so much borrowed time before that blancmange ceases to function.

I'll share them with you now, as I open a new file to write them down. (You're probably already aware of a few of them – you've been paying more attention than I have.)

Problem 1:	*Time delay between my death, my identification, and confirmation to the boys. (I want to be found and identified quickly.)*
Problem 2:	*Still two days to write up, and time is running out.*
Problem 2a:	*Unable to write up tomorrow's events on Sunday (?!)*
Problem 3:	*My writing (this week's and older) is accessible to me alone.*
Problem 4:	*Kieron and Conor will probably receive and read my letters to them today. (Lots of things here – what are they?)*
Problem 5:	*Car left stranded at bottom of hill.*
Problem 6:	*Caitlin???*

I need to get my head around these now. If I don't, they'll continue to take over, and before I know it, I'll grind to a halt and the day will descend into unhealthy self-recrimination and a bad exit.

When Caitlin surfaces about an hour later, I have the kind of smile on my face which might generously be deemed 'touched'. Borderline 'feel kid', in Trish's Doric vernacular. Anyway, whatever you want to call it, it draws a puzzled greeting from Caitlin, en route to her daily clothes wash.

Once she's back up, two coffees and Hebridean Smokehouse salmon gracing thick cuts of well-toasted rustic loaf, I'm straight in.

"Caitlin, I need to talk over a few things with you. But before I do, I really want to make sure that we're going to be OK with each other. I'm really, really sorry for how I treated you yesterday. Can you trust me to deal with a few things?"

I wonder how many of these words she's heard Sean use?

"Yeees? I guess so. But what is it? Should I be worried?" She clutches her coffee mug to her midriff, in that way that confirms a genuine defensiveness.

"Really, Caitlin, it's all right. Nothing's going to happen. It's just talk, right?"

This is getting us nowhere.

"So the sooner we do this, the sooner it's done. But first I want to ask you the question I asked you yesterday. About what you're going to do when you leave here. Where you're going to go."

She shrugs into a pose of bemused uncertainty. "I'm really not sure. Nothing's changed. I hate to say it, but I'm not sure I trust him. Da, I mean. I wouldn't put it past him to take Sean's side, and tell him to come and take me back with him."

"And your mum?"

Coffee overspills the lip of her mug. "What? *Really?*"

"Sean would never think to look for you there, though, would he?"

That shrug again. "Well, aye, there's that. But bloody hell."

"Is there anyone else you could contact? Old friends from when you worked in Glasgow?"

"Martin, I'm not trying to be awkward, but, come on, where would I start? I never really got to know that many folk from work, and my old school friends? I've got no idea where they'll be now – it's been more than ten years. I'd feel such a fraud. They don't need me turning up."

The coffee's no substitute for whisky, which is downstairs, but it'll have to do. No choice but to keep going. "I want to make some suggestions that might help you out. But to do that properly, I'm probably best starting by telling you a bit more about my own plans."

I keep it brief. Keep the tone of my voice even, particularly when it comes to the bit where I… you know. She just sits there. Says nothing.

"So I need your help, Caitlin. And I think that if we do this right, you could buy yourself quite a bit of time. Get your thoughts clear. And most importantly, stay safe."

I've done as good a job as I can, I think. Avoided a sense of the sensational or the downright creepy. Explained things in a way that suggests I'm still capable of unemotional analysis. As opposed, say, to being completely obsessed with myself and my selfish death wish, and willing to rope in just about anyone who can help.

I look across at her, confident of a constructive response.

"My clothes should be dry."

And she's off.

WHAT LARKS, PIP!

"Well, that's messed up the day, and no kidding."

She's pissed off. But she's back.

We go through things a step at a time. If she's happy to stay at The Schoolhouse, I'll write a last-minute email to Steve tomorrow and explain her presence there. I'll log onto the DVLA website and transfer the car to her (I brought all the paperwork with me to leave in the glove compartment). We can then book a slot through the CalMac website for the car ferry from Tarbert tomorrow evening. If there's a risk that someone might pick up on the car registration and tie it to the vandalism at Callanish, or yesterday's incident at the shop, then it's one we'll take. It's just a case of going for it. The same applies to any stay at The Schoolhouse. Caitlin just needs to know not to answer the door unless it's Steve (unlikely) or one of the boys (ditto).

I expected a lot more protest, or even shock, but Caitlin focuses on the details.

"But are you sure you want me to have the car? I mean, it's generous and everything, but that's just too much."

It's a drop in the ocean, frankly. The boys have already had one cheque each, and once the Will takes effect, they'll each get half of The Schoolhouse and whatever cash is in the savings account.

Money still needs to be discussed, though. "Listen, Caitlin. I know we've only known each other a few days, but I think you're all right. You know, I trust you. Use my debit card at the cashpoints on the way through tomorrow. There's plenty of money in the current account. Take out the maximum a few times, at Uig, Broadford, Kyle. Buy groceries at Kyle, and you should easily have enough cash and food to last a while. And you could always nip up the loch to Drum and use the machine there if you run short. To be honest, you could keep taking money out until the account hits the buffers. That should be enough to set you up when you go down to Glasgow, or wherever it is you head next."

We're back to no eye contact. Maybe she's not coping so well after all.

"You OK? Do you want me to slow down?"

"No. It's not that. It's just the other stuff you've told me. You know, what happens before that."

I really had no choice but to tell her, had I? We're only a day off.

I know what you might be thinking. Perhaps I secretly want to provoke a little drama. You know the sort of thing – have a young, attractive woman go down on her knees and plead with me not to deprive the world of my genius or my infinite capacity for love.

No.

That's not the case.

I just want this to work out. And now I know she's key to that happening. If she has the car, then there'll be one less physical clue pointing to me on the hill. I want Kieron and Conor to know my fate as soon as possible, but having the car parked at the bottom of the hill, with Kieron alerting his colleagues to track down my whereabouts, is too big a threat. I need a day – one with no outside interference or distraction – and I'll have my credit card on me for ID. There's no question. Caitlin's mobility will be really helpful for what comes next.

"So tomorrow, after I've written to Steve, I'll drop a note to Kathleen; tell her to expect your call or visit." Kathleen Ward, the published-author-turned-tutor on my first visit to the writing school, has already been really supportive in reviewing passages of *The Quarant.* She lives about forty miles from The Schoolhouse, up on the Black Isle. I show Caitlin her name in the acknowledgements of the copy she's reading. "I think she'll be prepared to take possession of all this stuff. It'll be a bit of a mess, but she might be able to work it into something that makes sense. She's worked with editors before, too, so maybe she'll know someone who might be good if she doesn't want to do it herself. Either way, I think she'll recognise why I want this to get to the boys, and make it happen. I'll give you details on how to contact her later, and how to access everything I've backed up at home."

I go upstairs, confident that I've unblocked the writing pipes. But no. It's like the tap's been turned off. Drips find their way onto the page, but dry up as soon as they land. I start to panic. I don't need this now.

Another half an hour. Nothing. I back off. No good getting flustered. I guess I shouldn't be surprised, right? I've carried the thought of tomorrow around with me for months. Stashed it away from the daylight, never once speaking it out loud. Not even to Trish.

Was I worried about how she would react? Not really. We always joked about walking together, while still just able to haul our old and failing bones up an ascent, and jumping hand in hand off Lochnagar (the Black Spout gully would do the trick), to save ourselves from a life alone for either of us.

That won't happen now.

I look down at her, at the polished sides of the urn. Is she aware of what I am doing right now? The supernatural is far from super, yet even so. *Even so*. I'm sure she has a view.

Where do *you* stand on all this? Love. Death. Suicide. 'The Afterlife'. I'd love to know. Discussing it might make you feel uncomfortable. But if we can't explore stuff like this today, when can we?

You saw in another one of my emails how Carol went for the nuclear option and wheeled out the vicar to help me 'see sense'? What better way to illustrate just how out of touch from each other we'd become? I'd shrugged off Christianity years before I met Carol, despite my submissive compliance with C of E Sunday ritual throughout our marriage, but she still believed a guest appearance from the clergy would swing things her way.

While on the subject of loose ends, I should follow up on how good it felt to finally bring an end to that other lie. The one to my parents, and Carol, that my 'fling' with Trish was short-lived and over by the time I took that plane north just before Christmas.

It took me the best part of two months to fess up to Mum and Dad, first on the phone and then in person. Even then, I hid (and still hide) behind the white lie that Trish and I had become an item only several weeks into my separation, hoping to spare them the need to confront the full-on adulterous behaviour of their son.

We drove down from Aberdeen to introduce her to them on an auspiciously sunny, still morning just after Valentine's Day. Things turned slightly surreal just below Glasgow; skies streaked with thick black smoke. Funeral pyres. Dozens of them, all the way to the border, dealing with the foot-and-mouth epidemic. Do you remember that? We'd already had the whole mad cow disease thing – chemical wash on our wellies, football matches cancelled in case any mad cows decided to throw sharpened coins from the visitors' enclosure – but here we were, just a few years on, driving through, possibly even *inhaling*, the charred remains of British agricultural credibility. Joking aside, it was pretty eerie.

We checked into a seafront hotel; the venue that, some fifteen years later, hosted Kieron's wedding. Our meal with Mum and Dad went well. Trish took her post-meal ciggie outside (as soon as our hillwalking hobby grew legs – *ha* – that was the last of the smoking), while first Dad and then Mum said they were happy for me.

For the next seven years, we travelled down to Lowestoft once every couple of months, staying at my parents'. Voluntarily, and then in response to threats of maternal restraining orders, I kept the boys out of Trish's company, usually taking them up to the match. Once, when the early summer weather was too bad to take them for a trip outdoors, Trish was exiled to the kitchen while I entertained the boys in the next room; a situation made worse by Dad's misplaced desire to keep Trish occupied by showing her, page after page, their photos of my wedding. Parents, eh?

We finally took the plunge, introduced the boys to her, and settled into an uncomfortable but necessary bimonthly rhythm. My secondment had been scheduled to end in April, but I was fortunate enough to secure a permanent transfer just before its expiry. In a manner demonstrating yet again my inability to do anything in the right order, we bought a flat in Aberdeen a month before I was confirmed in the role, but we got away with it.

Now that I'm back in that time, there's one more little story I want to share with you that shows just how charmed and surreal that time really felt.

A few weeks after our first Hogmanay together, our company had its annual dinner dance; one of the bigger black-tie dos in Oil City. There were a few rumours floating around the office just before that, suggesting that Trish had been seen in a shoe shop (of all places!) with me on a Saturday afternoon (of all days!). What was going on?

Still officially on the books of my home base, I didn't qualify for a ticket. But Trish did, and she decided we would attend together, as something of a 'coming out' ball. Our cover crumbling by the day, I liked the idea. In the spirit of making it a bit of a 'thing', we booked a room at the Ardoe House, one of the grander country piles on Royal Deeside converted to a hotel and events venue.

We arrived early, chilled out, and had a couple of drinks in the bar before joining our table. Things got under way without incident until Trish shuffled up to me to say that she'd split the back of her skirt on the dance floor. "I'm going back to the room to fix it. There's some needle and thread. Walk right behind me in case my arse hangs out."

I shuffled three inches behind her like a needy penguin seeking protection from the Antarctic chill, trying not, please

God, to look like I was about to mount her in some gross breach of ballroom decorum.

Upon our return some twenty minutes later, we should have thought. Should have pondered why the music had stopped and everyone was seated. But no. Oooooh no. Keen to retake our seats on the far side of the dance floor, and quell any clacking tongues regarding our paired exit, I opened the door and let her through in front of me.

Approximately five hundred heads turned from the senior manager calling out the raffle prizes, to watch us take our long, lonely walk, the sound of Trish's high heels corralling the attention of those who had failed to notice us by the door. Wouldn't want them to miss anything, eh? We made it back to our seats three geological ages later. Blood was just beginning to drain from my face when the top prize was announced – a state-of-the-art DVD player (this was 2001, remember). "And the winning ticket is…"

Trish's. No fucking way.

It was a great prize, and we were in the process of hunting for a flat together. What would *you* do? Well, I'll tell you what Trish did. She picked up her strip of raffle tickets, edged back past the folk around our table, and walked pretty much the entire length of the empty dance floor to the low stage where the CEO awaited the lucky recipient.

Is it possible to fall in love with someone when you're already in love with them? A kind of bliss squared? Re-approaching our table, her eyes firmly on mine, she strutted. *Strutted*, her head high and her eyes flashing their warning to anyone who cared to see it. *Make me feel embarrassed or defensive about being with this man, and I'll make you fucking sorry. And don't mess with my new DVD player.*

Anyway, back here in The Broch, still unable to get the words flowing, keeping that gorgeous look of defiance in the front of my mind, I take the easy option. Opening my mail system, I draft my email to Kathleen, leaving the addressee line empty to avoid any premature dispatch. I want to make sure I get this right. She's hugely generous when it comes to supporting aspiring writers, but this request is several orders of magnitude greater than any she'll be used to receiving.

What else will I need? A record of the sources of those subtitle headings and chapter quotes that are drawn from other books, songs or shows (I'll update that tomorrow, before I leave). A list, compiled since Wednesday, of all the characters I've mentioned in my story, and their contact details should Kathleen wish to talk to them. All the access codes I'll need Caitlin to provide.

Saving the email sends my thoughts back to sealing and addressing the letters to the boys. I shake it off.

Next, I pull up a web page headed 'Tell DVLA you've sold, transferred or bought a vehicle', and work through the options. It's easier than I thought it would be. Everything that's needed is in the car; I can tell Caitlin what else she has to do to make everything official and above board.

The ferry booking's another thing, though. The winter timetable's begun, and departures on Saturday look like they might not work. There's only one sailing back to Uig tomorrow, and it leaves Tarbert just before twelve. It's doable, but a bit tight if Caitlin's to drop me off at The Clisham. There's one leaving Stornoway a couple of hours later, but she shouldn't go back to Ullapool. Sean may still be around, trying to pick up any trail. Either we check out really early tomorrow, or Caitlin might need to stay on the island overnight. Sunday's not too great either, as the morning ferry, for some wanky reason, leaves from Lochmaddy on North Uist. God knows how you get across there to catch it. It all looks too bloody complicated.

I'm just thinking about going back downstairs to discuss it when I hear Caitlin coming up.

"Sorry, Martin, can we talk a bit? You know, a bit more?"

I follow her back down. I tell her how I've sorted her introduction to Kathleen, and all the car stuff.

"Have you booked the ferry yet?"

"Well, no."

Caitlin takes a deep breath. "But it's not too late to change things, is it?"

Where's this going? "But why would we do that? Don't you want to get off the island?"

"I do. It's just that I'd rather I wasn't going on my own." She blushes. "I guess what I'm really saying… what I think we should talk about… is that you leave here with me. We could do that, couldn't we? Just put two names on the ferry booking instead of one?"

She's almost crimson. I thought we were past this. But this? This is an intervention. She's trying to stop me.

Calm down. Don't just jump in.

"Are you worried about taking the car? I know you've not driven for years, but you'll soon get the hang of it again. Or is it about being stopped at the terminal because of the number plate? It's not you they're interested in. If you are stopped, I suppose you could easily travel as a foot passenger, get a taxi from Uig, and pick up cash the way we discussed."

"No, it's not that. Although now you mention it, I should've probably thought this through a bit more. But no." Her eyes drop to her lap; her fingers tighten around themselves. She looks at me directly. "I just feel really bad about taking you to that hill tomorrow."

All the pennies drop at once. Quite a din, right? A bucketful. *I'm right. She wants to fuck up the end of my life.*

I don't move. I don't speak. But she flinches. She's probably seen similar looks before. Time stands still. I'm inside here, fighting to hold it together.

How would *you* feel, setting out on a course of action, determined to make it happen, but knowing, deep down, that you're too cowardly by nature to see it through? That the only wise choice is to do everything within your power to sidestep anything that might dissuade you from completing it? To build walls and routines and, I don't know, barriers to stop you slipping back? I filled each of those little sachets, months ago, with just the right amount of ash to get me to the end of this week. To drive me along, push me to this point.

I know I'm a coward. I wasn't kidding when I told you that declaring my feelings to Trish, that night at the curry house, was, and remains, the single bravest act I have ever performed. Even now, I worry. About following it through. About *not* following it through.

And here I sit, with a woman I didn't even know existed three days ago, as she offers me a chance. No. That's not even it. *Asks* me to pull out.

I need a drink, but the Jack's upstairs. I dry-swallow. Screw things down inside. "Tell me, if you can and if you're happy to, why you feel you need company leaving the island. You've already shown how strong you can be when you have to be."

Caitlin has no interest in talking about herself right now. *She's not done with me yet.* "Are you sure this is what your wife would want? Maybe it's too soon for you to think straight."

I won't deny to you that she obviously has a point. You might well be nodding along with her. Trish sits just in front of me on the coffee table.

One look down at the soon-to-be-empty urn is all it takes. "I'm not doing this, Caitlin. You need to stop. I hear you, you mean well, but I'm not doing it. I told you everything because

I need you to know. I need your help. I *don't* need anyone, including you, shitting all over this."

I can see the effect of my rising voice. "Look. I don't want to bully you into doing things. Christ, you've had enough of that. But you need to stop. I really think you leaving here with the car, holing up at my place, for a few days at least, is a good thing. You can think about how to get out from under all this shit too."

Caitlin isn't finished, though. "But what if I can't get in touch with this Kathleen woman, or she just isn't interested in doing the stuff you want her to do? What then?"

"Then you'll have done your best. That's her decision to make. If all else fails, you can just get in touch with my friend Steve, or one of the boys. At worst, just leave the iPad back at The Schoolhouse on the desk in the snug with the same instructions you would've given Kathleen, and you'll be free to go anywhere you want after that."

This is horrible. I don't want to walk out, or to fight. We sit here, the two of us, weighed down by more unspoken pleas and wishes.

Seconds pass.

And then, the sound of my mobile phone, vibrating on the hard coffee-table surface. The bubble's pricked. We look at each other, then down to the phone, and then back at each other. I flick open its black-leather cover. Although locked, the centre of the screen displays a small photo of Conor. Just beneath it, a rounded green rectangle. 'Swipe to answer.'

Forget *walking* out.

It's time to run like hell.

FATHERHOOD REVISITED

We're fifteen minutes from The Broch, sitting on an outcrop

of rock above a small lochan. The rough track on which we walked here extends a further mile or two into the wide, rolling hills to our back. The air feels mild, while the breeze has yet to rob us of the heat of our hurried escape from that rumbling phone. The light here seems softer, somehow grainier above moorland greens and browns. My rucksack lies on the dense heather at my feet. Our breathing, heavy from a walk during which conversation was all but impossible, is back to normal.

We're agreed. Caitlin won't return to Ullapool. She'll drive back to Tarbert after she drops me off, and stay at The Backpackers Stop until Monday. On her own. If they're full, she'll park up the car and push one of the seats back. We'll make the ferry and hostel bookings when we get back in.

I'm gripping the Jack as tightly as I can. The world continues to constrict then expand, constrict then expand. I feel the need to explain.

"It's not that I'm a complete bastard. Really, it's not. He needs to talk, and I understand. But I really, really think he's better off if we don't. If we draw a line. Recognise it's already drawn."

We return to their letters.

"I know they're just marks on a page, but I thought through each line. Said nothing regrettable. Things come out of my mouth that surprise even me. I just start talking, and often have no idea what the hell's going to come next. Like now, in fact. I want to protect them from that. It's heartless, maybe. But what's the alternative? Tripping into something that'll hog-tie them the rest of their lives?"

This is all true, of course. But so is my fear that, like Caitlin earlier, they'll start to pick away at my decision.

I shift my feet around on the soil at the base of the rock. Look over the gently rippling water out and down to the bay beyond.

"I've told you a little bit about what it was like, Caitlin.

Those insane days I put myself and others through to be with Trish. But there was one evening, about three weeks before I left for good. I was staying in a hotel in Aberdeen. We'd gone to the Beach Boulevard after work to see a movie. When I asked at the reception desk for my key, they handed me an envelope. 'It's from your wife,' they said."

I mumbled my thanks, quickly ushered Trish from the lobby to my room, and opened the envelope. The message was brief. '*Time of call: 19.35. Please ring your wife at home urgently.*'

"My first thought was, you know, that one of the boys was hurt, or ill. Something terrible."

Caitlin nods, but offers no other response. I've no idea what she's thinking.

"Anyway, Trish went into the bathroom to give me some privacy. My chest was pounding by the time Carol answered the phone, and I blurted out some kind of apology. That I'd only just got the note. So what was wrong? I braced myself for the usual volley about how, of course, I'd been unable to call, given that I was out with my slut.

"Instead, the line went quiet, and then the next voice was Kieron's. It was nearer midnight than eleven, a school night, and Kieron was twelve years old. He was crying down the phone, and through the tears, from five hundred miles away, he said, 'Please come home. I just want you to come home. Don't leave us.'"

It's hard to decipher the look on Caitlin's face. If I had to guess, I'd say it's somewhere between empathy and accusation. I can't say I blame her.

"I didn't sleep that night, or the next. The anger I felt – *still feel*, even now – at their callous bitch of a mother, weaponising her own children.

"I went back south that weekend, and for the next two weekends after that. I had nothing to say to them. I had no words left; at least none that wouldn't make things worse. So I just held them. Hugged them wherever and whenever I could. I doubt it made them feel any better. I just tried to shut down. To roll past everything said to me. *At* me. Soak it up and take all that venom and anguish out of the house when I left, like a bag of rubbish."

Caitlin wonders, "Have you spoken to them about it since? About how all that happened? How they feel now, looking back?"

It took me fifteen years to ask Kieron. What he said surprised me. He said the main thing he felt, all the way through his teens, was anger. Not sadness, or bitterness. Anger at how I'd left him, the eldest, to handle his mother on his own.

"I don't want to make them angry again, Caitlin. Or hear their anger. They won't understand what I'm doing. I'm not going to hear them shout at me for abandoning them again. They're right. But I can't face it."

Caitlin shifts her weight to look me directly. She's heard enough. "So tell me a few of the nice things about them. About having them as your kids. I don't have any kids of my own, thank Christ, but give me something to offset all that bloody misery." She mock-punches me in the arm.

Urn or no urn, I could hug her right now. But of course I don't.

I'd always wanted children, although I'm not really sure why. No gorgeous nephews or nieces to set me on my way (Kieron was the first of the crop). No friends, having had their own, proclaiming the wonder and fulfillment that came from that decision. But I wanted them. I would load them up with all my cool thoughts and opinions without them having to work the same twenty or so years that I did to collect or amass them. I think every dad wants that, don't they? A semi-enlightened form of self-adulation? Cloning, but this time without Dolly.

Many of my favourite moments in their early lives occurred when one or the other of them did or said something as a direct result of my parental brainwashing. Hardcore indoctrinations.

Supporting Norwich City, dragging each of them to a game before the age of five, as my own father had done for me. Love of funk music (Kieron's gift to me, years later, of a signed book and a photograph of him with George Clinton at Glastonbury was one of my biggest birthday surprises and a strangely moving moment).

Many times, of course, I took pleasure in how they left me well behind in their own footsteps. Duke of Edinburgh Gold Awards. Playing American football at their Cambridge college (I'd only ever aspired to watch it from the sofa; the closest I've come to contact sport since school, if you don't count that ridiculous night when I floored Trish in the five-a-side).

About two years after Trish and I were married, Kieron arranged for me to borrow their childhood photo albums. It's buried, in each of those amateur snaps, that the heart of my love for the boys resides. I describe some of them to Caitlin. Runny noses in winter parks. Wide grins feeding the ducks. Infant faces covered in Bolognese sauce or ice cream. Echoes of unrestrained shrieks replaying in my head from visits to ball pools and fun factories. Birthday parties. Sitting proudly for the first time on bikes *sans* stabilisers, safety helmets at comically jaunty angles.

I turn to her. "And that's just me!"

Even the worrying times have their place; prove to me that once, as a dad, I could be there when it mattered. Holding an anaesthetic mask over Conor's contorted face, his back bare on a cold operating table at seven months, crying in large lungfuls of the stuff. Collecting him two hours later. Witnessing the real meaning of 'white as a sheet'. The ten years I aged on that day. Learning that Kieron, two terms into his school career, was being bullied by a fellow pupil deprived, as it turned out, of the kind of love and stability both my sons enjoyed. Or watching him stand on a football field, doing his best to look involved, despite never receiving a pass.

Neither of them went off the rails after I left, though God knows they could have. They simply refused to allow the world to dictate its demands to them. Kieron's now a well-respected, level-headed police officer back in his home town. Conor, never knowingly accused of level-headedness, will always be the hardest-working and most determined man I will ever know.

A CARNIVOROUS FLOWER

We're back in The Broch, booking Caitlin's ferry for early Monday morning. She's called and secured herself a bunk for the weekend.

My phone shows four messages and seven missed calls. Five from Conor and two from Kieron. I don't listen to the messages. Instead, I retreat upstairs with Trish, a new Jack, and a determination to get more writing completed before Ceremony time.

I know. I bloody know. I'm losing all my sharp corners.

The truth is, I'd have to tip the dictionary upside down and shake out half of the words to have any chance of selecting those that match any other more recognisable feelings. There's too many, all in one place. In me. Running, blending into some crappy, muddy mush.

I *do* know I'm anxious, if that helps. Keen that nothing gets in the way of leaving here tomorrow with this record finished, and the wherewithal to make the hike to The Clisham's summit.

Surprisingly, today is far from a total write-off. I'm glad, despite the fright earlier, to have spent time reflecting on life with the boys, and clarifying the logic of our departures. But now, I just want to sink into that space where words fill the screen. Apply the necessary analgesics.

I start with yesterday's details. How it felt to be driven to shape a past that has at times lacked any kind of recognisable pattern. How Caitlin makes sense of her early life in Glasgow. How she might help me as I help her.

It's not until the Jack's gone and I dig fingers into the muscles of my lower back that I notice the change. Outside, the view west has deepened into dark crimson skies. Someone's ignited the clouds. We were told of the extraordinary sunsets in this part of the world yet none, until now, have thought it polite to put in an appearance. But look at this! I lay back on the bed. Above me, the skylight looks like the Eye of Sauron. *I'm not exaggerating*. Oranges. Reds. Purples. I'm being sucked into it, like being stared at by a Rothko.

Is this how Caitlin felt, gazing into the eye of that huge, dying animal?

I catch myself (*before it's too late?*), and sit back up, facing the window again. But it's hard to shake off the weight of that circle of lava suspended in the skylight just a few feet from my head. I reacquaint myself with the rise and fall of the hills. Estate house lights. Taransay, pushing out into the bay. And the sky, stretching out beyond the illusion of that inverted caldera.

Sometime later, the room almost dark now, Caitlin comes up the stairs. Her hand is out, holding something. I instinctively reach out my own in response, and look down. It's my phone. And there's a live call open on it. I look at Caitlin. She says nothing, nods in its direction.

Oh no.

"Hello?" It's Kieron. "Hello?"

What to do?

"Hello? Dad?"

I kill the call.

If it's all the same to you, I'm just going to sit here for a few minutes in the dark.

We choose not to discuss it. Caitlin has no intention of apologising, and I've nothing to gain from bringing it up. I know why she did it, and so does she, but I don't have the energy for an argument. Instead, I explain to her how much more writing I need to complete.

She jokes. "So if we sit here in silence – say nothing, do nothing – does that mean you have to write less, or more?"

A good question.

"Very funny."

It's Ceremony time. The whisky, and the ritual comfort of the penultimate sachet (#26/10) has never been so welcome.

Brora 30 Years Old db (97)
n**24 that stunning Brora farmyard again, perhaps with a touch of extra fruit this time round. Beautiful structure, layering and harmony; **t**25 Gosh! Perfect or what? How can something be this old yet offer such a gristy sweetness? Chewy, smoky, barely oaky but 100 okay-dokey; **f**24 some late pear spice buzz adds a bit of bite to the smoke-fuelled serenity of this dram. A touch of something citrus helps thin out the layers; **b**24 here we go again! Just like last year's bottling, we have something of near unbelievable beauty with the weight perfectly pitched and the barley-oak interaction the stuff of dreams. And as for the peat: an entirely unique species, a giant that is so gentle. Last year's bottling was one of the whiskies of the year. This even better version is the perfect follow-up. **56.4%

These Highland whiskies are so muscular. All the way up the coast above Inverness – Dalmore, Glenmorangie, Clynelish, Old Pulteney – and then extending the line up to Orkney with Highland Park and those honey-hued Scapa drams.

This Brora is the tasting equivalent of a Harley Street makeover for mouth, nose and throat. The second glass, normally dedicated to targeted remembering, finds its way down my throat as the vehicle for an attempt at short-term forgetting. *(Even writing these details down in the small hours of Saturday morning, Caitlin asleep upstairs, I'm welling up, and having to take short, head-clearing breaks.)*

We talk more about my life with Trish. It's hard to gauge just how interested Caitlin is. She seems a little subdued, and I feel shitty going on about older, happier times; there's always that risk that she'll pick up on a subliminal, unintended brag. And that wouldn't be nice.

So I rein it in a little. We sit in the lounge, share a large plate of venison pâté and some toasted bread. A reconciliation of sorts. I resist the temptation to elaborate on the growing misery of my first marriage – it would overcome the bragging problem, but even that might come over as some half-assed attempt to state the blatantly obvious, *Look, I've been miserable too, you know*. The calibration of her experiences to mine can only lead to bad places.

I think she senses it too, the atmosphere. The fact that I didn't come bouncing down the stairs earlier to declare that I've reconsidered. That all plans are off, and we'll both head off the island tomorrow, searching for new ways to be.

No.

That moment, the passing of that possible outcome, is met now by solemn, reflective quiet. The Broch has seen its last Ceremony, and I need to get upstairs and get down today's events.

I think Caitlin's relieved when I head off. I suggest that she watch *Breaking Bad*, the final show on the list. She's already seen it, and says she'd rather just kick back on the sofa with another beer and read the rest of *The Quarant*.

"I'll let you know what I think of it when you come back down."

Sounds good. A suggestion of closure, of sorts?

I take Trish and the Brora with me, bracing for the challenge ahead.

As it happens, I surprise myself. I thought that, with just hours to go before departure (from this mortal coil as much as from this building), I'd find the writing hard. That the neck of the amphora from which words come would narrow, like the sphincter of a man in free fall. But instead, the telling of the day comes surprisingly easy. Like everything else I've written this week, the text is riddled with ugly sentences; missed or trite similes; the typos, misspellings and grammar of an untutored child. But I get it down.

I cleaned and buffed and polished every bloody paragraph to within an inch of its life when I first started on *The Quarant*. I was lucky if I could fill a couple of screens in a day. I was less a writer, and more a second- and third-guesser of myself. I completely overlooked the fact that writing a story for the first time should be fun. Blasting through scene after scene. Discovering how characters might interact with or respond to each other or the events around them. I learnt from that, and from then on just let my hair down. *The Puppet Master*, that first draft, was the most fun I'd ever had short of the need for contraception or the number of a trustworthy lawyer.

It's hard, though, to describe how these last two days have felt. How I feel right now, in fact. Sitting here on the bed, pressure is strangely absent. Short of a last-minute alien invasion, or the arrival of a triumphant Hebridean constabulary, there's not much else to record.

I'm almost there.

A FINAL WORD OR TWO...

So here I am, then. Up to date, pretty much. iPad fully charged. Everything backed up, ready for Caitlin to walk Kathleen around the material.

Heavy cloud masks what I believe is still a full moon. Lights from scattered crofts and a distant campsite pierce the otherwise empty landscape. It's quiet downstairs. Caitlin might still be reading, or have nodded off.

I close my eyes and drift.

I'm not sure why I'm suddenly so calm. So *accepting* of what today is. I would have thought, with all the upset earlier, I would be whirring around inside my own head, nerves on alert. But I don't feel it. Just the flow of warmth with each sip of whisky.

I've always been nervous about new challenges. Big meetings to run at work. Sleepless nights rehearsing difficult conversations. Further back, exams. Performance anxiety, they call it. But for me, they rarely felt like performances. They felt like judgements waiting to be delivered; outcomes that said something about me not as a performer, but as a person. I could never separate the two.

In our first few years together, Trish would go out of her way to assure me that all would be well, until even she finally gave up. I'd lose sleep, lose my sense of humour (unless biting the head off anyone coming near me within twenty-four hours of any such event counted as funny), and off I'd go. Succeed or fail, but never getting over that feeling that I was unfit for the next challenge, and the next.

Don't get me wrong. She could get nervous too. Short-tempered, even. She could be easily rubbed the wrong way. But moments like these were rare, and passed quickly. A good night's sleep would almost always be the answer, and then – ta-dah! – there she'd be, back to her old self.

I can't help but chuckle. On her worst day, I would still rather be with her than anyone. When I was a kid, in front of the TV with Mum as she did the ironing, she'd be watching *Mr and Mrs*. One night, a couple were introduced. They probably had one full set of teeth between them, and you could tell they were a little overawed by being in the studio. In answer to a question I no longer recall, the short, elderly man, wearing a suit that had clearly been bought when he was two stone heavier and six inches taller, responded with the phrase "Fifty-three years married, and never a cross word."

Many years later, much older and oh so much wiser, I'd relate what I'd seen that night to others, and run the couple down. "What a boring life those two must have had. I doubt if they've ever had even one meaningful conversation. *That's* why they never bloody disagree."

I was wrong. That's what I want to tell that couple now. That man could well have been telling the truth. Been part of something special. Two people truly meant for each other, and content in each other's company. Year in, year out.

I head downstairs. Caitlin has her feet up on the sofa, her head resting on a cushion placed at one end.

"Sorry, Caitlin. I didn't mean to wake you."

"No, no. That's fine. I wasn't asleep." Her hand moves behind her leg, and reappears with the paperback. "I've just finished. Imagining I was on that boat, leaving the lagoon."

She tells me how much she loved it. The story. The characters. How sad it was (she hadn't expected that). I don't care if she means it or not. Just getting to the end is quite something. And I never tire of people telling me I did a good job. Do you?

I ask her if she'd mind if I watched the end of *Breaking Bad*. "I promised myself I'd watch the finale. It's really something."

Caitlin shuffles over, and we put it on.

Walter breaks into an iced-over car, failing to kick-start it with his frozen hands and intermittent cough. He hunkers down at the oncoming police lights. Speaks to himself quietly, pleading under his breath for the chance to return home one last time. The police drive on, car keys drop from the sun visor, and a cheerful country-and-western song begins to play when the car starts up.

Although Trish and I watched the whole show together three times, I'm still shocked by just how confidently it plays out. Every shot lasts just the right amount of time. Every word counts. At no point does any character state how they're feeling. They don't need to.

Walter's dying, but has a few things left to do. Revenge to deal out. Schemes to implement. An endowment for his son Flynn to set up, under threat of death from his original nemeses, Gretchen and Elliot. In amongst all the melancholy, fear and bloodthirsty vengeance, black humour still hits the mark. Todd is still finding it hard to work out what the hell is going on, or why any action is needed.

Here's Walt's last conversation with Skyler, the wife he pulls into his criminal web. He admits what we as viewers have always known – that his descent into violence and drug manufacturing has been an entirely selfish act, giving him a sense of meaning and power and, yes, fun. His final view of Flynn, observing him unnoticed before he leaves for the last time, the camera staying on Walt as he turns away, is heartbreaking.

I don't let on, but I know Caitlin has turned from the screen and is watching me instead. The parallels are all there, I guess. I just hadn't realised. And all this before the last big scene in the Aryan Brotherhood's house. I won't spoil it for you, but the tension is beautifully crafted. Pure screen magic.

When the show ends, there's really not much to be said. There's nothing we can talk about that would realistically keep us away from the dangerous, emotionally charged themes of parental loss, suicidal throws of the dice, and the bonds between a husband and his betrayed wife. Caitlin knows it, and I know it.

The mood that filled the room earlier this evening has returned, and neither of us will confront it.

...AND THEN TO BED

We've swapped places. Caitlin's back upstairs, and I'm still sitting in front of the TV. I pick up Trish and sit her next to me. Cup my hand around the urn's surface. Have one last conversation with her.

And then I stop to think. Look around the room, out into the dark. I'm glad I came here. I'm glad I was part of that first discussion with Trish about coming to Harris, and saying, "To hell with it – why not?" when we booked this place. The two months we had, looking forward together to being here. Sharing daydreams of walking along golden beaches. Sitting on the lower slopes of hills, shoulders tightly pulled into arms, looking down on and beyond deep Atlantic waters. Huddled under covers, listening to each oncoming squall of rain, confident it will never reach us.

She would have loved it here. I love it for both of us.

Being with Trish, even on my worst days, when things got on top of me, or our tempers pushed us into that strange territory where we'd raise our voices, disagree, even (a handful of times) stomp heavily from the room; when I'd maybe forgotten something I'd promised to do, or done something I'd promised I wouldn't – even on those days, I loved where I was. Who I was with. What we were.

I was good at it, Trish. So were you. We were good at *us*. And tomorrow, I'll be more alive than ever, reaching out to join you. To still those ripping claws; enter the stillness where all I can hear is you calling me, telling me it will be all right.

I'll get that last thought down.

Oh, and goodnight, boys.

IMMEDIATE AFTERMATH
SATURDAY 20TH JANUARY 2018

It's a Saturday, so when the doorbell rings, he expects the substitute postie needing a signature. Or the sport that comes from driving off a pair of Jehovah's Witnesses, his triumph never in doubt.

"Ah, good morning, sir. Am I addressing Mr Rose?"

He shows the officer in. He wonders if he should ask him to take his shoes off – the black oak floor is unforgiving of outside dirt. He hears the quiet, telltale scritches and crunches of damp soil from the man's footsteps behind him. He confirms other things. His wife's name. Her date of birth. His own. Their car.

"And where do you believe your wife to be, sir?"

Then, the risk of mistaken identities cast off, the details flow. The crash is just a few hundred yards along the Skye road. Just inside the village sign. At the commencement of the lower speed limit. Before the playing field. Others, the officer tells him, are there "in attendance", with more to come.

He has heard enough. The officer only catches him at the door as he looks for footwear.

Outside, a long morning dawn meets an afternoon-long dusk. January in the Highlands. Blue and orange flashes scrape through the gloom. The colours of emergencies.

He runs until the wreck comes into view. Wrecks, actually. Two cars, one on its roof and both where they shouldn't be.

The Nissan is an origami of failure. Of both purpose and form. Of its obligation to protect its occupant from harm. The rear doors of the ambulance are sprung wide. A trolley stretcher is sided by two men in green overalls.

Movement to the left, over by the other car, draws his eye. Ken. Arguing with a different officer, wanting to walk back up his drive. His own movement registers with the man. Their eyes meet, one gaze wild, the other pleading. The real fear descends.

Martin approaches the ambulance. The policeman who came to the house calls his name, alerting the paramedics. They turn from their charge to face him.

"Sir? Sir, please."

His stomach, empty from the delayed lunch with his wife, churns like a dynamo, sparked into life by his defibrillating heart. He stands over the stretcher. Leans over and in. Sees the gash, a thin pulled-sugar-work ribbon. Lifeless eyes, shuttered and pale. Makes as if to touch her face, then pulls back, their life together racing past him, already forgetful and disloyal, back out and into the twilight day.

The policeman returns to the house for a jacket and his wallet. Hands him The Schoolhouse's keys.

He sits in the back for the drive up to Raigmore Hospital and the waiting paperwork.

CHAPTER 8

SATURDAY 27TH OCTOBER 2018
(FROM CONVERSATIONS WITH CAITLIN)

I did it for me. I liked it. I was good at it. And I was really… I was alive.

(Walter White, Breaking Bad)

LEAVINGS

Let's start by describing how they left what Caitlin calls "*that gorgeous place by the sea*".

All Martin's possessions are back in his case, with the exception of the urn and the opened but largely intact second bottle of Brora from last night. Both of these fit easily into his daypack, nestling comfortably in amongst his waterproof trousers and extra fleece.

Caitlin, with nothing of her own, of course, has watched him prepare. He tells her that anything in there that she wants is hers. They laugh. A case full of men's clothes, ready for the wash. Thanks very much.

He hands her the final two bottles of malt: the Ardbeg Ping

No. 1 Single Cask. "Offer these to Kathleen. A down payment, if she's prepared to help, or if not, just a gift to thank her for her support. They're worth at least a couple of thousand each, so make sure she doesn't use them to flavour her shortbread or donate them as a raffle prize."

Before the iPad goes into the case, he gets Caitlin to open his system and pull up his email to me, sent an hour earlier. The keycode to his iPad is the same as his four-digit cashpoint PIN. It's a good test for her, actually. He's thought this through.

Caitlin scans the text, her face calm and composed.

Martin, Saturday 27th October 2018, 7.18

Dear Kathleen,

I trust that you're well, and that your latest work is shaping up the way you hope.

For reasons that will become clear over the next few days, I'm writing to you in the spirit of a friend, and as one who, despite his absence for many months from the Sunday sessions on the hill, continues to believe in the power of prose to pierce even the thickest of skins and make the wild birds soar.

Were I to emphasise too much my wish that I'd got to know you better, other than through your wonderful writing, you might begin to harbour suspicions of insincerity where there should be none. Suffice it to say, then, that I can think of no one better to write to on this most peculiar of days.

So, to my point.

Sometime soon, a young woman will approach you. She will have with her my iPad, and details for navigating Scrivener. From this, it will be possible to access not only the first rough draft of some writing I have done this past week, completed hurriedly and with only cursory thought to flow and sequence, but also some older material (some dating back over the past twelve months, some longer), that I have earmarked in my draft for inclusion or substitution.

My request is a simple one, albeit substantial: it would be a great and lasting relief to me if you would take all this material and stitch it into a more coherent, considered whole. Please get all the help you might need from Caitlin, particularly as it relates to the second half of the week covered by the story, and any additional description of the events of this final Saturday.

I apologise in advance for the looseness of the writing. Please know that your every wince or grimace will merely reflect those more frequent and heartfelt of my own, knowing that I have not had time for even the briefest of revisits. I have never written at such speed, or with so much emotion, so please make allowances for all poor choices made.

My final request is that, even if all you are able to do is patch something together that honours the basic rules of narrative, you find a way to get copies to my two sons, Kieron and Conor, at the addresses listed below. If you feel able to do more, to turn this into something with commercial legs, please feel free to sprinkle your own magic dust over it, in any way you deem appropriate. Every choice you make has my blessing, although be aware that every character I have mentioned currently carries their real-world name.

It's been a pleasure.

Take care,
Martin x

Caitlin hands the iPad back, and it goes into the case with everything else. *Neither of them*, she tells me later, *seems in the mood for conversation.*

They eat their last breakfast together in silence, sitting around the kitchen table that's barely been used all week. Cheese. The last of the oatcakes. Some coffee from the Nespresso, its strong, nutty aroma climbing into the air around them.

"Don't forget the champagne, Caitlin."

She retrieves it from the fridge, untouched during the week, and places it by the door. When they finally leave, the bottle glistens with condensation.

Martin hands Caitlin the car keys. Shows her how to trigger the doors, and opens the boot for the case. He gestures to her to go to the driver's side. "Good chance to get used to the controls. You'll be fine," he says, pushing the passenger seat back and placing his rucksack in the footwell between his feet.

He shows her how to start the car. Explains that she needs her foot on the clutch for it to work. As she manoeuvres, Martin turns his head to take in the whole building. The grassed roof still spills slightly over the top line of granite in places. It could do with a trim in the spring, to preserve the smooth, modern lines of the glass. The sky into which the tower strains is high but overcast.

Caitlin makes a cautious way down the track to the main road, risking just one shift of the gears. Martin offers her a faint smile, and mumbles quietly. "*I'm not sure what he said*," she tells me. "*Something about 'hairy bastard' and 'next guests'.*"

A left turn, and they're soon opposite the large ornamental gates to the estate.

"It's OK. We can drive up to the office."

Robert comes to the door. (*"I felt him check me out over Martin's shoulder. God knows what he was thinking."*) Martin passes him the key, and they exchange pleasantries. An envelope, textured and creamy white, appears in Robert's hand. He passes it to Martin. Final smiles and handshakes complete, Martin returns to the car.

"Good," he says. "That was all a little bit wanky, but it's done."

When they turn back onto the road, Martin connects his phone to the music system. Mellow voice and acoustic guitar fill the car: Coldplay's *Parachutes*. Caitlin keeps her eyes on the road as they cross the first cattle grid on their way back to Tarbert. She's getting used to the clutch.

The land slips by, Caitlin staying alert for any oncoming vehicles, for the need to pull in. They allow the songs, short and shimmering, to substitute for words. "*The traffic*," until they drop back down to the east coast below Tarbert, she says, "*varied between sparse and non-existent, thank God.*"

Martin doesn't speak until they curve into and then up and out of the town. Tells her that there's a cashpoint a bit further down Pier Road, outside the Bank of Scotland. He changes the music. David Gray. "*White Ladder*. Old Wobbly Head."

The sky is lifting, the cloud thinning. Fence posts grow shadows, reaching down and leaning into the verge on their left as the car swings north.

Ten minutes more, and the details on the flanks of The Clisham and the hills around it crystallise. Martin points to where the hill disappears. "Hill mist," he tells her. "It should clear later. No problem." He pulls a plastic pocket from his rucksack, the sort with a green spine that fits an A4 binder. Two printed sheets are inside: one with narrow orange contour lines; the other a slightly skewed photocopy from a walking book. "That's where we'll park up." On the photocopy, several red lines converge at a large black dot. Curved black lines emanate from it in four directions, like a starfish's arms: ridges. A line of small triangles just above the dot: crags or cliffs.

They approach the pass. Martin eventually points to their right, where a narrow additional length of road runs parallel with the one they're on. "This is it," he tells her. "I checked it out on Monday."

Caitlin pulls up at the far end, just before three large rocks mark the end of the weed-strewn, weather-beaten tarmac. When she turns off the engine, the music stops, and silence floods in from the outside. They sit there for a few moments. Caitlin listens to the clicks from the bonnet.

Martin leans forward and pulls a small yellow handset from his rucksack. He pushes a button on its side and puts it on the dashboard. "GPS. I should have switched it on a bit earlier, but no matter. It'll soon pick up the satellites." He disconnects his phone from the player, presses back into the seat and pulls a pair of earphones from a trouser pocket.

The next few minutes involve Martin checking pockets, opening and closing his rucksack, moving backwards and forwards to the boot and removing a small bag. Walking boots and socks. ("*It was as if he couldn't put his mind to any one thing. Kept starting to do something, then changing his mind.*") He swivels on the passenger seat, swings his feet out of the car, and changes out of his trainers.

He's only just got his second boot on when he jumps out of the car, takes four or five hurried steps from the door and bends over double. Brings up his breakfast. "*And, by the sound of it,*" Caitlin says, "*several minor organs and a lifetime of pain. I don't know what was worse: hearing all that throwing up, or seeing the look on his face when he came back to the car. It must have taken him a good five minutes to do up his last shoelace. I think he preferred to keep his back to me for as long as possible.*"

When he's finally ready, Martin asks Caitlin to walk with him the few yards back to the main road. He's put on his rucksack, checked the GPS and put it in his coat pocket. The maps, folded in half, are secure in an inner jacket pocket. His earphones lie either side of his head, draped over his shoulders in readiness. He waves an earpiece at her. "Elvis and Burt. *Painted from Memory*. Our favourite."

He tells her his plan. Ascend above Monday's spur and onto the south-east ridge, and then follow it to the top. He's looked at photos and walk reports describing the summit, but remains a little unsure as to the precise nature and location of the crags. But with the hill mist likely to burn off as the morning moves on, he tells her, he doesn't think he'll have any problem finding them. "There should be plenty of juice left in the phone. Anyone using that device-tracking thing on Apple should have no problem."

There are no cars around. Martin begins to walk across the road. He stops before he gets halfway. Caitlin's rooted to the spot. She's still unable to explain exactly how those moments felt.

Just a few steps, and then he's back at her side. "I'm sorry. I'm not thinking. Well, not straight, anyway. So listen."

Caitlin sees him struggling for words. His eyes water. "*He snorted a bit at one point, and a couple of bits of sick came out of his nose. Got stuck in his moustache.*" He gives up, and shrugs off his rucksack. Bends, unzips it and takes out the Brora. She does her best not to roll her eyes as he rises, the bottle tipped tight to his lips. In fact, she says, him doing this gives her a brief chance to pull herself together. "*I was really close to losing it, and I didn't want him to see that.*"

The bottle goes back in the bag, and Martin straightens up. The vomit's gone. Then they just stand there. "*I thought for a moment that he was going to hug me.*" But he doesn't. Just one smile, and then he turns and walks back across the road. She sees him reach up and put in his earplugs, and then she turns back to the car.

The car feels empty. She turns on the radio, but there's no reception. *Better off without it*, she thinks.

She tells me that at no point did she decide where she was going. She just knew. It's easy to retrace the morning's drive; pass the point where the gravel of The Broch's track spills a faint brown stain onto the main road. She continues on to Northton, and the narrow byroad that bends back towards the Scarista sands. Past the low, circular stone of The Temple Cafe, and on to the small parking circle.

She lifts out Martin's spare jacket from the boot. She opens the suitcase. Takes out the champagne. It's lost most of its chill, but so what?

When she passes the end of the bracken and ferns, and moves out onto the open, flat spit of land, she's glad of the jacket. The hand in which she holds the champagne, and a significant part of the bottle, are draped in its overlong sleeve. She follows the path until it reaches the broad shank of the hill. The breeze strengthens, but she doesn't feel the cold. She unzips the front of her coat as her lungs stretch. The sides whip up and behind her in the wind coming in from her right; from the bay.

An hour, and she nears the top of the climb. Clouds are broken up into large white masses, fixed in place against the wide, featureless blue. *"I got to the trig point, and stopped to catch my breath. Looking north across the bay, to the hills I'd sat and stood beneath that morning, it looked as though all the tops were completely clear."*

Her breath slower, her mind turns back to where they parked this morning. The phantom road where, in the absence of all others, she and Martin did their stilted, reserved dance. Stepped in and out, nodded and glanced. Blinked away at moist eyes.

"He really was just a walking corpse," she tells me. *"I think that was one of the reasons why I accepted that it was right for him to do it. Part of him was already bloody dead. It was just that the rest of him didn't know what else to do about it."*

Later, she asks me, *"Can you imagine what it takes? To take something that you really love, and turn it into the weapon that kills you? What he knew about the whiskies; how he wrote best with the taste of Jack on his tongue, its heat in his belly. But then to use it to wipe out his brain, to handle the pain...*

"He really stank," she says. And she had to quickly learn to ignore his incessant mumbling. She couldn't hear what he was saying most of the time, but she always thought he was just a few words away from a full-blown argument – with himself, or with others who might be standing in front of him. Others, that is, visible only to him. *"Christ knows how he managed to still do stuff. Drive a car. Shop for things. And get all this stuff down on the screen."* She's no idea if I'll be able to make any sense of what he left for me.

But she really liked him, she says. Liked the way he was so fixed on doing what he felt was the right thing, no matter how twisted or selfish. He broke down in tears pretty regularly from the point he lifted her from the sands. How could he not attract her pity? And it's true, they shared some laughs. Sat in that gorgeous place, tight in against the weather, her sensing his wish to see her conquer her own difficulties, not go under, find some way through that didn't involve freezing to death *"on some fucking beach"* next to the stinking carcass of a whale that might have known, more than this strange, damaged man did, that it was already dead.

She stands back up. Brushes the damp soil off the back of her trousers. She's lost track of time. It's probably a good couple of hours since they parted. She walks a little further on, to a small cairn. The summit.

Stretched out before her, there's a scattering of white patches and bands; small accumulations of sand painted onto the canvas before her. Beyond them, looking north across numerous bays, one or two of the peaks rising up in the background sit under open sunshine. Including the tallest one.

She imagines him pulling up onto its ridge, stopping every so often to take another pull on his bottle; grab his sides or back from the intensity of the climb. She has no idea where he draws his strength from; how much it must hurt to coax his thumping heart on, to get himself up the hill but bring with him, with every thick, wrenching pull, all the pain he's been dosing himself against for months.

She makes no claim to know exactly when he might have reached the top. Whether he got his breath back sufficiently, once there, to sing along to one of his bloody songs. But she imagines him anyway, upright and unflinching in the unbroken sunshine, above some airy precipice. His bag at his feet, his eyes closed, the final sachet of Trish ("*#27/10, I guess*"), tipped into his waiting mouth. And the whisky, straight from the bottle, washing down his final communion.

She raises her hand towards the hill, moves the bottle above her head, knowing he won't see her but knowing also that, somehow, he will sense her actions. "To his kids," she says. She intends to open the champagne here; offer one last toast before his final leap. But the moment passes. She reminds herself instead to ring the police regarding Martin's whereabouts as soon as she gets into Tarbert.

She heads down the hill, the wind now behind her. Halfway back along the flats, she bears off to the south. The beach remains empty and pristine, swept clean bar a few scratched bird tracks just above the waterline.

But she remembers the whale. Falling into its eye.

She pulls the foil from the bottle, twists off the metal twine, and prises up the cork. Despite her walk down to the beach, its release barely registers above the remaining breeze and the steady arrival and retreat of the low waves.

She raises the bottle again. Makes a silent toast that she vows she will never share with anyone.

Then watches, a detached observer, as first some, then all of the liquid pours down and into the sand.

AFTERWORD

I'd like, if I may, to add a few more items of note that might bring the preceding story to its full conclusion. (To have done so in the foreword would have risked too much.)

But first I wish to put on record how much I have appreciated the cooperation and tolerance of the many people mentioned in Martin's story, as I've sought to clarify further some of the important aspects of his account. In the weeks following the recovery and return of Martin's body to the mainland, I had the opportunity to speak to a number of those who played a part in his life.

Geraldine and Iain, the close friends from whose home Trish was returning on the morning of her accident, have told me much to confirm the truth of Martin and Trish's life together. On the many occasions (and there must have been hundreds) they met, Trish never suggested anything other than that she and Martin still enjoyed each other's company. I won't judge the impact of Martin's attempts to keep her death from them. I suspect they will always wish that they could have offered their help and attended the funeral. They both confirm, however, that it would have been Trish's wish to be cremated, without any religious intrusion.

Steve and Donna gave me further insights into Martin from their time with him, both when visiting The Schoolhouse and when reciprocating Trish and Martin's hospitality on their visits south. Like Geraldine, Steve remains shocked at how Martin could have kept events from him, finding it almost impossible to believe that his friend stayed with them for five days that July, claiming that Trish was visiting her parents and sister in Aberdeen.

I also contacted Martin's friend Dennis in Austin, and explained to him the events of the past few months. At his request, I'll respect his privacy and leave you to speculate as to his reaction. He has since been in touch with Martin's sons.

It is only right, now, to properly acknowledge the forbearance and understanding of Kieron and Conor, and their partners. In particular, I want to acknowledge my continuing concern that my curiosity might have seemed untoward or intrusive. They have been most helpful in the latter stages of pulling this book together, and have offered many more insights into their feelings for and memories of their father. Kieron in particular was able to verify many of the details of Martin's departure from the family home at the turn of the millennium.

On that last Friday, Kieron was with Conor when they called their father's mobile. They tried many more times over the next two days to make contact, but none of their calls were answered. As Martin had suspected, Kieron immediately raised the alarm with his employers but, despite the existence of their letters from him, Martin was initially considered to be at only a medium risk of doing himself serious harm. It was not until twenty-four hours later, after all further attempts by his sons to contact him had failed, that the assessment was revised. Four hours later still, Caitlin contacted the police to confirm Martin's actions and approximate whereabouts. Two days later, a representative from John Fraser & Son, the undertakers on Chapel Street in Inverness, met the ferry at Uig to convey his body back to Raigmore Hospital.

After several conversations over the phone and on Skype, I finally met Martin's sons at Inverness Crematorium, just south of the city on Kilvean Road. Although they had visited their grandparents' residential home to tell them the news, their grandmother was too frail to travel, and Martin's father felt he should remain by her side rather than attend on his own.

It was one of those late autumn days, a month or so before Christmas, that can still surprise even the most established of residents. A high, clear sky; just a few degrees above freezing, but with still air. The open, tended grasslands of the complex felt uncluttered and peaceful. I introduced myself, and we walked into the main chapel together. In line with the wishes outlined in Martin's letters to his boys, we stood listening to Utopia's 'Love is the Answer' and then the growling, emotional delivery of Tom Waits' 'Somewhere'.

The morning before, the boys had received a visit to The Schoolhouse from Frasers. A young woman, one their managers, wished to pass on to them the possessions that had been found with their father.

After the service, we walked back to where Kieron had parked the car they'd shared on the drive up from Suffolk. He opened the boot and lifted out a black rucksack. He unzipped it, and pulled out a polished blue urn. It appeared completely undamaged. "They told us he'd fallen nearly a hundred feet beneath the north ridge of the next top on from the summit. It was broken in two, zipped into his coat. But they got it mended for us." He paused; glanced at his brother. "The sharpest edge cut into his chest." His accent reminded me yet again of his father.

Conor reached over and took it. "Let's get this back in there, so they've got it when they need it."

I don't know what Kieron and Conor will do with the urn once it's been refilled. But whatever it is, I'm sure that Martin would approve. Either way, I don't think I will push to find out. They deserve at least this last small concession to their privacy.

And what of Caitlin?

She had two official visits while staying at The Schoolhouse: the first from a young PC, and the second, three days later, from an official of the Scottish Fatalities Investigation Unit.

She told me that she had rung Kieron to explain who she was, and why she had his father's car and bank card. A day after that, she drove south to visit her own father.

I've met her perhaps four or five times since. Sean seems to have lost all interest in her, and she has decided to let things lie with him. She has no desire to see him again, not even across a courtroom.

She's another one, like Kieron and Conor, with her head firmly screwed on.

There's just one last thing I'd like to share.

You'll perhaps recall Martin's account of his confrontation with the man who caused Trish's accident – the old man with the slippers? Well, while working on reshaping his manuscript, I visited the village, and drove slowly past what I believe to be the bungalow from which Ken pulled into the road, and into the path of Trish. A 'For Sale' board stood at the foot of the drive. The place looked empty. I drove carefully on (there really is a slow, blind bend just west of the house), and then turned around at the next opening.

Remembering Martin's description of the resident's habits, I drove back into the village and parked outside the village store. I introduced myself to the man behind the counter. My luck was in: he was Terry, the owner.

"Oh, yes, that's right. Ken. Nice bloke."

I explained that his place looked empty, and inquired if he still lived there.

"Well no. No. We'd only just heard about the accident – you know, about how young Trish died – and then he called in here, just a couple of weeks later, to say that he was off down south to stay with his sister. To my knowledge, he's never been back. The place went up for sale in the autumn, but they can't shift it. Probably asking too much."

In his manuscript, Martin had been adamant that he'd confronted Ken, that day he finally left the village. He'd even castigated himself for being powerless to say anything to him.

So I just wanted to clear that up. I've decided to leave his account unchanged. It's him all over.

PS: I continue to wonder what became of Gallagher. I hope he's not too lonely.

PPS: For those of you who worry about these things, two bottles of Ardbeg roost safely in our drinks cabinet, ready to enable reflective moments of our own.

Kathleen Ward,
Fortrose,
Summer 2019

ACKNOWLEDGEMENTS

A number of people have been key to getting this book to this point in its existence.

Dennis Tardan has, as usual, offered his patient and insightful input and encouragement throughout the writing process. I've also had a significant amount of input from those writers I have befriended from my attendance at the Moniack Mhor Creative Writing Centre, including Cynthia Rogerson, a keen observer of human nature and a tireless supporter of the writing art. Friends Pam Macintyre, Annie MacDonald, Christine Hoy, Matt Wood and John Smith have been helpful with their thoughtful and supportive comments as the book took shape.

I'd also like to thank my editor, Faye Booth, for her meticulous grasp of how our language works, and protecting me from the kind of errors that no writer wishes to see aired in public.

On the subject of whale beachings and their treatment, I'd like to thank Keith Beaton of the Scottish Environmental Protection Agency for educating me on the cross-agency cooperation involved when dealing with such events, and Hector Low, the senior vet in Stornoway, whose many anecdotes of his own attendances were so enlightening and, in some cases, dramatic. Geoff Main, the head of the Scottish Fatalities Investigation Unit (North), was most generous with his time in advising me on the manner in which road accidents and their aftermath are handled in the Highlands and Islands, as was Sarah Maclean of Fraser & Son Funeral Directors in Inverness.

The Broch itself is one of a number of beautiful holiday rentals on the Borve Lodge Estate on West Harris. I wish to thank the owners, Cathra and Adam Kelliher, and the estate services manager Camille Craven, for their support in allowing me to set my story there. Also Victoria Harvey, the manager of the Callanish Visitor Centre, for advice on the operation of the site. Three other places are certainly worthy of mention: Munro's of Tarbert, the An Clachan Community Shop at Leverburgh, and Emma Davies' IV10 cafe back on the mainland in Fortrose, all of which serve their communities well.

Finally, and as always, thank you Joanne for your continuing love and support.

PERMISSIONS

The epigraph is a verse from Prefab Sprout's song '*I Remember That*', from the album *From Langley Park to Memphis*. It has been reprinted by kind permission of Paddy McAloon, and Keith Armstrong of Kitchenware Records.

Jim Murray's tasting notes and rating system from *Jim Murray's Whisky Bible 2007* have been used with permission by Jim Murray and Dram Good Books Ltd. As an aside, I remain convinced that the scoring can be applied just as accurately to people as to drams.

'Wisely and slow; they stumble that run fast' is from Shakespeare's *Romeo and Juliet*.

'What larks, Pip' is from *Great Expectations* by Charles Dickens.

I am also indebted to the creative and haunting power of the novel *Cloud Atlas* by David Mitchell, and the makers of the following incredible television shows, from which brief quotes are respectfully used: *Justified* (2010), *True Detective* (2014), *Battlestar Galactica* (2004), *The Sopranos* (1999), *Sons of Anarchy* (2008), *The Wire* (2002), *Breaking Bad* (2008) and *Travelers* (2016). While all efforts have been made to contact copyright holders of material used in these works, any oversights will be gladly corrected in future editions.

To Joanne.

ALSO BY THE AUTHOR

THE QUARANT

January, 1348. They say bad things come in threes...

The day after an earthquake and tsunami have ravaged Venice, Malin Le Cordier, a successful English maritime trader, sails into the city with plans to mature a coup on behalf of Edward III and Genoa. His time? Short. His guilt? Strong. Keeping the coup a secret from those he loves most weighs heavy on his soul. But Venice is a place with secrets and revenge flows through the city like its canals. For his sake and those he is bound to, it is best he learn to navigate it. And quickly.

Unbeknownst to Malin, there is someone powerful in the city who seeks revenge on Edward III on behalf of his family. Well-situated, he operates under covert circumstances, monitoring Malin's every move - and playing his own long game, merely waiting for the perfect time to strike.

Combining greed and guilt, revenge and undeclared love, this is one trip that Malin may not live to regret.

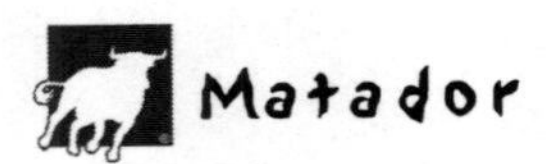
Matador